Praise for *Hold Back the Dark*

"Carr's romantic suspense debut starts off like a rocket. . . . The characters are engaging and distinct, with complex motivations, and the pacing of the thriller is so inexorable it almost overshadows the romance."

—*Publishers Weekly*

"Suspense lovers will be delighted with Carr's tightly woven and tense plot. The chemistry is tangible and realistic, and the intricacies of the murder plot are masterfully crafted. Carr will have instant fans."

—*Romantic Times*

"Gripping suspense . . . a heart-pounder."

—Roxanne St. Claire,
New York Times bestselling author

"A definite winner in the romantic thriller category."

—John Lescroart,
New York Times bestselling author

"An excellent addition to the genre."

—Kwips and Kritiques

"If you're looking for good romantic suspense, look no further."

—Book Binge

This title is also available as an eBook.

ALSO BY EILEEN CARR

Hold Back the Dark

VANISHED
IN THE
NIGHT

EILEEN CARR

Pocket Books
New York London Toronto Sydney

Pocket Books
A Division of Simon & Schuster, Inc.
1230 Avenue of the Americas
New York, NY 10020

This book is a work of fiction. Names, characters, places, and incidents either are products of the author's imagination or are used fictitiously. Any resemblance to actual events or locales or persons, living or dead, is entirely coincidental.

First Pocket Books paperback edition August 2011

POCKET and colophon are registered trademarks of Simon & Schuster, Inc.

For information about special discounts for bulk purchases, please contact Simon & Schuster Special Sales at 1-866-506-1949 or business@simonandschuster.com.

The Simon & Schuster Speakers Bureau can bring authors to your live event. For more information or to book an event contact the Simon & Schuster Speakers Bureau at 1-866-248-3049 or visit our website at www.simonspeakers.com.

Designed by Jill Putorti
Cover design by John Vairo Jr.
Woman running © Jan Mammey/STOCK4B/Getty Images; forest © Nacivet/Getty Images

Manufactured in the United States of America

10 9 8 7 6 5 4 3 2 1

ISBN 978-1-4391-8387-8
ISBN 978-1-4391-8391-5 (ebook)

*To Debbie, Naomi, Marian, Elizabeth, and Kathy
and all the many nurses I've been blessed to know.
You are my heroines every day.*

Acknowledgments

Thank you to my sister Diane, who gave this book its original title. We didn't get to use it, but it kept me focused as I wrote the story. Thank you to my sister Marian, who devised ways to kill many of the victims in the book. Thanks to Susan and Virna for help in fleshing out the story, coming up with nicknames, and providing general moral support at a very crucial moment. Of course, many thanks to the usual suspects—Andy, Spring, Deb, and Carol—who talk me down, cheer me up, create backstories, and generally keep me sane.

As always, many, many thanks to my wonderful editor, Micki Nuding, who keeps me from disappearing down too many literary rabbit holes, and my ever-patient agent, Pamela Ahearn, for encouraging me to explore some of them.

VANISHED IN THE
IN THE
NIGHT

1

Whoever the poor bastard was, he'd been dead a long time. All Sergeant Zach McKnight of the Sacramento Police Department could see in the bottom of the hole were bone and some hair held together by a few shreds of cloth. Crap, was that a 49ers jersey? He hadn't seen one of those since 1989.

This case was beyond cold. It was freaking arctic.

His partner, Frank Rodriguez, came to stand beside him at the edge of the construction pit. "I think the first forty-eight hours have totally passed."

"Gee, Frank, what was your first clue? The nearly total decomposition? Or the rotted clothing?" Zach slid down the side of the pit to crouch next to the body, which rested on top of a ripped black plastic bag on the dirt. Morning dew shimmered a bit on the exposed bone and dampened the red-and-gold jersey.

A dump job, for sure. No way had this skeleton been buried in this pit. Somebody had put it there.

"I'm going with the decomp. That's always a dead giveaway." Frank pulled the collar of his coat up around his ears. It was chilly this early in the morning.

All around them crime-scene techs combed the area, gathering bits of garbage that would probably amount to nothing, but which had to be collected and cataloged. Outside the chain-link fence the construction workers loitered, trying to figure out if they were going to have an unexpected day off or not. Uniformed cops were asking questions and looking for familiar faces amidst the crowd that had gathered.

Zach scanned the remains. The likelihood that he'd find anything helpful was between slim and none, but the job was 80 percent going through the motions, 20 percent making a difference. On a *good* day. "Who found him?"

"Foreman." Frank slowly descended into the pit. "Swears on his mama's grave that it wasn't here at the end of the day yesterday. Then poof! It magically appeared overnight."

"Magically? He said that?" Zach glanced up with narrowed eyes. Did he have whack jobs on his hands? Satanists digging up dead bodies? Halloween was right around the corner, so it wasn't totally out of the question. At least he'd be looking at a crime that had happened recently enough that someone might care. As it was, would anybody give a rat's ass about this poor son of a bitch? Zach would be lucky if he could even get an ID on the dude.

"Of course not, I'm embellishing slightly to make the story more compelling, moron. He didn't swear on his mama's grave, either. Keep up, will you?" Frank folded a piece of Juicy Fruit into his mouth and crouched next to Zach. "At least he don't stink."

Amen to that. The lack of *eau de corpse* was about the only advantage to working a cold case. Pretty much everything else about them sucked. Most people couldn't remember what they were doing last Tuesday, much less some random day five, ten, or fifteen years before. Most of the forensic evidence had probably rotted along with the flesh off the body. "They have security cameras? A guard? Anything?"

"They're getting the tapes from the security cameras together for me now. There's a rent-a-cop who drives by all their sites in the area. I got his name and number. Uniforms are canvasing, but there's not much to canvas."

True enough. They were in the middle of downtown Sacramento; nobody lived down here. There were administration buildings, offices.

Frank shook his head. "It looks like a dump job to

me, but why bother dumping it after all these years? And why here?"

Good questions. Zach looked around. "What's this site going to be, anyway?" You didn't see much construction anymore; nobody had the cash.

"Some kind of medical office building."

Figured. The only people with money to build something these days would be doctors.

Something shiny near the leather belt that hadn't fully rotted caught Zach's eye. Reaching down with a pencil, he fished a metal chain out of the shredded fabric around what must have been hips.

Military dog tags flashed in the weak morning sunlight. They were dirty and a little corroded, but Zach was pretty sure a little cleaning would make them readable. His day brightened slightly. "I think IDing him just got a little easier."

"Nice," Frank said. "I'll call in the crime-scene geeks and see what else they can find."

The two of them scrambled out of the pit. Outside the construction fence, the media was starting to gather. Zach saw Marianne Robar from Channel 4 climbing out of a van with a giant satellite apparatus on top of it, and sighed. He couldn't really blame them; it was more interesting than covering what little weather Sacramento had. But it would be a pain in his butt on a case that would be a pain in the butt all on its own.

To the side of the news vans, he spotted Ben Ste-phenson from the *Sacramento Chronicle.* The guy had been born in the wrong era. He should have been working at a newspaper back in the days when report-ers smoked cigarettes and drank whiskey, not when they sat behind their desks and tapped computer keys all day.

Ben gave him a little-two finger salute. Zach nod-ded back. It was good to know that if he needed a friendly outlet in the media, he'd have one. He'd pay for it in insider information and a scoop or two, but the price wouldn't be exorbitant. He'd probably get a free beer out of it, too. Ben did an awful lot of his investigative reporting in bars.

Ducking the reporters yelling questions, Zach got into the unmarked car with Frank and headed back to the police station. They'd let the crime-scene techs do their thing and figure out what to do after that.

Meanwhile, he had the tags. Maybe this wouldn't be quite as big a pain in the ass as he'd thought.

Veronica Osborne saw flashing lights up ahead—it looked like J Street was blocked off. That was going to make the morning commute charming for most people. Luckily, she did the reverse-commute thing. An hour before the capital area filled up with government officials in suits and ties, she was on her way home from her eleven-to-seven shift in the emergency room.

It was one of the many things she loved about working the night shift. There was also getting to go to the bank and the grocery store during uncrowded daytime hours, and a great reason to leave blind dates early. The easy commute was just gravy on the fluffy mashed potatoes of her life.

As she drove closer to where the road was blocked off, she saw news vans. It must be something juicy. But no ambulances were screaming in or out, so it wasn't anything life threatening.

No one needed her to leap out of her car and stop the bleeding or administer CPR, so she might as well go home and get some sleep. She turned on her blinker and cut to the left. She'd swing around to Alhambra and avoid the whole mess. It didn't have anything to do with her, after all.

Several hours later, Zach stared at the computer screen in his cubicle at the Sacramento Police Department headquarters. He should never have told Frank it would be easy to identify the body; he knew better than to taunt the Investigation Gods. Pride goeth, indeed. Might as well have tugged on Superman's cape.

The dog tags had belonged to a Jamal Shelden. A

quick database search revealed that Shelden had been born in Sacramento to Lois Shelden on March 3, 1949. He died in the jungles of Vietnam on February 23, 1974, a few months shy of his twenty-fifth birthday. He was awarded the Purple Heart posthumously and his remains were buried at the Veterans Memorial Grove Cemetery in Yountville. Jamal's mother had died in a car accident in 1987. He had no siblings, and no father was listed on any of the paperwork Zach could find.

Zach supposed a quick drive by the cemetery was probably in order. He'd call the police department up in Yountville and ask them to check into it, though some-one probably would have mentioned it if a veteran had been dug up recently. Things like that tended to piss people off. He didn't have much hope that the bones at the bottom of the pit were those of Jamal Shelden.

So . . . whose were they? And if they hadn't been attached to Jamal Shelden, how the hell had his dog tags ended up in the construction pit?

Mr. Shelden's next of kin at the time of his death was his wife, Celeste Shelden, also of Sacramento. After bouncing around a few databases, Zach learned that she had died in 2003, after giving birth to two children. Max Shelden had been born in 1974, a few weeks after his father died in Vietnam. Celeste had remarried a George Osborne in 1979 and had given birth to a Veronica Osborne in 1983.

Before Zach could start looking those two up, his talkie buzzed on his hip. "Yeah?"

"Come to the AV room. I got something to show you," Frank said.

Zach pulled a roll of Tums from his desk drawer, pounded down two of them, then headed downstairs.

He found Frank in front of a television screen with a cup of bad station-house coffee and the previous night's surveillance tapes from the construction site. Frank looked up at Zach as he walked in, his eyes bloodshot from staring at the screen. "I found the dump."

Zach slapped his shoulder. "Nice."

"Yeah. Don't get too excited." Frank hit the play button.

A blurry image of the construction site came up in grainy black and white. Based on the angle of the view, Zach figured the camera must have been on top of the office trailer. After a couple of seconds, a figure wearing a dark hooded sweatshirt with the hood up and baggy, shapeless sweatpants came into the frame pulling something behind itself. Its burden looked like it was wrapped in a black plastic tarp or maybe a big yard-size garbage bag. The figure pulled it to the edge of the pit and rolled it in, brushed the dirt off its hands, and walked out of view.

"Not exactly Oscar material, is it?" Frank mused.

"I'm not giving it a thumbs-up." The tape gave them damn close to nothing. The figure was shapeless, featureless, sexless. Maybe, if they were lucky, one of the lab geeks could figure out approximate height and weight.

Frank snapped the tape off. "Whoever it was knew the security guard's schedule pretty well, too. Showed up about half an hour after he swung by and about forty-five minutes before he'd be by again. Optimum time for a dump. That's no accident."

"Not looking up at the camera was no accident, either." Zach rubbed his hands over his face. Not much about this smelled like an accident. He came back to the question Frank had asked him earlier. "Why dump this body there now? You think there's something special about the site? Or was it just convenient?"

"It's as mysterious as the Loch Ness monster," Frank pronounced.

Zach gave him a baleful look.

"Big Foot?"

Zach remained silent.

Frank shrugged. "I'm just sayin'."

"Where do you think the body was before this?" Zach sat on the desk next to Frank.

"How the hell should I know? Let's go talk to the lab rats and see if they found anything good we can chase down."

*   *   *

"I don't care what the dog tags say. There's no way this body belongs to a man of twenty-five." Eric Dinsmore shoved away from the autopsy table and rolled backward on his wheeled stool. Dinsmore was six feet and three inches of skinny forensic pathologist. Freckle faced and pale as a ghost, he also had a wicked jump shot that made him wildly popular with most of the squad. He also knew what he was talking about, and was accurate and efficient. "Whoever he was, he was still growing. The growth plates in the long bones hadn't fused yet. He was definitely under twenty-one and probably younger than that."

Zach wasn't surprised; he hadn't expected the bones to be Jamal's. "Any idea when he died?"

"Not yet. But I've got enough teeth that I should be able to get a positive ID eventually. I'll have more later today." Dinsmore turned back to his bench.

The dog tags had to mean something. Zach knew exactly where his dad's tags and old police shield were: in a box on top of his dresser—high on the list of what he'd grab on his way out the door if his apartment caught fire. "The guy had a kid I haven't been able to track down yet. The name was Max Shelden. See if that helps."

"Got it," Dinsmore said, scribbling the name on a pad of paper. "When did the kid die?"

"He hasn't, as far as I know. I didn't see any death certificate on file."

Dinsmore looked up at him. "The kid in the pit is really most sincerely dead."

"I noticed. The lack of actual flesh on the bones was a dead giveaway." He shrugged. "It's what I've got so far."

Dinsmore nodded. "I'll call when I get more information. There's a lot to process here."

"We'll take whatever you've got as soon as you've got it," Zach said as he and Frank headed toward the door.

They'd found him. They didn't know who he was yet, but they'd found him. Susan Tennant leaned back in her chair and snapped off the small TV in her office. The local news stations had been playing the tape of the shapeless body bag being loaded into the coroner's van over and over since eight o'clock that morning. Every news program throughout the day had led with it, and she wouldn't be surprised if they led with it again tomorrow.

Something else was bound to happen somewhere that would bounce Max off everyone's radar. It was the story of his life, in a way: too much attention when it would be better to be ignored, and not enough when he needed it.

With the TV off, the clinic was silent. Susan was the last one here. The staff was used to her being first in and last out, since it was her operation. Her baby.

She hadn't doubted that they would find Max right away; they could hardly have missed him. She couldn't have done much more to make sure of it, short of planting spotlights over him.

Of course, they'd been missing him for almost twenty years. Maybe "missing" wasn't the right word. Someone would have to have been searching for him to have missed him. No one had even been looking for Max. She shook her head. It was too easy for someone to fall through the cracks. Even now, with all the computers and linked databases, people slipped off the face of the earth and no one noticed. No one cared. Too many people were deemed dispensable. Half the people who came in and out of this clinic every day were people no one was looking for, who could cease to exist one day and no one would notice.

But *she* would notice. She would care. That was the vow she'd made to herself. Twenty years ago, she'd been too frightened and too stupid to act, but she'd tried to make up for it. She thought she had in many ways, but she could never fully erase what had happened all those years ago. It would always haunt her soul.

She was finally doing something for Max now, though. She had brought that terrible secret out of the grave along with those bones, and exposed it all to the world. The police would have to care now, too. Bones showing up in construction sites forced people to pay attention.

Susan sighed and pushed back from her old metal desk. There was nothing more she could do now. Not without destroying everything she'd worked so hard for—the clinic and all the people she helped. The legacy of her cowardice had ended up being a pretty good one.

It was the least she could do to make up for the things she hadn't done, for not having stopped the things that still haunted her dreams and made her wake up gasping and sweat drenched, heart racing. It didn't undo the things she'd done and seen done, but it helped balance things out. She hoped and prayed, so, anyway.

She also hoped it would stop more wrongs from being done. Some people should never be allowed to have power over others. Their true natures came out, and nature wasn't always pretty. It was often harsh and brutal.

"Rest in peace, Max," she whispered. "Finally, rest in peace."

2

Oh, joy of joys. Cops on her doorstep at seven o'clock in the evening. They were illuminated by her porch light and by the little blinking pumpkin lights she'd hung outside.

Veronica could tell the two men were cops without seeing their badges or their guns. The shoulders were a little too square. The jaws a little too set. Their attitudes a little too alert. She'd seen it enough in the emergency room.

She'd seen it enough away from work, too. She'd dated one or two cops, but no more. She and Tina had sworn off them. It was like giving up sweets or white flour. At first you felt deprived and a little desperate, but you knew you'd feel better in the end.

Then, of course, there was the time she spent with

cops because of her father. You hadn't really lived until you'd used your condo as collateral to bail your father out of jail. And this visit was probably about dear old Dad.

What had he done this time? Seven P.M. was a little early for a fight. He didn't usually loosen up his fists until ten o'clock or later—all the better to drag her out of work. It wasn't too early for a DUI, though. Dad occasionally laid down a base buzz at home before he ventured out to the bars. It was more economical.

Whatever it was, she wasn't going to be sucked in this time. She was going to stand firm. She'd had enough. She'd warned him and warned him and warned him. This was it, though. She was drawing her line in the sand.

The short dark-haired cop, who looked like a mournful basset hound, was sniffing around her stoop as if flying monkeys might pop out of her Halloween decorations. The taller one wasn't as jumpy. Maybe he got it all out at the gym, where he clearly spent a lot of time.

The tall one rang the bell again. Maybe she could pretend not to be home?

He rang a third time. Tenacious bastard, wasn't he?

Veronica opened the door. "Can I help you?" She pulled her sweater tighter around herself and crossed her arms over her chest.

"Veronica Osborne?" the short one asked.

She nodded. "You got her."

"Could we come in?"

She took a deep breath. "Look, I don't know what he did this time, and I don't care. He's a grown man. He can take care of his own troubles. I'm not bailing him out."

Both men went carefully blank faced. "What him do you think we're here about?" the tall one asked.

Could she have this wrong? She knew that blank-faced look. She'd said something unexpected, and they were not reacting until they figured it out. Total cop behavior: assess the situation, give nothing away.

"My father. George Osborne. This isn't about him?"

"No, ma'am," the tall one said. "This is in regards to your brother, Max Shelden."

"Max?" she gasped and took a step backward. "If it's about Max, I guess you'd better come in."

Zach glanced around the living room. Would any of the furniture hold his weight? It all was made out of that woven wicker stuff he associated with fancy patios. He chose the chair by the end of the glass-topped coffee table. Sure enough, it creaked beneath him as he lowered himself into it. If Veronica Osborne had a boyfriend, he was a little guy.

She looked like the kind of girl who would have a boyfriend, the sort of girl who would have a regular date for Saturday night. She was cute. No more than five foot four. Button nosed, with a spray of freckles, and big hazel eyes peeping out from under reddish-brown bangs.

He hadn't been surprised when Eric Dinsmore had told him his hunch about Max Shelden had played out. If anyone would have a man's dog tags, it'd be his son. So if the bones couldn't belong to Jamal, they probably belonged to Max. How or why the bones and the tags ended up in that construction pit still eluded him, but an investigation like this was all about baby steps.

Dinsmore had gotten the ID straight from the dental records. There were a buttload more tests to be done, but it was pretty certain that the bones in the pit belonged to Max Shelden, son of Celeste and Jamal, brother of Veronica. According to Eric Dinsmore, Max had died when he was somewhere between sixteen and twenty-one, which made the bones somewhere between thirteen and twenty-one years old. He'd attended McClatchy High School, but apparently hadn't graduated.

Veronica Osborne, the half sister, was the closest they could find to a next of kin. Luckily, she'd been easy to locate. A little *too* easy. A woman who lived alone should consider security more seriously. She'd been in the freaking white pages, for God's sake.

"You found Max?" she asked. "Where is he? Where has he been?"

"Maybe you should sit down," Frank suggested from where he sat on the sofa.

She shook her head. "Please, can I see him? Is he in trouble?" She twisted her hands. No ring. So if there was a boyfriend, it wasn't serious.

"Ms. Osborne—" Frank started.

"Could you just cut to the chase?" She threw her hands in the air. "Please?"

Frank glanced at him and grimaced. Zach rolled his eyes. Rodriguez could take down a belligerent drunk, bust in a door, and drive a squad car 110 miles an hour through traffic, but give someone bad news? Especially a woman? He turned into a whimpering puppy.

"There's no easy way to tell you this." Zach leaned forward and braced his elbows on his knees. "A body was found this morning in a construction site in downtown Sacramento. We have reason to believe that the remains might belong to your brother, Max Shelden."

The hands flew to her mouth and the hazel eyes got even bigger. "Oh." She swayed a little.

Zach stood up and led her to a chair. "I'm terribly sorry for your loss."

"No. Oh, no. Oh, poor Max. What happened? How did he . . . die?" She choked a little on the last word. Her eyes brimmed.

"We don't know yet. It might be a while before we figure all of that out." Zach looked around and saw a tissue box on the coffee table. He grabbed it and handed it to her.

"Do you need me to . . . do I have to . . . identify him or something?" She looked up at Zach, her face full of questions.

He squatted down next to her so she wouldn't have to crane her neck to look at him. "He's been, uh, gone for a while. There's really nothing for you to identify. The medical examiner will be making the ID based on dental records."

She blinked rapidly. "I don't even remember what dentist Mama took him to. I went to Dr. Stanzig, so maybe he did, too, as a kid. I don't know who he went to later."

"Later?" According to Dinsmore, Shelden had died when he was still a kid. There shouldn't be a "later."

"Yeah. You know, after he ran away."

This wasn't making sense. It didn't help that her brain was buzzing with a white noise that made it seem like the police officer's words were coming from far away, distorted with static. It wasn't as if she hadn't considered that this might be a possibility—that someday some official person would show up on her doorstep and tell her Max was dead. She had acknowledged that it was possible that Max would never come back.

Somehow she'd thought she'd know, though. She'd known the moment their mother died. Veronica had been asleep in the chair next to the hospital bed, and it was as if she'd been slapped awake when the rasp of her mother's labored breathing finally ceased. It wasn't the absence of noise that woke her from her fitful sleep, but a feeling—a new absence in her life, a new rock to carry around in her chest. She had known the instant it had happened.

She'd really thought the same thing would have happened with Max, that there would have been some ripple in her soul when he was gone forever.

Veronica had hoped, dreamed, that one day Max would show up on her doorstep, arms open wide with forgiveness and love. If Max *was* going to find her, he probably would have done it a long time ago. Still, she always listed her telephone number, even though most of her coworkers didn't, especially the women who lived alone. People fixated on nurses in unhealthy ways sometimes.

But she'd wanted to make herself easy for Max to

find. Plug her name into Google. Pick up the white pages at the local library and flip it open to O. She'd be there, waiting for her prodigal brother to come home and be greeted with a feast.

She could quit all that now. Change her number, her name. Move to a different city. Max was never going to come find her. Never going to come home and forgive her.

"I'm sorry. Why isn't there anything for me to identify?" She shoved her bangs aside and looked into the steady, dark eyes of the detective crouched in front of her. What was his name? McKnight?

"The medical examiner is still working on the time of death. It's been . . . a while." He took her hand.

His was big and warm and a little rough. Patients always teased her about her hands. Blocks of ice on the best of days. They felt brittle now, as if they might break.

The cop let her think over what he'd said about Max being dead for a long time. The little one was getting antsy, but the big one with the deep, dark eyes was just breathing with her. She swallowed hard and stilled herself. She knew how to focus. She was quite capable of pushing her emotions into the background and functioning.

Had he said a construction site in downtown Sacramento? Had that been the flashing lights she'd skirted this morning on her way home? Had that been where they'd found Max? Not only had she not felt anything when he'd died, she'd been that close to where he was buried and only felt irritation at traffic being rerouted.

"What can I tell you? What can I do to help?" Her voice sounded thick and clogged, but steady. She'd shed her tears in private after they left. She didn't know anyone who would share her grief with her. She'd release it alone. Like always.

"Do you remember the last time you saw Max?" the shorter one asked. Rodriguez. His name was Rodriguez.

Did she remember the last time she saw Max? Yes, of course she did. She'd never forget it. The men had come in the middle of the night. They'd hauled Max out of his bed. He'd fought them, of course. What boy wouldn't have? Max had been tall and broad shouldered already at sixteen. Not quite a man yet, but on his way there. He'd done some damage.

Veronica's heart pounded as she remembered the damage the men had inflicted back. It hadn't taken long for three grown men to subdue one adolescent boy. She remembered the kick to the ribs that one of them had administered after Max was already face-down on the floor. Their mother had screamed, only to be hauled back by Veronica's father. He'd told her to shush, that it was for Max's own good.

Veronica was only seven, but even she knew he was lying.

They had cuffed Max's hands behind his back and hauled him in pajama pants and stockinged feet to the door. He never stopped fighting, so they had to drag him. As they took him out the door, he turned back and begged, "Mama, don't let them take me. Mama, don't do this. You know this isn't right, Mama. Don't let them."

But Mama had turned away, like she always did. Dad got his way and Max was gone. Had he known Max would be gone for good? Had her mother? Would it have changed anything? She put her face down in her hands, her heart like a rock in her chest.

"Veronica? Ms. Osborne?" It was McKnight again, quiet but tenacious, dragging her back to the here and now. "Do you? Do you remember the last time you saw your brother?"

She nodded. "The last time I saw my brother was when they came to get him." She couldn't force any more words past the clog in her throat.

Again, she got the carefully blank cop face. It was enough to bring her back to earth. "Do you want a glass of water? I need a glass of water." Whiskey was also tempting, but smacked of how her mother and father would have dealt with the situation. If she had a life motto, it was to never, ever deal with any situation the way her mother or father would.

McKnight let go of her hand and stood. "Sure. Water would be great."

"None for me," Rodriguez said from the couch.

Veronica stumbled into the kitchen, hoping to be away from their prying eyes for a second or two, but McKnight was right on her tail. She filled two glasses with ice from the freezer and then water from the tap and handed him one.

"You're what? A sergeant?" She took a long drink of water, letting the ice-cold liquid slide down her throat, closing her eyes and willing the buzzing in her head down to a manageable level.

"Yup," he said and drank, too.

Was he mirroring her to make her comfortable? She did that sometimes with flustered patients. She would stand with the same posture they had or sit with her legs crossed the way theirs were crossed. It was somehow reassuring, calming to them. Was McKnight manipulating her, or was it instinctive?

It didn't matter—she was calming down enough to think straight.

"The last time I saw Max was when the men from the Sierra School for Boys came and took him. It was 1990. Sometime in the spring. I'm sorry I can't be more helpful. I was only seven."

"He never came home?" Rodriguez asked from the kitchen doorway.

When had he gotten there? Veronica took a step backward and pressed against the wooden cabinets at her back. She wished they'd both take a few steps away and quit crowding her. "No. He never came home. He ran away from there less than a year later. Once he turned eighteen, Daddy said it wouldn't matter if we found him again or not. He'd be an adult and out on his own, anyway."

McKnight nodded. "So he was a runaway? From some kind of school?"

"Sierra School for Boys. It was up near Blairsden. It was, well, like a reform school, I guess." Veronica rubbed her eyes. "I don't think it was a real juvenile detention facility. It was more like one of those places you send a bad kid before he ends up in juvie, a reform school."

McKnight scribbled some notes down on a pad he'd taken out of his pocket. "So Max was a bad kid? He'd been in trouble?"

"That came out wrong. Max wasn't an angel, but he wasn't exactly a problem, either. He was just a kid, doing the stuff that kids do. He and my dad, they didn't . . . they didn't get along too well. It made little problems seem bigger."

"So he wouldn't have a record, or anything?" Rodriguez asked.

Veronica shook her head.

"So he was sent up to this Sierra School in 1990 and ran away in 1991. Is there anybody who might be able to nail the dates down a little more for us?" he continued.

Hoo, boy, here we go. "Possibly my dad, but Max isn't exactly a topic he likes to discuss."

Zach looked up from the notepad and nailed her with those big brown eyes. "Your dad's the one you thought we were here about when you answered the door."

"Yeah."

"He got a record?" Rodriguez asked, still from the doorway.

The guy liked his records, didn't he? Veronica shrugged. "Yeah, he does. Nothing major. He's had to pay some fines and spend a night or two in the drunk tank."

Keep it even. Stay focused. You can get through this if you stay in the moment. Don't relive the hearings in your head. Don't replay the mental pictures of your father stumbling out of a jail cell, reeking of vomit and urine. Stay here in the clean kitchen with the nice police officers.

"And he didn't get along with Max," McKnight said.

"No. He didn't. Max was my mother's son from a . . . a previous marriage." That made it sound so

civilized, so modern. So entirely different from how
it had really been.

"So he was your half brother." McKnight's gaze on
her was unwavering.

She'd always hated that. Half of Max wasn't her
brother. *All* of him was. She was certainly all his sister,
with her whole heart. That wasn't what the cop was asking, though. There wasn't a check box on a form for how
much a little girl loved her big brother. She nodded.

"What was the beef between him and your dad?"
Rodriguez came fully into the kitchen.

She blew out a sigh. "I wish I knew. From the time
I can remember, they were always fighting. I don't
think Dad was all that crazy about raising someone
else's son, especially one who was part African American. Max's biological father was black. He died in
Vietnam before Max was even born."

The cops exchanged glances. She knew that look;
they already knew all about Max's dad. They'd made
her hop through those hoops just to confirm the information for them.

"So after Max ran away, what did your parents do
to try to find him?" Rodriguez pulled out a chair and
sat down at the kitchen table.

"I wish I could tell you. I was only eight. I remember my mother crying and my father yelling." Of
course, that could be pretty much any day from her

childhood. But it didn't matter now. Max was dead. Her mother was dead. She'd learned to deal with her father, and was trying to learn not to let him get too close. She wasn't always so successful.

"Any chance we could have your father's contact information? It would help us narrow down the time frame we're looking at."

Veronica rattled off her father's address and phone number.

McKnight snapped his notepad shut. "Thanks for your help. If you think of anything else that might help us figure out when Max ran away from school, or where he might have gone, would you contact me?" He pulled a card out of a case and handed it to her.

"Of course."

Did she have anything that might help? "Do you want a picture of Max?" she asked. "Would that help at all?"

"We were gonna ask your father for one," Rodriguez said.

She shook her head. "He won't have one. I have the only photos of Max that are left. I'll get you one."

"A little jumpy, isn't she?" Rodriguez leaned against the kitchen counter while they waited for Veronica to bring back the picture of Max.

"She just got some heavy bad news. What do you want her to do? Go all Zen?" Even though she hadn't seen her brother since she was little, she had obviously loved him. It sounded like she might have been the only one who had.

"I'm not talking about that. I meant about here in the kitchen. You see the way she backed up against the cabinets when we followed her in here?" Rodriguez asked.

"A woman alone with two men. She might have felt threatened."

"Two *cops*—we're the good guys. Chicks aren't supposed to be afraid of us. They're supposed to dig us."

Not everyone would appreciate that. "You think she's got a problem with cops? Maybe she thinks we're picking on the father?"

Rodriguez shook his head. "Nah. I don't think it's cops. I think she's got a problem with men."

Zach allowed himself to remember Veronica's backside as she'd walked away. It had been hard not to notice it, encased in well-fitting jeans, and he was not made of stone. "That would be a damn shame."

Frank nodded his agreement. "I bet the father's going to be a piece of work."

"That would be a sucker bet." Her defiant stand at the front door had told him plenty about her father, and her description of his record filled him in on the rest. He'd met dozens of men like George Osborne.

"Yeah, I think she was sugarcoating it. I bet he's even worse than she made him sound. So, you ever heard of this Sierra School for Boys?"

Zach shook his head. "Can't say as I have. You?"

"Nope, and I've heard of most of those kinds of schools. We bust enough of their graduates. I'm betting it's not around anymore."

Zach's view of those schools wasn't as jaded as Frank's. Some of them really worked. He was living proof of that.

3

Veronica pulled the box out from underneath her bed, removed the lid, and unwrapped the album from the sweater she had wrapped around it. She didn't need to hide it anymore, since she'd moved into the condo, but it was habit. She'd kept her treasures hidden for most of her life. It had been the only way to keep them safe. She doubted she'd ever stop hiding them now.

The cover was bubble-gum pink and was emblazoned with the words YOU AND ME in acid green. She ran her hand over the scratched cover and drew in a shaky breath. There was no time for this kind of stupid sentimentality now. There were cops in her kitchen. They were waiting. Still, she hesitated. What good would an old picture do them anyway?

She flipped the book open and found the picture she was looking for. Sixteen-year-old Max, all gangly arms and giant Adam's apple, building a sand castle with her at Capitola. She would never forget that day. They'd played in the waves, built sand castles, and drunk chocolate milk shakes. It had been just her and Max and Mama. She couldn't remember now where her father had been that day. If he'd been drunk and angry, it was with someone else. The photo had been taken three weeks before the men from the Sierra School came for Max in the middle of the night.

She peeled back the clear protective sheet and pulled the photo off the page. Then she rewrapped the album, tucked it back inside the box, and slid the box under the bed. It was too precious to leave out, especially now. It was all she had left of her brother. And whose fault was that anyway?

She bowed her head, laid it against the bed for a moment, and closed her eyes against the rush of tears. Max wasn't coming home. Ever.

There would be no homecoming. No joyous re-union. No forgiveness. She was stuck with that rock in her chest forever.

When Veronica walked back into the kitchen, she was even paler than when she'd left. Wordlessly, she handed Zach a photo. It showed a light-skinned African-American boy with a little blond girl on a beach.

"Is that you with him?" he asked.

She nodded. "It's the last photo I have of him."

"Thanks. This'll help a lot." He couldn't take his eyes off the two kids, clearly having a great time. There were probably a dozen or so photos at his mom's house of him and his sisters, looking just like this. Smiling up at the camera, enjoying the day, not thinking about anything else. Certainly not thinking that he would end up as a set of bones at a construction site. "Do you know why your parents sent him away?"

Everything about her went still. He'd touched some kind of nerve, that was for sure.

"They, uh, found marijuana in his room." She looked down.

A residential school for a little bit of weed? That seemed harsh, especially in the early nineties. "That was it?"

"It was enough for Dad. He said we were doing Max a favor by getting him away from bad influences before it got any worse." She turned away and began to restack some envelopes on the counter, her movements stiff and jerky.

"Do you have anybody you want us to call? Or

that you could call so you don't have to be alone right now?"

She turned around and smiled at him and shook her head. "That's okay. I have to go to work in a little while. Besides, it's not like this is so terribly shocking. He's been missing for twenty years. I knew it was possible that he was dead. I'd just always hoped . . ." Her voice trailed off.

The family always hoped. Everybody talked about giving the family closure when someone was missing, and finding a body did that, in a way. They could stop worrying. They could stop waiting. They could start grieving.

But it also killed all the hoping, and maybe having a shred of hope alive in your heart was worth the worrying.

"Where do you work?" Rodriguez asked.

"I'm a nurse in the emergency room over at St. E's. I work the night shift." She glanced up at the clock. It was close to eight o'clock now. "I have to be there in a few hours."

"Okay, well, thanks again for this photo. We'll make a copy and get your original back to you as soon as possible. We'll also keep you posted when we learn anything concrete. In the meantime, feel free to call if you can think of anything."

She nodded and showed them to the door.

As they walked to the car, Zach looked back at the condo, strewn with fake spiderwebs and strings of pumpkin lights.

"I say we go talk to the stepfather next," Rodriguez said.

Zach got in the car. "Damn straight."

They were gone. Veronica sat at the kitchen table and laid her hands flat against the wood, trying to soak up its stillness and stability. How much more horrible was this going to get? McKnight had said Max had been dead for a while. A year? Ten years? They probably didn't know themselves yet. Had he been trying to get back to her when he'd somehow ended up in that construction site? Or had he still been running away?

Would she ever know?

If there wasn't enough left of Max for her to ID, was there enough to start an investigation? Veronica didn't even know what to hope for. Knowing he was dead was bad enough. Having to probe back into those days when he was still around? Pretty much the opposite of priceless.

Some kids learned to block traumatic memories, and she often wished she was one of those. It would be nice to settle a hazy curtain over her childhood.

She didn't need it blocked out entirely; she'd learned some valuable, if unpleasant, lessons. How to calm an angry drunk. What to feed a person with the mother of all hangovers. When to duck and when to hide. She sure as hell didn't need to remember it in the kind of detail that she did, though. She didn't need to replay it in her dreams. She didn't need to flash on it at work when things got crazy.

Most of the time, she kept the door shut tight on the past. At the moment, that wasn't so easy. Images flooded back to her: Her father's face distorted with rage, spittle flying from his lips as he roared at Max. Max's head snapping to the side after a hard slap, his screams when his arm was twisted up behind his back. The racial slurs. The insults. Her mother's tears. Her brother's shame and quiet courage.

Things had calmed down some right after Max went away. Her father had seemed harder to set off. There'd actually been some family dinners where nothing had gotten thrown at anyone and no one had ended up in tears. It hadn't lasted, though. Dad never went after Mama with the ferocity that he'd gone after Max, but Veronica understood now that the focus of the anger was really secondary to the anger itself. Something burned inside her father. Something hard and fetid and nasty.

She hadn't understood that as an eight-year-old.

She'd been terrified that Dad might send Mama away next and the only target left in the house would be her. The slight nausea of shame crept up her throat. Her mother had been a human shield for her; could anyone blame her for dulling the pain with booze?

At first it was wine. Then Celeste had discovered vodka, which is not nearly as odorless as everyone says. By the time Veronica was thirteen, she could recognize when her mother was on a bender by the scent when she walked into the house.

Eventually the booze had killed Celeste—and it had probably killed Max, too. If she hadn't been drinking, maybe Mama might have looked for Max. Maybe it wouldn't have been too late. Maybe they would have found him before he ended up nearly unidentifiable and alone in a construction site.

Maybe he would have told Veronica that it was all okay—that he didn't blame her for anything.

She finally laid her head down on the table and cried.

It was well past dark by the time Zach and Frank got to Veronica's father's house. The porch light was off, but there was a light on inside and the blue flicker of a television set. The yard needed to be raked, but

Zach liked the smell of the leaves as they crunched underneath his feet.

Frank kicked the leaves aside as he marched up the steps and rang the doorbell. He jingled the change in his pocket and glanced over at Zach as they waited. "Takin' him long enough."

"It's not like he's expecting us," Zach observed. They hadn't called ahead because they'd wanted to see Osborne's reaction to his stepson's death up close and personal.

Frank rang a second time. This time Zach heard footsteps heading toward the door.

The porch light was flipped on and the door opened. According to his driver's license, George Osborne was in his late fifties. He hadn't exactly aged well. He still had a full head of hair, liberally sprinkled with gray, but it didn't look clean. His face was slack and heavily lined and a lit cigarette dangled from his fingers. His paunch stretched the T-shirt he wore, and even in the dim light of the entryway, Zach could see the network of spiderlike veins across Osborne's face. That might have to do with the beer bottle that dangled from his hand. Not exactly a poster child for clean living; more of a terrible warning than a shining example.

"What do you want?" Osborne leaned against the door frame and looked from Zach to Frank.

"We'd like to have a word with you, Mr. Osborne." Zach flashed his badge. "May we come in?"

Osborne didn't budge. "Not without a warrant." He gave a little snort, as if the situation was funny.

Frank stepped up onto the top step so he was toe-to-toe with Osborne. "You got something to hide in there?"

Osborne didn't move a muscle. "Maybe I do. Maybe I don't. Either way, you're not coming in." He turned his head to the side and spat into the bushes.

"It's about your stepson," Zach said.

Osborne looked confused for a moment. "My what?"

"Your stepson," Zach repeated. "Max Shelden."

Osborne's eyebrows went up a little and he stood up straighter. "I haven't heard from that kid for twenty years at least. I got nothin' to do with him." He moved back into the house and started to shut the door.

Frank stuck his foot in the doorway. "That's because he's been dead about that long."

Osborne froze for a second and then said, "That would explain it."

"Can we come in and talk to you about it?" Zach asked again, stepping up behind Frank.

Osborne looked at Zach, narrowing his eyes a bit. "I still don't see any warrant."

"You really want us to come back with one?" Zach leaned in. He was tired of the crap.

Osborne was a tough guy—he got it. But if they all had to drop trou right now and pull out rulers, Zach would win because he had the badge and the gun. He knew it. Frank knew it and clearly Osborne knew it, too, because he decided to back off. Classic bully. Zach would bet his left nut that Osborne only picked on people he thought he could beat. People who were smaller and weaker. People who backed down in the face of confrontation or were bound by rules and regulations. Zach had seen Osborne's kind before plenty of times. He didn't like playing their games and he didn't like them.

"All right already. You don't have to make a federal case out of it." Osborne stepped back from the door and walked inside. Zach and Frank followed.

It wasn't a bad place. A little on the small side, but what wasn't in California? It wasn't much different from the house Zach had grown up in. Osborne walked directly into the living room. Zach could see the dining room and kitchen beyond it. He assumed that was where the faint sickly smell of garbage was coming from.

The place wasn't immaculate, but it wasn't trashed, either. There were some newspapers on the floor by a well-worn recliner, a plate on the end table next to it. But the dishes weren't piled up.

"So the little shit's been dead all this time?" Osborne eased into the recliner, which sat directly in front of the television. He didn't bother turning it off. The Kings were up for once.

"Where'd you think he was?" Frank asked.

Osborne shrugged. "The kid turned eighteen a month after he ran off. He wasn't my responsibility anymore. The wife cried about him every now and then, mainly on his birthday, but that was about it. Truth was, it was more peaceful around here with him gone." He turned away to look at the game.

Zach ground his teeth. "So when was the last time you saw Max?"

Osborne turned back toward him and blinked a few slow blinks, almost as if he'd forgotten they were there. Maybe the man was drunker than he looked. "You seriously expect me to remember something that happened twenty years ago?" He turned back to the TV as if the question wasn't worth thinking about.

"Yeah, I do. It was the last time you saw your son. I expect it to stick in your head." Zach kept his voice pleasant. It was an effort.

"Stepson," Osborne corrected. "Not my kid."

"You married his mother. He was your responsibility," Zach shot back.

Osborne came up out of his chair. It was meant to be an aggressive move, but the waver in his balance made it more pathetic than threatening. "And

I met my responsibilities. I put a roof over the brat's head. I put food on the table. What do I get in return? A juvenile delinquent bringing drugs into my house where my little girl could find them.

"You want to know the last time I saw him? It was when they came and took him up to that school. I never laid eyes on him again after that, and that's just fine with me."

Frank glanced over at Zach, eyes narrowed. "What kind of drugs?"

Osborne sat back down and waved the question away as if it was inconsequential. "Marijuana. In a Baggie with a pipe and some matches."

"So you never went to visit him up at the Sierra School for Boys?"

"Nope. The wife did once. Came back weeping and wailing. I wouldn't let her go again after that." Osborne's attention was back on the game. The Kings had let their lead dwindle to six points. Typical.

"How long was he there?" Frank asked.

Osborne shrugged. "A year. Maybe a little more. Why's it matter?"

"We're trying to nail down a time frame here," Zach said. "Your daughter indicated that Max had run away from the Sierra School."

Osborne looked at him sharply. "My daughter? You've talked to Ronnie?"

"If you mean Veronica Osborne, yeah. She was listed as next of kin after your wife."

"What'd she say?" Osborne sat very still.

"Not much. She seemed pretty shocked." And sad, and a little frightened. Beyond that moment of hesitation at the front door, Max's death didn't seem to shock Osborne in the slightest.

Osborne shook his head. "She worshipped that kid. It was part of why I had to get him out of the house. He was a bad influence. She was a little girl. She doesn't know anything about this. I don't want you talking to her again."

"So when exactly did Max run away from Sierra?"

"I told you, it was around twenty years ago. What do you think, I made a notation in my diary? 'Dear Diary,'" Osborne said in a singsong voice. "'Today I heard that my piece-of-shit stepson took a powder from the place that was supposed to be kicking some sense into his good-for-nothing head.'"

"How 'bout you, Osborne? You ever try to kick sense into Max's head? You knock him around a little?" Zach got into his face.

"Maybe." Osborne didn't meet Zach's eyes. "No more than was necessary."

It was damn tempting to knock some sense into Osborne's head, but the satisfaction wouldn't be worth the consequences.

"So you never saw Max after he went to Sierra? He didn't come back here after he ran away? Maybe stop by to ask for some money?" Where else did the kid have to go? Blairsden was a far piece away. It couldn't have been easy to get away from there.

Osborne snorted. "The kid wasn't stupid. He knew if he showed his face around here, I'd kick his ass back up the hill with pleasure."

"So you've got no clue as to exactly when Max went missing?" Frank asked.

"You want a clue? Go dig it up yourself. You're the detective, aren't you? Go detect. Start with detecting the missing persons report that the school filed." His eyes still glued to the television, Osborne waved his hand as if to dismiss them.

"A report was filed? Up in Blairsden?" Zach hadn't seen that when they ran Max's name through the databases, but not everything from back then was computerized.

Osborne spared them another glance. "Wherever. They filed one at the school. Said it was protocol or something."

Zach had a nagging suspicion the man knew more than he was letting on, but they weren't going to get anything more from Osborne.

"Thank you for your time, Mr. Osborne. We're very sorry for your loss. We'll see ourselves out." He turned to go.

"Don't let the door hit your ass on your way out," Osborne called after them.

"Classy," Frank said as they got into the car.

"True that," Zach said. "What do you think? Could he have done it?"

Frank leaned back in his seat and loosened his tie. "Kid could have shown up with his hand out for money. Osborne could have taken a swing. Maybe things got out of hand and the kid ended up dead. Doesn't explain how he ended up in that construction site, though."

"Even if Osborne didn't see the kid, maybe the wife did. Maybe she gave him some money. Or the sister," Zach added.

Frank shook his head. "The sister would have told us. Osborne, though, I'm not so sure. You have a feeling he knew more than he was letting on?"

Zach nodded and buckled his seat belt. "I did. Let's go back to the station and check out Osborne's record. Then let's run it past the lieutenant. Seems like we might have enough for a warrant."

"Sounds like a plan." Rodriguez tossed Zach his cell phone. "Text Sheila for me. Tell her I won't be home."

"Okay, but I'm not sexting for you."

"Asking you to tack xoxo to the end of a text is not sexting, Zach. You're such a prude." Frank started the engine and pulled away. "Here's what I don't get about Osborne, though. If you didn't want to put up with a woman's kid, why marry her in the first place? There's lots of fish in the sea. Why not hook up with one who doesn't have a kid? Or at least doesn't have one who bugs the crap out of you just by being the color he is?"

Zach shook his head. "I don't have an answer for that. Why does anybody marry anyone? It's a mystery."

"Spoken like a true bachelor. Just you wait. You'll meet the right one someday. Then you'll be building picket fences in your head and you'll understand why men get married."

"Just like you, Frankie?"

"Just like me."

"Which time exactly? The first one? Number two? Or number three?" Zach razzed him.

"All of them, Zach, all of them. What can I say? I give my heart too easily."

It wasn't his heart that Frank gave away with such abandon, it was another body part entirely. In all fairness, he did seem pretty happy with number three. Zach had never met number one, but two he had met. He might still have the scars from it, too. Doreen was a hard, hard woman.

4

Veronica walked up the steps to her father's porch, a McDonald's bag in one hand and a coffee cup in the other. She'd gotten off work at seven, driven through McDonald's to pick up breakfast for her and her dad, then come straight here. She wasn't sure if the cops had talked to him or not yet, but either way, she figured she should stop by.

It was something of a routine anyway. She showed up once or twice a week, usually with a sausage egg McMuffin and a black coffee. She figured the booze would kill him long before the fat and cholesterol did. He already had the facial veins and the swollen nose of the habitual drinker, not to mention the distended stomach. She hated to think of what an ultrasound of his liver would look like, so she just didn't. She had long since perfected the mental equivalent of plugging her ears and chanting "la la la."

She knocked on the door, even though she didn't expect an answer. It was a courtesy and a reminder to herself that she didn't live here anymore. She could walk out the door anytime she wanted and she never had to come back. She was here by choice. Sort of.

She'd left at eighteen, despite her mother's begging and her father's threatening. She'd only gone to San Jose to attend nursing school, but you would have thought she'd been leaving for Borneo, never to return, the way her mother had wept. And after all her father's bluster and threats to cut off support—as if she'd ever expected any—he'd gone silent. As she'd walked out the door that August, he'd growled, "You'll be back."

He'd been right about that, although not in the way he'd meant it. Her mother had been diagnosed with pancreatitis only a few months after Veronica graduated from nursing school. She'd moved back to Sac to look after her.

It hadn't done any good. Her mother had kept on drinking and ended up killing off most of her pancreas, developing an infection and dying as Veronica sat next to her bed. She should have moved back to the Bay Area then—it would have been the moment to make a clean break. But somehow she hadn't. She'd gotten a job here at St. Elizabeth's, made friends, and bought a condo.

Veronica knew what compelled her to stay here; she'd gone through Al-Anon and a few stints of therapy. He was still her father. Despite everything, she wanted to love him, even if he made it damn near impossible. She could only do what she could do. So she stopped by with McDonald's every so often, called a couple of times a week, but generally kept a safety zone between them. Kind of an emotional DMZ. It was what she had to do to be able to live with herself. It probably wasn't good for her. Hell, it probably wasn't good for her dad. But without her, he'd have either hit bottom by now or gotten himself killed. Or both.

She juggled the bag and the coffee and pulled her keys out and opened the door. "Dad," she called. "It's me. Ronnie."

No one else called her that anymore. Just him.

"You bring coffee?" she heard him call from up-stairs.

When had she walked into this house without coffee in the past ten years? "Yeah, Dad, I got coffee. And breakfast."

"I'll be right out."

She pulled the food out of the bag and set the wrapped sandwiches on place mats on the kitchen table. Then she started her rounds.

First she emptied the garbage from the kitchen and the hall bathroom. She could hear the toilet flush in the master bathroom. Then she gathered the piled-up newspapers and magazines and catalogs from the living room and dumped them into the recycling bin. She'd run the vacuum cleaner around the place after they'd eaten. She could hear the water running now; he'd be out in a minute or two.

She started gathering up the bottles. It was almost like a perverse kind of Easter-egg hunt. Where had Daddy hidden her treats this time? Oh, look, it was an empty bottle of Early Times under the sofa. And what was that peeking out from behind the dusty silk plant in the corner of the living room? Oh! It was an empty Bushmills bottle. She found only four bottles. It could have been worse, she supposed. Hell, it *had* been worse at other times.

"What brings you around?" her father growled as he stomped into the room.

He didn't look good. His eyes were red and his face looked puffy; his hands trembled at his sides. Still, he was standing and he looked sober.

She countered with her own question. "Have the police been here?"

He nodded and headed into the kitchen, sitting down and unwrapping a sandwich without waiting for Veronica to join him.

She followed behind him. "And?"

He chewed and swallowed. Washed down the bite with a sip of coffee. "And what?"

Her McMuffin had already gone cold. She set it down. "They told you? They told you about Max?"

Her father looked up at her. "Yeah. They told me. Been dead this whole time. Your mother wasted a lot of tears on that kid." He took another bite of his sandwich and made a face. "Cold."

Veronica tightened her lips. The tears hadn't been wasted. Self-pitying, maybe. But there was no point in arguing with him about it. She picked up their sandwiches and put them in the microwave. "I wonder what happened. I wonder how he died."

"Nothing that kid ever did made sense to me. I doubt whatever happened to him'll make sense, either."

The microwave beeped and Veronica brought the sandwiches back to the table. "We're not talking about some random kid here, Dad. We're talking about my brother."

"Half brother." Osborne picked up the sandwich and dropped it immediately. "Too hot."

"My brother," she said again.

"Whatever." Osborne drank a little more coffee.

Let it go, Veronica. Don't react.

Her father must have seen something in her eyes, though. "Oh, here we go again. Are you going to preach the gospel of St. Max to me again, Ronnie? Because I'm not interested." He pushed back from the table and walked into the living room.

Veronica swept the remains of their breakfast into a garbage can. "That's it, then? That's all you have to say?" Her voice was calm and steady.

"Christ, Ronnie, what do you want me to say? The kid was no good from the start. He ran off. Now he's dead. There ain't much more to it than that."

"He died out there, maybe alone. Probably frightened. Doesn't it bother you? Even a little?" She shoved the garbage can back under the sink. To hell with it.

"No. It doesn't. I'll tell you why, too, Veronica Gail. That kid was no good from the second he was conceived."

"That's not true." Max had been funny and kind and patient.

He waved her away. "You don't know. You don't remember. You were a little girl."

"I remember plenty, Dad." It was both her blessing and her curse. It kept her from following in her parents' footsteps. On the other hand, it kept her up a lot of nights and maintained a steady burn in her stomach that was more than likely the beginning of an ulcer.

It wasn't as if her childhood had been that horrible. She saw plenty worse nearly every day in the emergency room. Her father had never raped her or pimped her out to earn money for the family.

But Max had been backhanded at the dinner table so often that Veronica had thought that one of the family members getting slapped was the way everyone knew that dinner was over. And that hiding in the closet until Daddy wasn't mad anymore was what most little girls did.

George and Celeste Osborne had been what Veronica and her colleagues at the emergency room often referred to as "volatile."

On the other hand, her father always had a job. He moved around a fair bit because his temper tended to get him in trouble. Still, he always found a new job. He was good with his hands, and that was still valued in a lot of places. There was food on the table and a roof over her head. She saw plenty of kids every day who would count a childhood like hers as an incredible luxury.

"So did the police ask you any questions?" She walked into the living room. Her father was tying his shoes. She glanced at the clock. It was after eight. In a few minutes, he'd be heading to the Jiffy Lube, where he'd change oil and check brakes for the next eight hours.

He shrugged. "A few."

Veronica perched on the arm of the sofa next to him. "Like what?"

He shot her a look. "Like why I still have to tell my grown daughter not to break my damn furniture by sitting on the arm."

She stood. "Seriously, Dad, what did they ask? Do you think they're even going to try to find out what happened to Max?"

Osborne finished tying his shoes and stood. "How the hell should I know, Ronnie? Why the hell should I care? Why should you?"

"I care because he was my brother. You should care because he was your son." She crossed her arms over her chest as if that way she could keep her heart from cracking.

"He wasn't my son. Wouldn't take a rocket scientist to figure that out. Max wasn't even light enough to pass."

Veronica clenched her fists. It made her almost physically ill when her father said things like that. "When was the last time you saw him, Dad?" She'd never asked before because Max wasn't exactly a topic you brought up for fun.

"Same time as you. When they hauled his sorry ass out of this house and up to that reform school." He stood, hitched up his uniform pants, and headed toward the door. "You coming? Or are you going to hang around here a little?"

"You never heard anything from him again? What about Mama? Did he ever call or send a letter or anything?" she pressed.

"Ronnie, don't dig into this. What happened, happened. As far as I'm concerned, it's good riddance to bad rubbish. The cops stopped by. They asked their questions. They're probably going to drop the whole thing and forget about it. I mean, what else can they do?"

Veronica followed him toward the door. "Don't you want to know why, though? Don't you want to know what happened to him?"

"Why? It wouldn't make any difference. Besides, it's not like he was going to find the cure for cancer or make peace in the Middle East. He was a fuckup and was going to stay a fuckup. It was probably some giant fuckup that landed him wherever they found him. Let it drop, Ronnie. Nobody cares what happened."

They were interrupted by a loud knock on the front door. Osborne threw his hands in the air. "*Now* what? I'm going to be late for work."

He marched to the front door and pulled it open.

Cops on the doorstep. Again.

Veronica's presence made Zach pause for a second as he served his search warrant. "George Osborne, I have a warrant here to search your home." He handed the papers to Osborne and then shouldered past him. "Good morning, Ms. Osborne. Nice to see you again."

She pressed her lips together and moved out of the way. She was wearing scrubs and looked tired. Right, she worked the night shift at St. Elizabeth's. Her hair was pulled back into a no-nonsense ponytail.

Zach nodded to his small group of officers and they fanned out through the house. He didn't have a lot of boots on the ground since this case was so cold.

Osborne gave him a disgusted look. "I'm going to work. Don't break anything or I'll sue your asses from here to kingdom come. Ronnie, lock up when they leave." He marched out of the house.

Veronica sank down on the couch as if someone had let the air out of her. "Have at it. I don't know what you think you're looking for, though. Max hasn't been here in twenty years."

Most likely, Max hadn't been anywhere in twenty years. Zach headed out to the backyard. It was too much to hope to find a freshly dug pit there, but he had to check.

Frank followed him. "She has a good question, Zach. What precisely do we think we're going to find here?"

Zach stood in the yard with his hands on his hips, taking in its complete lack of places to hide a body. "We don't go in looking for something specific. We gather evidence and let the evidence point us in the right direction. Remember?"

"That does ring a bell."

"We have the stepfather of the victim with a drinking problem and a violent background." Veronica had been truthful when she said her father had a minor record. It looked mainly like bar fights. Most of the time, charges had been dropped after Osborne agreed to make reparations. Still, it was a pattern of solving your problems with your fists, and it would be irresponsible to ignore it.

On the other hand, say Max had come back to this house after he ran away from the Sierra School. What evidence would there be of that? Hairs and fibers didn't hang around for twenty years.

"Plus, this'll shake Osborne up a little. That's a pleasant by-product," Frank observed as he walked toward a toolshed at the back of the yard. "How 'bout we see if Osborne's been digging recently?"

It was as good a place to start as any.

McKnight hadn't expected to see her here. Veronica had noticed his careful, blank expression when he'd seen her behind her father, and his momentary hesitation. It gave her a small sense of satisfaction. He'd shaken her up plenty in the last twenty-four hours. She was glad to have her turn.

McKnight hadn't answered her when she'd asked what they were looking for. She hated that. She hated not knowing. It didn't make her a control freak; she just needed information. It was her number one frustration in the emergency room. Patients lied. Or they left things out. Or they played things down. Or up. She could deal with anything the world threw at her, if she had the information necessary to process it.

She needed information now. What were they looking for? What did they need? She glanced at her watch. It was eight forty-five, and she longed for her memory foam pillow and the Tempur-Pedic topper on her bed. She heaved herself up off the couch and went out to the back porch in time to hear Rodriguez tell McKnight that it would be nice to shake her father up a little.

She stared after them in disbelief as they headed into the toolshed. The bastards. All they wanted to do was yank her father's chain? *That* was what this was about?

She marched after them to the doorway of the shed. "You can't seriously believe that my father is a suspect, can you?"

Rodriguez and McKnight both turned to look at her. "What makes you think that he's a suspect?" McKnight asked.

"Because you're searching his house. That was kind of my first clue." Did he think she was dim?

"It was also Max's last-known residence before he was sent away. There might be some clue as to where he would have gone after he ran away." McKnight came to the doorway of the shed, blocking her view into it and her entry.

"In my father's toolshed?" She knew he was trying to get her to back away from the door by standing so close. To hell with him. She stood her ground.

"In your father's toolshed, under your father's floorboards, behind your father's dryer. Wherever we need to search." He didn't raise his voice, but he didn't back down, either. "We have a warrant. You need to let us do our jobs."

Fine. She could be reasonable, too. "Look. I understand that my father is . . . difficult."

She heard Rodriguez snort from inside the shed and ignored it. She knew another side to her father, though it didn't come out much. "He wouldn't have done anything to Max. If he says Max never came back here, then he never came back."

"With all due respect, Ms. Osborne, you know full well that your father is a violent man. How many fights has he been in over the past six months? Is it him paying off the bar owners, or is it you? What about bail? Who posts that? Based on how you greeted us yesterday, I'm pretty sure it's you and that you're tired of it. With your father's track record, yeah, he's a suspect." He looked down at her. His eyes were not unkind, but they were unflinching. "Coupled with what you already told us about your brother and father not getting along . . ."

She couldn't believe what she was hearing. "You're

using my words against my father? Isn't there some kind of law against that?"

"You're thinking about husbands and wives in a court of law. They don't have to testify against each other," Rodriguez called from the back of the shed. "Not applicable in this case."

The urge to tell them both what they could make applicable to themselves and where they could apply it was damn near overwhelming. She walked away, her clenched fists down at her sides.

Zach watched her walk away. Not many women could fill out a set of scrubs in a way that interested him. This one did. Too bad she was clearly furious. It would have been so much better to meet her, say, through work. Maybe he'd be coming in to question a gunshot victim and she'd be there. Their eyes would meet, and . . .

Damn, his fantasy life was nearly as pathetic as his actual love life. He'd just gotten bored. Hookups with Badge Bunnies were too easy and didn't mean crap. He'd rather watch the game than deal with the drama and the bullshit that seemed to go along with it.

He turned around to Rodriguez. "Anything?"

"Nothing that looks like it's been used recently, except the lawn mower. I don't think Osborne is a member of the garden club." Rodriguez exited the shed, blinking in the sunlight. "Wanna see what's doing inside? Or do you want to hide out here and try to avoid the dragon lady?"

"You scared of that little thing? The ex-husband of Doreen Winston?" Zach grinned at him.

"It's not me I'm worried about, bro. You're the one who went all tongue-tied." Frank started toward the house.

"I wasn't tongue-tied. I was being serious. It's important she understand the gravity of the situation." Zach followed him.

They walked in through the back door. "Anything?" Zach asked the first uniform he saw.

"No. Nothing obvious. But what did you expect?" The uniform shrugged and kept walking.

Zach wasn't sure. Three people had asked him what he'd expected to find here, and he didn't have a good answer for them. Still, it was the place where they needed to start. They needed to get to know the victim.

"Hey," he called after the uniform. "You find any old yearbooks or anything like that?"

"Yeah. I think there's a box down in the basement."

It would probably be a whole 'nother load of nothing, but they should take a look.

*   *   *

Veronica was sure Max had never come to this house for help.

So where *would* he have gone if he'd come back to Sacramento? Who would he have asked for help?

Max had had lots of friends. He was one of those kids who was good at sports, and smart but not freaky smart. He was normal.

As she drove home, Veronica tried to remember their names.

On the radio on her way home, she heard: "A preliminary identification has been made of the bones found in the construction site in downtown Sacramento yesterday. Stay tuned for more."

She sighed. Max had often told her he would be famous someday, a rock star or an NBA player. But his fame had come from a pile of bones trying to get his story told.

The cops were probably done with whatever investigating they could do. They didn't seem to know when Max actually died, so how the hell were they supposed to figure out why and how?

Veronica still felt like she should have known, somehow. It had to have been after he ran away from that Sierra School. She made the turn into her condo complex and pulled into her assigned parking space. Instead of getting out, though, she shut her eyes, trying to remember the names of friends and teammates she'd heard him talk about. Faces floated in front of her eyes and a few first names occurred to her. She'd been so much younger that their social lives hadn't intersected. Max hadn't brought friends around their house, nor had she. It hadn't taken long for her to figure out that other little girls' mommies didn't take those long naps on the couch with empty bottles nearby.

She'd search through the mementos she had of Max. Maybe there would be something there. Because if the police weren't going to try to find out what happened to her brother, then she would. If Max had come back to Sacramento, *someone* must have seen him. She just had to find out who that was.

Because her father couldn't have killed Max. He wouldn't have killed Max. Oh, dear God, *could* he have killed Max? Could he have lost his temper and by accident killed Max and dumped his body downtown somewhere?

She couldn't believe it, wouldn't believe it. The police had to be on the wrong track. She'd find out who'd seen Max when he'd come back to Sacramento and convince the police that her father was innocent.

And if she was wrong? Well, she needed to know that, too.

5

"You're not going to believe this, but the basketball coach is still at the high school." Frank stood up and stretched. "He said he could talk to us after school at about four thirty."

It had taken a little over five hours to search George Osborne's house. They hadn't found much that was interesting. No one was surprised, though Zach was a little more disappointed than everyone else.

They had come away with only a box that held Max's high school yearbooks, where he'd been prominently displayed with the rest of the junior varsity basketball team.

"Does the coach remember Max?" This could be helpful. Coaches tended to know the kids in their charge pretty well. Zach remembered a long string of soccer coaches who seemed to know exactly what had made him tick. Most of them took some extra time with him, and he hadn't questioned why at the time. He'd been too damn grateful for the attention. He supposed they knew that.

How many men had stepped in to fill the void after Zach's father had died? Quite a few.

"He seemed to remember the kid. I guess we'll know this afternoon." Frank glanced up at the clock. "You hungry? I could use a burger. You want one?"

"No, thanks. I want to find out about that missing persons report that was supposedly filed."

"Suit yourself." Frank ambled out of the room.

Zach picked up the phone and dialed, got a receptionist, and waited to be put through to someone who could actually help him.

Janice Lam, a deputy sheriff in the Plumas County Sheriff's Office, picked up. Zach identified himself and told her what he wanted.

"You're looking for a twenty-year-old missing persons report?" she asked when he finished. "How the hell is that going to help?"

He laughed. "I have no idea. I'm hoping there's something in it that will give me a direction to go."

"I'll dig it up and fax it to you."

"Thanks. You know anything about the school?"

"I know that it's a pain in my butt. It's been closed for

years and we constantly have problems with the property. Kids hang out there to drink and make out. There's vandalism and parties. It's off the beaten path enough that we don't get too many complaints about noise and such, but it's also far enough off the road that it's out of my deputies' way to patrol it very often. One of these days someone's going to fall through a rotten floorboard, and everybody's ass is going to get chewed out."

"Who does the property belong to now?"

"Near as I can tell, the bank, and they don't give a rat's ass about the place. Aaron Joiner owned it before, but he died in ninety-eight and the place has been empty since then. He didn't have any kids to leave the property to, and the school closed a year or two before he died."

That wasn't going to make it easy. "So what's up there?"

"A bunch of empty, half-falling-down buildings. Well, except the stone ones. Those'll still be standing when we're dead and cockroaches are ruling the earth. Apparently they brought a bunch of Hopi Indians up from Arizona to build them back in the thirties. They're gorgeous. Too bad the place is such a pain to get to. Someone could have probably made something of it. A resort or something."

Lam said she'd give him a heads-up when she faxed the missing persons report, and they hung up. He figured he'd try to find out a little more about the Sierra School. Maybe someone from there would know something. Even if all they knew was Shelden's shoe size, it would be a damn sight more than he knew now.

Lyle Burton stared down at the newspaper. What the hell was going on?

He'd been expecting the article about himself; he'd written the press release publicizing his promotion to director of Child Protective Services. The agency had had some black eyes and he was going to come in and fix all that. He'd worked hard to get the job. He'd worked hard to make people recognize him. This was his time. His moment of glory.

And his picture was on the front of the Our Region section of the *Sacramento Chronicle*, with an article about his appointment.

But below the fold was another photo. Max Shelden at seventeen, smiling as if he hadn't a care in the world. It didn't make any sense. How in hell had Max Shelden's body ended up in a construction pit in downtown Sac?

Burton threw the paper down on his desk. He would get to the bottom of this, one way or another.

*   *   *

Gary Havens pushed his big-wheeled trash bin into Mr. Osaka's classroom. "Hey, Mr. O."

The teacher looked up from his desk. "Hey, Gary, how's it going?"

"Not bad. Not bad." He liked his job at the school. Maybe being a custodian wasn't prestigious, but he was making a contribution. He was helping. He grabbed the trash can by Mr. O.'s desk and emptied it into the big bin. "You finished with that paper?" He pointed to the newspaper on the edge of the desk.

"I am. You want it?" Mr. O. asked.

"Would it be okay?" He liked the comics and the sudoku, but a subscription was a lot of money for something that seemed to always come his way for free. He didn't really care if he did the Monday sudoku on Tuesday or spent the whole week on the Sunday crossword puzzle. His life wasn't like that. He wasn't like that.

He was nothing if not patient. He knew how to wait. He'd learned that a long time ago, sitting as quiet as he could in the dark, waiting and praying for the morning light to come, waiting and praying that no one would notice him.

"No problem at all," Mr. O. said, then glanced up at the clock. "Your mom should be here by now, Cedric."

Gary hadn't even noticed the little boy. "How's it going, Cedric?" he asked. He liked Cedric. He was a nice little boy. Small for a fifth-grader, and Gary knew how that felt. He'd been a scrawny little thing, too. A late bloomer. He wasn't scrawny anymore. He was tall and strong, and he worked hard to stay that way.

"Okay." Cedric smiled at him as he gathered up his books. He looked at the door and swallowed hard.

"Do you want me to walk you to the curb?" Mr. O. asked Cedric.

Cedric shook his head. Gary glanced over at Mr. O.

"Cedric's been having trouble with some of the junior high kids while he's waiting for his mother to pick him up. She can't get here before four, so I told him he could wait here in my classroom. That way he won't cross paths with them so much," Mr. O. explained.

Gary nodded. The teachers weren't really supposed to do things like that. The school had an after-school program. It wasn't cheap, though. And you paid the same whether your kid stayed for half an hour or for two hours. Gary also knew that Cedric's mom was a single mother and probably didn't have a lot of cash to spare.

He picked up his newspaper and said, "Come on, Cedric. I'll walk you out to the curb. I have to dump this in the Dumpster."

Cedric blinked furiously. "Yeah, okay," he mumbled.

Gary felt a little clutch in his heart. Poor kid. Terrified of getting picked on. Terrified of asking for help.

Embarrassed. Ashamed. Praying for help, but not sure how to accept it. Gary had walked that walk. He pushed the trash bin toward the door and gave Mr. O. a wave.

They stepped out into the sunshine. Gary loved the way they'd set up the school, all the classrooms opening on to the outdoors. He didn't like closed-in places. Cedric scuttled along next to him along the wall as they walked toward the Dumpsters.

"Can you open the gate for me?" Gary asked when they got there.

Cedric nodded and stood on his tiptoes to reach his skinny little arm over the top of the gate and unlatch it. It would take nothing to twist that arm up behind his back, shove him into the garbage enclosure, and do anything he wanted. No one would be there to stop him. The kid would probably be too scared to even cry, and certainly too scared and too ashamed to tell anyone. It could go on for a year or two, and no one would ever be the wiser. Gary's breath started to come a little faster just thinking about it.

Despite the bullying he had already received, the kid was way too trusting.

Gary knew all about that, too. He knew how getting pushed around could make you look for someone bigger and stronger than your enemies to protect you. He knew how that could turn on a guy, too.

People who were bigger and stronger than your

enemies were bigger and stronger than you, too. Strength and size didn't guarantee benevolence. People who were bigger than you just had an easier time pushing you around.

Cedric turned and smiled at him, and Gary pushed the trash bin on through. He dumped the garbage in the Dumpster and said, "Let's go see if your mom is here."

A gray Toyota Celica with a dent in the rear-passenger side pulled to the curb as Gary and Cedric came around the corner of the school. Cedric cried out "Mom!" and sprinted toward the car.

Before Cedric could get to the car, two older boys, jeans drooping halfway down their asses, dirty flannel shirts over T-shirts, came out from behind a tree. The smaller of the two bumped Cedric as he ran past, sending him flying.

Gary was moving away from the building in a split second. The first boy had turned to snicker with the larger boy, trying to impress him by picking on someone smaller than he was. Gary knew this dynamic all too well. And he was bigger than all of them. "Hey!" he yelled. "What do you think you're doing?"

It was very satisfying to see the boy jump. "I . . . I . . . nothing. It was an accident." He started to back away.

Gary took a few more steps toward him. "Then help him up."

The boy froze. "What?"

"I said help him up. Now."

"Okay, okay. Don't have a coronary." The boy walked over to where Cedric lay sprawled on the sidewalk and held out his hand.

Cedric glanced over at Gary, confused.

"Let him help you up, Cedric."

Cedric swallowed hard, but took the kid's hand. The kid hauled him to his feet.

Cedric's mother got out of her car. "Hey, everything okay over there?"

"Just fine," Gary called back to her in a friendly tone. "Cedric will be there in just a second." He turned back to the bully. "Now tell him that you're sorry," he growled.

The kid shot him a defiant look.

"Now." Gary crossed his arms over his chest.

The kid took a step back and turned to Cedric. "Sorry."

"Now tell him it won't happen again."

The kid cast a disparaging look at Gary but said, "It won't happen again."

"Now get off the grade school property," Gary said. "Is there something wrong with you that you're hanging out with little kids? Can't you make any friends your own age?" he taunted.

The kid picked up his backpack, and he and his friend slouched away.

Cedric had already run over to his mother's car. Gary followed.

"I hung out with Mr. O. and then Gary walked me over here," Cedric told his mother.

Cedric's mother looked up at Gary, her brow creased. "We don't mean to be a bother."

Gary waved her concerns away. "I needed help getting the Dumpster gate open. It's hard to do when you're wheeling the bin at the same time. Cedric was a big help."

She shot him a look of gratitude. "Thank you so much."

"No problem." Gary leaned down and looked in the car window. "See you tomorrow, Cedric."

"Yeah, Gary. See you tomorrow."

They pulled away from the curb and Gary shook the paper out from under his arm. Then the bottom dropped out of his stomach.

The picture of a boy stared up at him from the printed page. A boy with café-au-lait skin and light brown eyes. Gary knew that face. He hadn't thought he'd ever see it again. Not after the way it looked the last time he'd seen it. Bile rose in his throat as he remembered the blood, the head tilted at such an unnatural angle.

He shook the paper open more. There had to be a reason for the photo being there. There had to be a story that would explain it. He saw the headline: BODY DUMPED IN DOWNTOWN CONSTRUCTION SITE.

How could that be? It was all so long ago. What had happened? Why would it be there now?

He opened the paper up fully and saw the second photo.

He knew *that* face, too, and felt even sicker. He would have recognized that face anywhere. The jaw was thicker, the eyebrows heavier, but there was no mistaking it.

He stared from one picture to the other. What bizarre twist of fate had brought those two pictures together on the same day? Was there anyone else in Sacramento who would see this and know it was significant? A chill ran down his spine. Maybe that was the point. Maybe it was a message for him. Maybe *he* was supposed to do something.

There would be no more bullying on his watch. He had stood by once before and done nothing, and someone had died. Someone good. Back then Gary had been small and weak, but he was a man now. He would act like a man, not like a child.

Max was whispering for help, just like Cedric had been silently praying for someone to help him. Gary could do that. He could be the one who helped. Pride swelled in his chest. He could be that person. He would be that person. He would do it for Max.

*   *   *

Coach Jackson lived in the 300 block of Parkshore Court, in a house he'd either bought in the 1980s or with money he'd inherited. No way had he purchased a two-story sweetheart in Greenhaven on a teacher's salary these days. Same with the Lexus in the driveway.

Maybe his wife made piles of money. Zach had met plenty of women who made more money than he did as a cop; his youngest sister was constantly fixing him up with women from the bank where she worked. They all had fatter wallets than he did. They all also had perfectly done hair, flawless makeup, and designer clothes. None of them made his heart hammer.

Frank rang the bell of the coach's house. "Pretty nice place for a teacher," he observed.

"I was thinking the same thing." There was a reason he loved working with Frank. "Guy's a source of information, though, not a suspect. Old information, to boot."

Frank gazed at the trees in the front yard. "A yard like this takes some time to cultivate. I checked and he's been here since the late eighties."

Zach looked around the yard. The trees and bushes looked like they'd been planted at least that long ago.

The man who answered the door looked like a former basketball player. Derrick Jackson was tall, lanky and loose limbed, with a full head of graying hair. Otherwise, he didn't look much different than he had in the yearbook photos. A few more wrinkles around his eyes, and his jowls hung a little lower, but he'd obviously kept in shape.

"Derrick Jackson?" Frank unclipped the badge from his belt and held it up.

The man nodded. "That's me. You must be the officer who called earlier. Come on in. Both of you."

Two teenage boys sat on the couch in the living room, game controllers in hand and a combat scene playing out in front of them. One of them looked as if he'd had the entirety of his last growth spurt in his neck. The other was a little more solid looking.

"These are my sons, Danny and Rusty," Jackson said as he walked past.

The boys didn't even look up, but gave an acknowledging grunt. It was about as communicative as a lot of teenage boys got.

"Come on into the kitchen." Jackson continued to lead the way. "I'm getting dinner ready."

It smelled good; Zach's stomach growled. The kitchen was nice. Really nice. Lots of brick and wrought iron. It had the look of a kitchen that got a lot of use, too.

"So you want to talk to me about Max Shelden," Jackson said as he stirred something on the stove. "It's been a long time. I'm not sure what I can tell you at this point."

"Tell you the truth, we're a little worried about that ourselves." Frank pointed at one of the kitchen chairs. "You mind if I sit? My dogs are barking."

Jackson bit back a smile. "Sure. Take a load off. Haven't heard that phrase in a long time."

Frank shrugged. "I'm kind of an old-fashioned guy." He pulled one of the chairs out and sat down heavily. Zach stayed leaning against a counter.

"So do you remember Max at all?" Frank asked.

"You bet." Jackson turned from the stove. "I had him on the squad for two years before his parents took him out of the public school system."

"What kind of kid was he?" Zach asked.

Jackson twisted his shoulders as if to work out a knot. "In what way?"

Why the sudden caginess? "Coach Jackson—"

"Call me Derrick," he interrupted.

Zach started over again. "Derrick, we're trying to find someplace to start investigating what happened to Max. Nothing you're going to say is going to hurt him now. I'm sure you know that."

There wasn't a news outlet in town that hadn't led with Max Shelden's identification. The picture that Veronica Osborne had given them was running on pretty much every major news outlet today.

Jackson thought for a moment. "Max was a pretty ordinary kid. He was good at basketball, good enough to make the team, but it wasn't going to get him a free ride to a university. He wasn't stupid, but he wasn't exactly a brainiac, either. He was a kid."

"So if he was so normal, why'd his parents yank him out of the school and send him up to that Sierra School?" Zach pressed. Most parents didn't send their kids off to residential schools unless it was really necessary.

Jackson snorted. "Have you met Max's stepfather? *Him* I remember all too well."

"We've had the pleasure," Frank said dryly.

"Well, I think he's your first clue as to why Max got sent away. He was always looking for any excuse to knock Max down a few steps. There's a lot of hate in that man." Jackson leaned back against the counter and crossed his arms over his chest. "I only met him a handful of times, but I sure haven't forgotten him."

"You have run-ins with Osborne?" Zach asked, more interested now.

Jackson dropped his head. "I wish they were just run-ins. It's more like I got run over. I was a relatively new teacher back then. Nothing they taught me at Sac State prepared me for a man like George Osborne. The man charged into one of my practices looking for Max. He was livid. There was some chore

Max had been supposed to do before he came to practice—something stupid like taking out the garbage or
sweeping the porch. Anyway, Max had blown it off.
Osborne hauled him out of my practice practically
by his hair, screaming obscenities at him the whole
time."

Jackson looked over at both men. "You know how
there are moments in your life when you have to act
fast to do the right thing? If you hesitate, the moment's gone and you've blown it?"

Frank and Zach both nodded. Zach knew those
moments all too well. His days were full of them.
Every cop's were. His nights, too, sometimes. Nightmares where he reacted too slowly to save someone, or
too quickly and his rash behavior endangered someone. Too often it was a lose-lose proposition.

Jackson said, "This was one of those moments. I
didn't know what to do. I'd never been confronted by
a parent who acted like that. Before I could do anything, they were gone. I'll always regret not stepping
between them, not protecting Max from Osborne."
He shrugged. "I choked. The game was on and I
didn't even throw up a brick."

"Did you ever see Max again?" Zach asked. An un-
swept porch? He remembered some of the things he'd
done as a teenager. The car he'd stolen from a neighbor's driveway. The CD he'd shoplifted from a store.

"He was back the next day, acting like nothing had happened. What else could he do to save face? He laughed it off." Jackson turned away from Zach and Frank. "And I let him. I didn't ask for more information, and Max sure as hell didn't volunteer any."

"Did Osborne show up a lot?" Zach asked.

Jackson shook his head.

"What about the mother?" Frank asked, his head cocked to one side like a dog waiting for a treat.

"Pretty much never." Jackson turned back around from the sink to face them again, his face composed. "But really, what good is this now? What does it have to do with how he died?"

"We're trying to figure out where he may have gone after he ran away from the school. We were hoping that you might have some ideas about that." It seemed completely possible that Max could have turned up on his coach's doorstep, looking for help.

"I never saw him after they transferred him up to Sierra." Jackson's forehead creased.

"What about his teammates? Was there anybody he was especially close to?" A kid who'd learned to mistrust adults might be more likely to turn to another kid for help.

Jackson thought for a moment. "Absolutely. Let me think for a minute. It was a long time ago, and names and faces tend to run together."

"We brought along a yearbook," Zach said. "In case it might help."

"It would. It would help a lot."

Fifteen minutes later, Jackson had given them a list of five boys who were good friends of Max's back in the day. He had no idea where any of them were now.

One of his sons, the more solid one, poked his head into the kitchen. "Hey, Dad, what's for dinner?"

"Meatball subs. They'll be ready in about five."

"Excellent," the boy said and ducked back into the living room.

"We'll get out of your way, then." Frank stood up, scraping the chair legs on the floor. "Thank you for your help."

Jackson took in a deep breath and blew it out. "I wish I could do more. I wish I *had* done more. It's a shame. He was a good kid."

He saw them out, and as they walked down the sidewalk to the Crown Vic, Zach heard him call his sons in for dinner. "You think he's righteous?" he asked Frank.

"Yeah. He seemed on the up-and-up."

Zach had thought so, too. "What about the names? You think we should run 'em down tonight?"

Frank looked at his watch. "I think they've been sitting for twenty years; another night won't hurt."

"Okay if we run Veronica Osborne's photo over to her at St. E's on our way home?"

Frank glanced at his watch. "Just barely. Sheila will be getting antsy. Tonight's our ballroom dance class."

Zach's eyebrows went up. "Ballroom dance?"

Frank scratched his belly. "It's very romantic. Sheila loves it. I spend two hours cha-chaing once a week and then I get laid without even taking her out to dinner. Plus it's good exercise."

"Sounds like a win-win to me."

Frank pointed at him. "There are not too many of those in life, my boy. Pay attention. Grab every one of them that comes your way."

6

Susan Tennant was a careful and precise woman. Paying attention to things was part of being a good nurse. You had to notice things that other people might not notice, see things that other people might not see. A slight bluish tone around the lips, or a slight dip in a blood test or in blood pressure—little details that would slide right by the average person could mean the difference between someone's life and death.

So Susan noticed the car idling down the street from her house when she got home. It was already dark. She rarely ever got home when it was still light out at this time of year. But she actually welcomed the dark. The long, light evenings of summer made her melancholy.

Susan couldn't make out the color of the car in the dark or its license plate, but she noted that it was a big solid sedan with an expensive purr to its engine. She wished whoever was inside would turn it off. It was a waste of gas and was making extra pollution in the air that Sacramento definitely didn't need. "Spare the Air" days came around plenty without any extra help.

Susan set her emergency brake—just in case—got out of the car, locked it, and let herself into her two-bedroom, one-bath ranch in the Arden-Arcade neighborhood.

She liked it here. It didn't take her long to get downtown, but the tree-lined streets made the ugliness she dealt with every day seem far, far away. Sometimes it even made the past seem far, far away.

It *was* pretty far away. All that unpleasantness had happened years before. She'd practically been a girl, young and green and trusting. Not anymore. Those days were definitely gone.

She took the badge from around her neck and dropped it in the bowl by the front door; her keys followed. She stowed her purse in the cabinet and plugged her cell phone into the charger. Her shoes went into the closet on a rack, and she put on her slippers.

As she walked into the kitchen, her cat wound between her legs. She scooped him up and burrowed her face in his soft fur. "Hello, Patches, how are you tonight?"

He replied with a little chirping meow. She set him

down next to his bowl and filled it with food, then filled up the kettle to make herself a cup of tea.

The doorbell rang. She set the kettle on the burner, turned it on, and went back to the front door. Who would be ringing her doorbell at this time in the evening? A neighbor needing a favor? Certainly not a salesperson. Maybe one of those people out collecting for a cause.

She peered through the peephole, but could make out only a square, distorted head. She opened the door and said, "Can I help you?"

"Hello, Susan. Long time, no see." He pushed into the house past her and locked the door.

That was the moment that Susan Tennant realized that in trying to confront her past, she might have closed off her future.

"What I need," Tina said to Veronica, rubbing her lower back, "is a big juicy code. Something dramatic that brings everyone running."

Veronica shook her head. "You are a sick puppy, you know that?" She turned back to the lab results she was entering in the chart.

Tina grinned. "Yep, and you're one, too. 'Fess up. You're as big an adrenaline junkie as me, and it's been too damn slow around here."

"Careful what you wish for," Veronica warned her, but she knew what Tina meant. "Why don't you go try to get Donny to shut up again? He's cussing out those two women who brought their mother in. It's not nice."

Donny was one of St. Elizabeth's frequent fliers. He was a Vietnam vet living on disability who, on a fairly routine basis, got rip-roaring drunk and started threatening people downtown. He'd added the very special trick of using a broken bottle this time, so he was handcuffed to a gurney waiting for a psych consult in bay number 3. In bay number 2, two middle-aged sisters had brought in their mother, who had clearly had some kind of minor stroke.

Every time the sisters started to talk, Donny let loose a string of obscene epithets, the most recent being "stupid retard fucking bitches." Amazingly, the sisters found this hysterically funny—Veronica was glad to know someone else on the planet laughed inappropriately in times of great stress—and kept giggling. This was whipping Donny into grander and more elaborate strings of obscenities, which just made the sisters laugh harder.

Another night of saving lives and defying Darwin one drunk at a time.

One of the real problems with working the emergency room was how few actual emergencies they got.

The car crashes and gunshot wounds were few and far between; the vast majority of the cases barely even qualified as urgent care.

Nothing really got the heart racing like someone showing up in full cardiac arrest.

Or looking up from your paperwork to see Sergeant Tall, Dark, and Dangerous striding through your emergency room.

"Ooh, even better than a code. Armed and hot and coming straight at us," Tina whispered.

"Ms. Osborne," McKnight said as he walked up to them.

Tina shot her a look. "Holding out on me, Osborne?"

Veronica gave her a quick shake of the head. "Sergeant McKnight, how can I help you?"

He glanced around the nurses' station. "My sister works night shift, too. Up in cardiology."

"Your sister?" She ran through the possibilities in her head. There was a nurse named McKnight she'd met at an in-service training. "Your sister is Rhonda McKnight?"

"Yep. That's her." He smiled. He had a nice smile. "Bossy as hell."

Veronica loved a nice smile. She had a soft spot for broad shoulders and well-developed biceps, too. Not this one, though. This one thought her father might have killed her brother. This one would need more than a nice smile and a well-developed set of guns to impress her. "We've met."

"I came to return your picture." He handed her the photo of Max.

Tina was looking back and forth between the two of them, wide eyed. Veronica turned, glared at her and made a shooing gesture. Tina backed away slowly, but not without pointing to her own eyes and then to Veronica. She was being watched. Whatever.

She stared at Zach. He had a lot of nerve, doing this where she worked. "You're done using all the information I gave you against my family, then? Gosh, thanks."

He clenched his jaw. "I'm sorry you feel that way about it. We're trying to find out what happened to your brother. I know you want to know, too."

"I do. I just don't want to have to hire legal representation while you do it. Especially because of something I might have said during a moment of great emotional distress."

"I don't know what you want me to say. I'm sorry. I really am. Even you have to admit that we would have been derelict not to look into your father as a suspect."

"Is he still a suspect?"

McKnight didn't answer.

Veronica took in a deep breath and blew it out slowly.

So her father was still a suspect. What's worse was that McKnight was right. It didn't make her feel any better, though. Especially since she was the one who had made the police look at her father in the first place.

McKnight broke the silence. "I'll be going, then. You know where to reach me if you think of anything else that might help."

"Yeah. I'll be real sure to do that." Every word dripped more sarcasm than a leaky IV dripped saline.

McKnight walked away.

Tina was back in a second. "I thought you'd given up cops."

"And paramedics. I'm thinking a nice accountant would be restful."

Tina took the ponytailer out of her hair and shook out her curls. "Too nitpicky. You sure you don't want to make an exception for Tall, Dark, and Handsome? He's got a nice rear view."

She hadn't missed that. It was nearly as impossible to miss as the way his shirt stretched across his shoulders and chest. "I'm sure."

"So what was he here for?" Tina asked as she rewound her hair into a messy bun.

Veronica shook her head.

"Are you going to make me guess, or are you going to give up and tell me? You know I won't stop until I know."

That was true. There was no point in trying to keep

anything from Tina. "They found my brother's body. McKnight caught the case. He wanted to ask some follow-up questions."

Tina sat on the rolling stool next to the counter, her eyes wide. "I didn't even know you *had* a brother."

That stung. In a lot of ways, Veronica hadn't had a brother for twenty years. He wasn't at family dinners. He didn't borrow money, or help clean the gutters. He didn't do the usual brother things. He hadn't been able to. He'd been dead.

In her heart, though, Veronica had always had a brother. He'd been alive there, kept that way through hope. A hope that had proved to be pathetic and ridiculous. She couldn't decide if she was better off knowing the truth or if she had preferred operating in blissful ignorance.

"He disappeared a long time ago. When I was just a kid. They found his body in a construction site."

Tina's eyes went wide. "Wait. Your brother was the body they found downtown the other day? The bones in the pit? That was your brother?"

Veronica nodded.

"Wow." Tina's brow creased. "But wait. The picture they're showing of that kid. He's, well . . ."

"Black?" Veronica finished for her.

"Yeah. I think we're supposed to use African American now, but you got the gist."

"He was my half brother." There it was again. "He was from my mother's first marriage. Max's dad died in Vietnam."

"Correct me if I'm wrong, but isn't your dad pretty racist?" Tina's brow furrowed deeper.

"You could say that." Oh, boy, could you ever say that. Although Veronica suspected that if Max had been Caucasian, her father would have found some other reason to hate him. It was what her father did best.

Well, second best. He was damn good at drinking. They were intertwined. Maybe he wouldn't hate quite so much without the booze, or drink so much without the hate. She'd given up trying to parse that one out years ago.

"That must have been fun." Tina stood up and started riffling through the case files. "You want the five-year-old breathing emergency in two, or the Natasha Richardson case?" Ever since the actress had hit her head while skiing and died a few days later, every Tom, Dick, and Harry with a head bump came to the emergency room.

Veronica shot her a look.

Tina handed her the file. "Five-year-old it is, but you owe me." She swished away, but turned before she went behind the curtain. "And if you don't want Tall, Silent, and Studly, I'm more than happy to take your sloppy seconds."

Veronica snorted. As if Tina had ever had to take anyone's sloppy seconds. She went in to check on the five-year-old with asthma, but before she could take two steps, all the buzzers and whistles started to go off. She looked over at Tina. "I guess you got your wish."

"Let me guess. She was thrilled to see you. She accepted the photo and expressed her deep, undying gratitude for how seriously you were taking her brother's case," Frank said as Zach got back into the Crown Vic.

"Yeah. Then I proposed and we're hoping for a June wedding. Save the date, will you?" Zach shot back.

Frank snorted. "Gave you a hard time, did she?"

"It's shocking, but she resents the fact that we consider her father a suspect. Can you believe that?" Zach buckled his seat belt.

Frank started the car, waited until the ambulance that was pulling into the lot, lights flashing and siren blaring, had gone past, then pulled out of their space. "Absolutely shocking. So what's next?"

"I say we start looking at this Sierra School. Maybe we can find someone who might know something that would give us a lead." Zach leaned back in his seat. *Please let them stir up a lead somewhere.* Lord, he hated cold cases.

"Sounds like a good plan for tomorrow." Frank pulled onto I-5. "Have I mentioned that I hate cold cases?"

"It's like you're reading my mind, Frank."

Zach closed his eyes. He wanted a hot shower and a cold beer, perhaps at the same time. He wanted a black, dreamless sleep undisturbed by sexy little nurses or old bones clutching military-issue dog tags.

The case was getting to him, and he knew why. He hadn't exactly been a perfect teenager. After his father died, he'd been angry.

The problem was, there wasn't anyone to take that anger out on. The cops found the drunk who had hit his dad during a routine traffic stop, and the man had gone down for vehicular manslaughter. Maximum sentence, maximum outrage from the community, solidarity from his father's brothers in blue.

Without a target to focus his rage on, it had diffused throughout Zach's world. He'd started cutting classes, gotten in some fights, experimented with booze and grass. Really, it had been a classic pattern. It had ended with him coming damn close to being arrested for breaking into a neighbor's garage. His plan had been to steal a stereo system to get money to buy some weed.

Overwhelmed with her own grief, his mother

hadn't had a clue about how to deal with her angry son. That's when some of his father's friends had stepped in. A collection was taken and Zach had been sent to the Mount Hood Academy.

He was pretty sure it had saved his life.

It hadn't been easy. The first few months had been pure, unadulterated hell. They had broken down every defense he had, one by one, until he felt as if there was nothing left of him. Every bit of anger and defiance had been drained from him. Then they'd started to build him back up again.

Had Max been one of those kids who were so sure the rules didn't apply to them? Zach remembered that type. The ones who thought they were special, that they shouldn't have to wait in the line or do the work or earn the privilege. He still dealt with them every day. Talk to your average criminal and you'd hear the same story. They shouldn't have to earn their own living. They should be able to take someone else's stuff. They shouldn't have to abide by the rules of society. They were special, special snowflakes and should be treated as such.

Right.

All snowflakes had to abide by the rules, or Zach was going to help society melt them.

*   *   *

Tina stripped off her gloves and threw them in the garbage can. "How many times do we have to tell them?"

"Don't start, Tina." Veronica knew what she meant, though. If the person was dead, why bring them to the emergency room? It's not as if CPR was going to bring them back when they were already stone cold.

Tina glanced up at the clock. "We spent forty-five minutes trying to resuscitate that woman when we all knew it was pointless. For God's sake, her pupils were totally blown before they walked in the door. Why can't they just call the morgue or something?"

"She had a pulse."

Tina and Veronica both turned. One of the EMTs was filling out paperwork at the nurses' station. He didn't turn around. The view wasn't half bad, although he looked a little old for Veronica's taste. She had Daddy issues and she fought them as hard as possible.

"And she was still breathing," he continued without looking up. "At least a little."

"Ever heard of agonal breathing?" Tina fired back.

The body wants to breathe. Even when the brain is basically dead—and the code they'd just spent forty-five minutes laboring over was definitely brain dead what with the hugely dilated and unresponsive pupils and all—the body will still try to gasp in air.

"Ever heard of paramedics calling a code in the field if there's even the slightest sign of life?" He was giving as good as he got, and he was getting it pretty good. It didn't seem to ruffle him, though. He turned around from his paperwork. The front view was fine, too. He had a little salt mixed in with the pepper of his close-cropped hair. It wasn't Veronica's thing, but Tina seemed damn near speechless.

"You new here?" Veronica asked. She knew most of the EMTs, at least by sight.

He stuck out his hand. "Yeah. I just moved down from Truckee a few months ago. I'm Matthew Cassel."

"Veronica Osborne." She shook his hand. "My testy friend here is Tina Rivera."

Cassel smiled over at Tina. "I don't blame her for being testy. It was a lost cause from the beginning. Nothing anybody could do about it. Except their jobs."

"True enough," Veronica said.

Tina just stared as Cassel headed out the door.

"Wow," Tina said. Then she whirled back on Veronica. "I don't care *how* cute he was. It was still a waste of my time, and you know how I feel about that."

Veronica did know. Anyone within earshot of Tina knew exactly how she felt about having her time wasted, the latest set of contestants on *Dancing with the Stars,* and the *Eat Pray Love* movie.

"Just think of all the money the emergency room is

going to charge her insurance company. It'll pay your salary for the entire year," Veronica told her, patting her on the back.

Tina grinned. "You always know the right thing to say."

Two cops approached them. They were in plain-clothes, but they were undoubtedly cops. The man was a nice-looking guy. Tall, broad shouldered, the whole bit. The woman was striking. Long, curling hair clasped back in a barrette. Flawless mocha skin. Beyoncé with a gun. Well, Beyoncé before the Master Cleanse diet. The woman had some dangerous curves going for her and baby totally had back.

"Hi, I'm Detective Josh Wolfe. This is my partner, Elise Jacobs," the male cop said.

"I take it our vic didn't make it," Jacobs said.

"Sorry, no. She was long gone before she got here."

Wolfe ran his hand through his hair. "Yeah. It looked that way. It was a weird one, though. Any idea what happened?"

"She choked on her own vomit," Tina chimed in. "Very *Spinal Tap,* except the part where she wasn't a drummer."

Elise snorted, but Josh just stared at her. His partner jabbed him in the ribs with her elbow. "It was a joke, Josh. Smile."

"I got it. Right." He turned to Veronica. "Any-

thing else? We got nothing so far. Nice neighborhood, no sign of forced entry. A neighbor noticed
her door was open and walked in. Found her tied
and gagged."

"Could it have been sex play gone wrong? Maybe
her partner panicked and took off." Veronica had
seen a lot weirder stuff than a little bondage, and a lot
of things way weirder than someone running when
they'd accidentally killed their S and M playmate.

"Didn't look that way." Elise flipped open a notebook she'd taken out of her jacket. "She was fully
clothed. There wasn't anything at the scene that indicated any kind of sexual rendezvous."

"What? No candles or Barry White? No glasses of
wine?" Tina asked.

"Nope." Elise glanced at her notes. "One cup of
chamomile tea with milk and a Lean Cuisine."

"Ouch. Sounds like my place," Tina said.

"I hear you, sister." Elise flipped her notebook shut.

"Maybe the doc's got something more," Wolfe said.
The two detectives started down the corridor to
where the attending, Dr. Mahaffy, was talking with
a colleague.

Tina looked at Veronica. "He was cute, too. It's
practically raining men in here tonight."

"No sense of humor, though," Veronica pointed out.

"Maybe he was just tired." Tina stretched and

yawned. "I'm tired, too. Maybe I wasn't as funny as you thought I was."

Veronica shook her head. "I thought we'd sworn off cops."

Tina turned and watched the detectives talking to Dr. Mahaffy. "That's you. I'm not swearing off anything, cops or paramedics."

"Do me a favor and check to see if the next one is married before you throw yourself at him." There'd been one incident this year that had left her fun-loving friend weeping for six weeks. Veronica wasn't sure she could survive another breakup like that one.

Tina gave her a sidelong glance. "Where's the fun in that? By the way, there's a constipated eighty-year-old available now."

Oh, man. That did not sound like any kind of fun whatsoever. "What happened to the asthmatic five-year-old and the Natasha Richardson case?"

"The five-year-old got a breathing treatment and went home with an inhaler. Natasha decided that her head didn't hurt that bad anymore and left. Gave one of the chairs in the waiting room a pretty good kick on her way out, too, according to Linnea. I believe she may have also impugned our sexual reputations and several people's mothers."

All in all, just another night in Emergency Room Paradise. Veronica looked at her watch. "It's time for my break." If possible, it would always be time for her break when there was a constipated eighty-year-old within a mile radius.

"Mine, too." Tina smiled at her. "Rochambeau?"

"You have got to be kidding. You want to do rock paper scissors for a patient?" Veronica shook her head, although she'd seen worse ways of deciding who had to deal with a less-than-ideal case.

"We could flip a coin." Tina's smile got bigger.

"Forget it. Go enjoy your break. I'll go disimpact the eighty-year-old."

"Have fun." Tina wiggled her fingers at her and headed for the nurses' lounge. She stopped then and turned around. "Did that woman who coded look familiar to you?"

Veronica wracked her brain. In all honesty, she wasn't even sure what the woman looked like. She'd been too focused on starting an IV and trying to get her heart going again to look at the woman's face. "I don't think so. Do you think you know her?"

"Not sure." Tina bit her lower lip. "I felt like I'd seen her somewhere before. You sure she didn't ring any bells for you?"

"I'll look at her chart later and see if I can figure it out." If Tina said she was familiar, chances were she was familiar. The question was, what difference did that make? Regardless of who she'd been in life, she was tits up now.

*   *   *

Matt Cassell stood by his rig out in the ambulance entry and reminded himself to breathe. When he'd moved to Sacramento, he'd thought he was moving farther away from his past. Then tonight he'd landed smack-dab in it.

"You doing all right out there?" Matt's partner, Jason, stuck his head out of the back of the ambulance.

"Great. Terrific," Matt replied.

"Then what say you hop in here and help me clean up some of this mess?" Jason's spiky-haired head disappeared back in the rig.

Matt climbed in and began to pick up some of the trash left behind after desperately trying to revive Susan Tennant.

He had tried, hadn't he? He went over everything he'd done. Would anybody be able to fault him? Would they be able to say that he'd let her die? That he'd watched her choke on her own vomit and hadn't felt one ounce of pity or remorse?

No. He was pretty sure he'd covered all the bases. From the second that he and Jason had gone into the house, he'd done everything he was supposed to do.

It had been quite a shock, though. He hadn't laid eyes on Susan Tennant for twenty years, and she most definitely had not been the one who'd been restrained in their last encounter. Obviously someone else in town knew exactly how Susan had treated boys at the Sierra School.

"You're kind of quiet," Jason observed.

Matt glanced up. He didn't want there to be anything suspicious about this night. "I was just thinking about the two nurses I met in there. Late twenties, maybe. One looked Latina, with curly black hair. The other was a short reddish-haired chick."

Jason laughed. "Oh, you got an eyeful of the Tina and Veronica show. Careful, buddy, you wouldn't be the first one to step on his dick rushing toward that goalpost."

"Is that so?" Interesting.

"Oh, yeah. They're a feisty set. I hear they're worth it, though."

As Jason continued to talk, Matt tried to figure out what the hell he was going to do about Susan Tennant.

7

Zach looked over the missing persons report that Janice Lam had faxed to him. There wasn't much to it. The kid had been there at lights-out, but was missing the next morning. The school staff searched for him for a few hours before they called it in.

He stretched. He hadn't had the most restful night's sleep. Everything about this case bugged him. From the fact that this kid had been dead for two decades without anybody realizing it, to the effect Veronica Osborne had on him whenever she was nearby.

And then there were the parallels with his own life. What if things had turned out differently for him? What if *his* mother had gotten remarried to some alcoholic asshole who had wanted him out of the picture? Max Shelden's bones came with more than a little taste of "there but for the grace of God" for Zach, and he didn't want to contemplate those pathways.

He picked up the phone and called Lam. "You get the report?" she asked after he tracked her down through a couple of telephonic gatekeepers.

"I'm looking at it right now." What there was of it.

"There's nothing I can add. That was long before my time."

The date on the report was before his time, too. He would have been what? Nine? Ten? His world had been perfect then. Oh, he would have whined about Ms. Reeves, his teacher that year. She hadn't liked Zach and the sentiment was returned many times over. Still, life had been pretty much perfect. He'd had a mother and a father, three older sisters who doted on him, and a roof over his head. He hadn't known how good he had it.

He did now, and he tried to be thankful for it on a regular basis.

Zach turned his attention back to the report. "Yeah, I figured you wouldn't know much about it. The officer who took the case, Ray Stoffels, he still around?"

"Yeah, he's around. You want to talk to him?"

"Sure." It seemed like grasping at straws, but you never knew. A lot of stuff happened that never made it into reports. The odds of Ray Stoffels remembering that particular case and that particular kid weren't great, but it was worth taking a chance. "What's this Stoffels guy like?"

"Ray? He's okay. He'll talk your ear off, but he's all right." Lam snapped her gum.

That described most of the retired cops Zach knew. There was nothing they loved more than swapping old war stories, and hopefully Stoffels was the same. "Any chance I can get his number?"

"Let me give him yours instead. He can call you if he feels like it. I don't like giving out people's personal information without their permission."

Zach bit back a growl of frustration. He was a cop looking for information, not a telemarketer trying to sell magazine subscriptions. But arguing with Lam wouldn't help. He gave her his number and hung up.

"We get anything new from Dinsmore?" he asked Frank.

Frank riffled through his notepad. "Not really."

Zach rubbed his face. "You dig anything up on that school?"

Frank shook his head.

"We're running out of places to look, Frank." They needed to drum up some more leads. "I keep hoping somebody saw that kid when he came back here."

"Yeah, but who? The coach didn't see him. The

stepfather. The sister. We can go talk to the high school buddies, but they were just kids then, too."

"Let's do that tonight."

"It's a date."

Lyle Burton stared at the copy of the *Sacramento Chronicle* sitting on his desk. Susan Tennant was dead. Murdered in her home last night.

A cold bead of sweat slid down his back. Maybe it was just a weird coincidence. A woman living alone was an automatic target for weirdos and rapists. Then there was the nurse thing—lots of guys had things for nurses. Hell, the kinky stores were filled with sexy nurse uniforms.

Lyle understood that. He remembered quite well how Susan had looked in a white nursing uniform back in the day. Someone could have fixated on her and followed her home. Someone could have been watching her, waiting for her.

Slowly and carefully, he folded the newspaper shut. There was nothing he could do about this right now. It might not have anything to do with him. He'd have to wait and see what happened next, and then he'd make a plan.

This might even be the end of it. Already, the news of Max Shelden's bones had faded off the front pages of the newspapers and off the TV news. He might never hear the names Susan Tennant and Max Shelden again. He definitely might never hear them uttered in the same sentence.

He smiled. This was right in his wheelhouse. He knew how to wait and plan, and strike when the moment was right.

Feeling back in control, he dumped the newspaper into the wastebasket and went back to work.

Gary smoothed out the pages of the newspaper that he'd pulled from the trash. So the Whore was dead. The newspaper didn't go into detail, although it did mention that she'd been tied up.

He should feel bad; he knew that. He was pretty sure he would later. It would sink in. But not right now.

She'd fought against the rope used to bind her wrists and feet. She should have known that was pointless. How many times had she told the boys she tied up not to fight? She'd tied them so tight that their wrists and ankles would be marked for days. You always knew by the angry red marks which kids had been to see the Whore.

Gary rubbed his wrists as if those marks were still there. For a second they seemed to burn again, the way they had all those years ago. There was nothing there, though. Those wounds had healed a long, long time ago. There weren't even any scars there.

The Whore had tied Gary up only a couple of times—restrained him, was what she'd called it. That made it sound more refined, but it was like being trussed up the way you'd truss up a pig for slaughter. Gary hadn't been the kind to fight back. The defiant ones, those were the ones who walked around with marks on their wrists and ankles all the time.

He still remembered it, though. He remembered the terror. Lying there, tied up, unable to even wince away from anything they might want to do to you— and they wanted to do a lot to you.

There were boys who were so scared that they did exactly what the Whore had done—threw up. She'd put them on their sides and wipe their faces off with a rag when that happened.

It had choked her when she'd done it.

Gary had never understood how those men could have done what they did. They weren't protecting themselves. Even the biggest of the boys, like Max, weren't big enough to take on a whole group of big, powerful men with ropes and bats. He supposed if they'd all ganged up together they could have done something, but the boys weren't like that. They didn't group together. The men pitted them against each other in so many ways. Gary understood that now.

He hadn't then. He'd just known he couldn't trust anyone, that the other boys would turn on him in a flash. None of them could be trusted. Except Max.

Strong, handsome Max with the easy smile. Max, who had been kind to Gary, who had protected him, who had talked to him. It had been such an incredible thing to have someone to talk to. Someone who wasn't constantly putting him down or terrifying him or getting information to be used later.

Max had tried to make the other boys see. He had tried to get them to protect each other, stop turning each other in, stop fighting, stop picking on each other. Gary shuddered when he remembered what it was like in that dormitory. The lights would go out and the terror would start all over again. Whatever mistreatment one boy had received that day was passed down to a smaller, weaker boy, one like Gary.

He shook his head. You would think that knowing what it felt like to be a victim, a person wouldn't want to make anyone else feel that. Why would anyone wish that gnawing shame on someone else? Why would they wish the pain, the humiliation, the terror on anyone else?

But they did. They did it all the time.

No one wanted to feel like a victim. Everyone wanted to be the big, strong one. He had never wanted to be like those men, though. They sickened him.

Gary wasn't a religious man. He had spent too many hours praying for rescue as a child, first at his own home and then at the Sierra School, to think there was anyone or anything out there watching over him. At least nothing benevolent. If there was a higher power out there, it didn't give a rat's ass about Gary and Gary didn't give a rat's ass about it.

Nor did he believe in fate. Shit happened. That was all. A person could spend days and weeks trying to make it make sense, and it still would just be random.

This, however, felt different. The Whore had choked on her own vomit, tied hand and feet. Something was leading him. But what? Who? Max was nothing more than a pile of bones. A pile of bones couldn't tell anyone anything, could it?

He would have to think about that. Gary rubbed his thumb over Susan Tennant's watch, in his pocket, and headed home.

Okay. She had a list of names. Veronica had managed to remember first and last names for three of Max's old basketball buddies.

She flipped on her computer. Google was an amazing and terrifying tool. Could anybody really hide anywhere anymore? It didn't seem possible. We all left too many trails behind us in cyberspace and on paper.

She found listed phone numbers for two of them. She could call. That seemed somehow wrong, though. "Hey, I don't know if you remember my brother, but they found his remains in a construction site. I was hoping that maybe you'd seen him."

No, it should be done in person. She hit a few more search buttons and found an address for one of the two guys she'd found a phone number for. It looked like he still lived in the old neighborhood, possibly in his parents' old house.

Veronica took a deep breath. Did she have the guts to do this? Then she thought about the cops crawling all over her father's house, and her own lingering doubts. Could she live like that? Not knowing? Not being sure? It didn't seem like much of a choice.

A few hours later, Veronica shivered inside her car and watched Jimmy Delacroix's house. Once the sun went down, everything turned dark and cold. Normally she didn't mind it, but sitting in her cold car, watching the lit-up house in front of her, made her feel frozen from her head to her toes. Golden yellow light poured out of every window. She could see all the people inside as they went from room to room, carrying drinks and bowls of food between the kitchen and the living room, slapping each other on the back and laughing.

It looked like a whole group of her brother's old

friends was there. She was a little surprised. It had been twenty years, after all, and not everyone wanted to live in Sacramento forever. She sure hadn't.

Max had loved coming to this house. She knew how happy he was whenever he got an invitation to have dinner there or spend the night, or just hang out and watch a movie. Jimmy Delacroix's parents had been his benchmark for what parents should be. At one point, her father had slapped Max across the mouth because he'd heard the words "Mr. and Mrs. Delacroix" one too many times in one evening. Max had stopped saying their name, but Veronica didn't think it changed the way he felt.

Mr. and Mrs. Delacroix now apparently lived in a condo a few miles away. They'd "sold" their house to Jimmy when he'd started his family. Jimmy had space for his two little girls to run around, and his father didn't have to mow the lawn anymore.

Jimmy might have his old basketball buddies over to watch the game. That had been the way it was back in the day, too. This was the house that all the kids had hung out at. The one where the mom baked cookies and kept an eye on things. Not the one where the mom might lurch into the living room and vomit on the floor right when the game was starting.

Veronica steeled herself to walk up to the door, feeling uneasy and embarrassed. She was being ridiculous. They'd want to help her figure out what had happened to Max. They'd cared about him, too. Jimmy Delacroix had stopped by the house looking for Max after he'd been sent away. Veronica cringed when she remembered how her father had "welcomed" him. It hadn't been pretty.

But that hadn't been her and it had been a long time ago. Maybe he didn't even remember. She got out of the Honda, then marched up the sidewalk to the front door and rang the doorbell.

It felt like forever before the door opened, but was probably only a few seconds. Jimmy would be listening for the doorbell. He was expecting a few more people, probably, and he wouldn't want to keep them waiting. He had been that kind of kid, considerate and more thoughtful than most teenage boys. And in Veronica's experience people didn't change that much.

"Hi," she said, looking up into Jimmy's face. "I'm Veronica Osborne, Max's sister."

Recognition flashed across Jimmy's face. "Ronnie Osborne," he said. "Max's little Pop-Tart."

She blushed at the nickname. Max had said her freckles reminded him of the sprinkles across a frosted strawberry Pop-Tart, one of his favorite foods. She'd loved it when he called her that; it had made her feel special and loved. She hadn't heard it in years.

"I was wondering if I could ask you a couple of questions about my brother." She hadn't spoken loudly, but something in Jimmy's posture must have communicated itself to the other men in the house. Conversations halted, and eyes turned toward the open door.

Veronica recognized four of the men. A few others seemed a little familiar, but four looked enough like their high school selves that she recognized them. In addition to Jimmy, she saw Caleb Herbert and Pernell Moore and Justin Tran.

Jimmy crossed his arms over his chest. "You want to ask me questions about Max?"

"If it's not inconvenient," she ventured, feeling uncomfortable.

"Who is it?" Justin called from inside the house and started walking toward the door.

"It's Ronnie Osborne." Jimmy didn't move out of the doorway.

"Max's sister? What's she doing here?" Justin stood next to Jimmy. Caleb was there now, too.

"I'm not sure you know," Veronica said, stumbling over the words a little. "They found Max. They found his . . . his bones."

Why was it so hard to say? She dealt with death every day. She fought death every day. It was a war she'd always lose in the end, but she fought each battle as if it might make a difference.

She was too late to make a difference for Max, but

she had to do something. She couldn't just sit there and let the police railroad her father. Maybe, just maybe, Max had come to one of these boys after he'd run away from the Sierra School. If so, maybe Zachary McKnight would start looking for what had actually happened to her brother.

And maybe her heart would stop ratcheting up its rate every time he came within a ten-yard radius of her. That would be nice, too.

"Kind of hard not to know about that, Ronnie," Jimmy said. "It's been the lead on the news."

"I was wondering if maybe one of you had seen Max after he was sent away."

"Sent away?" Caleb took a step forward. "That's not how we heard it went down. We heard that a goon squad dragged him out of your house kicking and screaming and begging for mercy in the middle of the night."

Justin took a step down out of the house now. "We heard that they did it because your father found out that Max was smoking pot."

Ronnie dropped her gaze to the ground. What did they see in her face? Did they see her shame and her guilt? How could they not? She pressed on. "Did Max come to any of you for help? I was hoping that one of you might have seen him and might have some idea of where he was headed after he ran away.

Maybe that would give the police someplace to start looking. Maybe they'll be able to figure out what happened to him."

Pernell's eyebrows rose and he looked at Veronica. Pernell had aged well. Dad hadn't liked any of these men back when they were boys, but he'd hated Pernell with a special intensity. He was the only other African-American kid in the group besides Max. George had hated Justin and his quiet Vietnamese parents, but he'd hated Pernell much, much more. "Kind of too late now, isn't it, Ronnie?"

"I know. I thought I'd ask anyway." She should have been here years ago asking questions. She hadn't been, though. She hadn't asked because she'd hoped Max would come to her of his own will someday. She hadn't wanted to hunt him down and force him to be her brother again. She'd wanted him to come back to her all of his own accord. "Did he? Did he contact any of you?"

None of them spoke for a moment and Veronica held her breath.

"What makes you think he would have come to us?" Jimmy asked, leaning against the door.

"Well, the police think he must have come back here after he ran away from the Sierra School. He wouldn't have had any money or a place to stay. He would have had to go to somebody for help." She looked again from one face to another, hoping to see a glimmer of something.

"Oh, I get it now," Caleb said. He turned toward his friends. "My mom told me the cops were crawling all over old man Osborne's place the other day. They must think he did it. They must think Max showed up to ask his old man for help."

"Max wasn't that stupid," Justin said. "No one's that stupid."

"So none of you ever saw him? He didn't come to any of you for help?" Veronica pressed.

"Sorry, Ronnie. None of us ever saw him." Jimmy turned to go back inside the house.

Veronica turned and walked right into Zachary McKnight, who grabbed her by the arm. "What the hell are you doing here?"

8

In seconds, McKnight had her marching back to her car, his hand on her elbow. Rodriguez was talking to Max's friends.

"What the hell were you doing back there?" he demanded.

"I thought one of them might have seen Max after he ran away from Sierra. What are you doing here?"

His jaw tightened and he didn't answer.

She wrenched her arm away. "You're here for the same reason? You were going to ask them if they'd seen my brother after he ran away?" Perhaps she hadn't given Zachary McKnight enough credit.

"Ms. Osborne," he said, looming over her a little. "It is not your job to investigate what happened to your brother. The police department is doing that. At worst, you're going to get yourself hurt. At best, you'll screw up this investigation and we'll never be able to figure out what happened to your brother."

"So I'm supposed to sit around and not worry my pretty little head while you accuse my father of murdering my brother?" Part of her anger was from the adrenaline coursing through her system, but it didn't make it any less righteous. Plus, if he thought he could intimidate her just by being taller than she was, then he had no idea what it was like to go through life at five foot three. It didn't bother her one bit. She took a step toward him so they were toe-to-toe.

"I wouldn't have put it that way, but yes." He threw his hands in the air. "No one is railroading anyone. Of course we're looking at your father as a suspect. We always look at the family as a suspect. The fact that your father has a record, a drinking problem, and anger-management issues pushed him to the top of the list. His daughter saying that her daddy wouldn't do such a thing is neither an alibi nor a reason not to investigate him. That does not mean, however, that we aren't exploring all avenues. We are investigating this crime. Please stay out of our way and let us do our jobs."

Oh, crap, he was right. Suddenly all the fight went out of her. "Am I free to go?"

"Of course." McKnight stepped back.

She clicked the button to unlock her car and Mc-Knight opened the door for her. He leaned into the car after she got in. "Let us find out what happened to your brother. If there's anything you can do to help the investigation, we will ask. Until then, please stay out of it."

She hated to be sidelined, hated to sit around and wait for answers. But she could understand what he was asking. Nothing irritated her more than well-meaning family members getting in the way in her ER. She couldn't count the number of daughters she'd had to ask to shut up for ten seconds so their elderly mother or father could answer a question.

"I'll think about it," she said.

"It's a start," he said, and unexpectedly flashed a big grin at her. Then he shut her door, giving her a tap on the roof as an all clear.

Zach watched Veronica Osborne drive down the street in her Honda. Frank walked up next to him. "I wasn't sure if you two needed a room or a referee."

"I wasn't, either." Zach shook his head. Generally, he didn't go for crazy; he didn't want the drama. And he was pretty sure Veronica Osborne was packing a big ole suitcase full of crazy and bulging with drama. So why did he feel this little zing every time he looked down into those big brown eyes? It made absolutely no sense. "Did you learn anything back there?"

Frank scratched his belly. "That the Kings suck, that nobody ever saw or heard from Max again after the goons hauled him away in the night, and that everybody and their brother blamed your girlfriend there for him being sent away."

Zach turned and looked at Frank. "Any particular reason?"

Frank nodded and started walking back to the Crown Vic. "Yeah. She was the one who ratted out her brother. She found the Baggie of pot in his room and gave it to her father. That was the reason he kicked Max out of his house."

"Interesting," Zach said as he climbed into the car. She probably blamed herself, too. A big pile of guilt on top of finding out that your brother had been dead for twenty years? That could make almost anyone act a little nutty.

Frank tossed the *Sacramento Chronicle* on Zach's desk. "We dropped to page three of the Our Region section today. That nurse who got murdered last night is bogarting our spotlight."

"We need to take back our place, then. I keep hoping somebody will come forward. Somebody saw something or heard something, even if they don't know it. They just haven't made the connection. We need to keep this in front of people." He tapped his pencil against his desk.

"What are you thinking, Zach?"

"I'm thinking we need to get the word out."

"How do you propose to do that?" Frank asked him.

"What about a press conference?" You had to hand the reporters a story. They didn't have the time to go digging stuff up anymore. Hell, they barely had time to write the articles.

Frank snorted. "You hate talking to the press."

That was true. He also sucked at it. They tended to twist him around and make him lose his temper. "Not me. The sister."

Veronica was coming back from the grocery store when she found Zach McKnight standing in front of her condo door. Sadly, even if your life was turned upside down, there was still a need for Diet Coke and kitty litter. Laundry also had to be done. It actually shocked her a bit that all the mundane little tasks were still there for her to do. Her brother was dead. Shouldn't the world stop? Just for a moment or two? She paused, balancing one of the bags on her hip. "What is it that you need, Sergeant McKnight?"

"I'd kind of like it if you'd call me Zach." He flashed that grin at her again, the one that made his dimple come out.

She found herself grinning back at him. Dammit. She'd spent a few years giving her heart away far too quickly. She'd learned the hard way not to do that anymore. Heaven protect her from a man with both good looks and charm, especially one who had already said that he wanted something from her.

"You drove all the way over here to get me to call you by your first name? I'm pretty sure you could have done that over the phone." She unlocked the front door and went in.

He followed her in, walking to the kitchen. "Your brother went somewhere after he left the Sierra School. We're trying to figure out where that somewhere might be. It's the first step in figuring out what happened to him."

"I've told you everything I know. I don't know what else I can do to help." She shoved the milk in the refrigerator. "In fact, I'm pretty sure you told me to stop helping. Remember?"

"It's not that we don't want your help. We just want it to be constructive. So we were wondering if you'd be willing to do a press conference." He started unloading the bags, setting items out on the countertop for her to put away.

"What good would that do? It's already been in the paper. TV even covered it a little."

"It would give what happened to Max a live, human face. A plea from the family often gets the media's attention, and what grabs the media's attention grabs the city's attention. Maybe we'll luck out and someone who saw Max that night will see how much you want to know what happened to your brother, and come forward."

Veronica chewed it over for a minute. The thought of standing in front of a microphone with a dozen TV cameras aimed at her was not particularly appealing. She didn't even like getting her photo taken for her employee badge. She definitely didn't want to talk about Max, not even to her closest friends.

But it might help find out what had happened to him. It might provide information. It might get her father off the hook. In the end, how important was what she did and didn't want to do?

"Would I have to answer questions?" She'd seen how the reporters screamed questions at people and she couldn't handle that. It wasn't that she didn't operate well under stress. She was amazing under stress. Give her a myocardial infarction and a cranky ER resident and she would shine like a freaking diamond. The quick-with-a-comeback thing? Not so much. She sat down at the kitchen table.

McKnight sat down across from her. "Maybe a few questions, but we'd make sure it stayed mellow. It's not like you're a politician who's been caught in a sex scandal. You're a grieving family member asking for the public's attention." He kept those caramel brown eyes trained on her, steady and calm.

She leaned forward and looked directly into his eyes, her face inches from his. She could feel his warmth from across the table. His lips were so close. If she leaned forward just a fraction and he leaned forward just a fraction, the gap between them would disappear. She wondered what his lips would feel like on hers, what he would taste like. "You don't have to treat me like a spooked horse," she said.

He jerked back. "I wasn't aware that I was treating you like any kind of horse."

She leaned back in her chair, satisfied at having rattled him. "I know all the little tricks of the trade. I use them in the emergency room every freakin' day. Talking down meth addicts and calming car accident victims is my job. I know how to mirror people's posture and keep my voice low and steady. I don't like having the same tricks used on me. Just talk to me like a person. Not like a resource to be managed."

Ooh. She'd made him blink. Score one.

He shook his head and laughed. "You're right, I'm

sorry. It's an occupational hazard. I do it to my mother all the time. It pisses her off, too."

She smiled. "It's okay. I know. I'm constantly triaging people in my head. You have no idea how many diseases I've diagnosed walking through Arden Fair Mall. Only my nursing buddies will shop with me anymore. Now. About the press conference. Tell me what I need to do."

Gary Havens chopped the green onion. He liked to cook. He found it interesting to see how things came together, how different flavors complemented each other, what things went together and what things didn't.

It had started out as a necessity. He had to learn to cook to feed himself when he was finally out on his own. It was either that or a steady diet of McDonald's, and he'd had more than enough of institutional food for a lifetime. He'd found an old copy of the *Joy of Cooking* in a thrift shop and a whole new universe had opened before him.

After a while, cooking had become less of a necessity and more of a hobby. He cruised the farmer's markets now, often driving into Davis on Saturday mornings to get the freshest produce. Then he'd scour the Internet looking for recipes for things to do with the magical things he'd find. Fava beans? Who had ever heard of fava beans? They were a revelation with their double pods and strange fibrous insides. And he'd never even heard of chard, much less eaten it. Now he had it all the time when it was in season.

Everything was best in its own time. You had to be patient. Wait until things were at their peak and then seize your opportunities when they presented themselves.

He switched on the evening news while he cooked. He preferred Channel 14, largely because of Marianne Robar. She was one of the reporters, and she was on almost every night.

It went without saying that she was very pretty. What television newsperson wasn't? They were all pretty, with thick hair and perfect teeth and flawless skin. Gary knew some of it was makeup. Sometimes when they got in super close on Evelyn Martinez, the anchorwoman, you could see that her skin had broken out under the pancake makeup.

Marianne never looked like her skin had broken out. Or like she hadn't gotten enough sleep. She had a great laugh, too. It wasn't phony sounding, like most of the newspeople's laughs. Marianne really sounded like she was enjoying herself, even when they made her stand out by Interstate 80 up in Truckee to broadcast about the latest winter storm. Gary snorted. As if snow in the Sierras in January was breaking news.

Sometimes Gary imagined that he was making dinner for Marianne as he watched her on TV and cooked. He liked to pretend that she would come over after she was done at the station and they would have dinner together and talk about the broadcast. She would tell him funny stories about what the cameramen had done and he would tell her what a great job she'd done. Then she'd look up at him with those beautiful dark eyes and tell him that his opinion meant more to her than anything else.

One time, he'd actually gone to the television station and waited outside. He'd followed her when she left. He hadn't been able to follow her all the way home, though. She'd pulled into a gated community, and Gary couldn't figure out how to get in after the gates had pulled shut behind her. It was a shame. He'd hoped to see where she actually lived. He thought maybe he'd come and watch over the place sometime, maybe do little repairs that he could see needed doing without telling her. He'd be like her special guardian angel.

He diced the green onion very thin. He was sure Marianne would like it better that way. She came on now, and Gary picked up the remote to turn up the volume.

"We're here live at the press conference now, Evelyn," Marianne said. "The victim's sister is going to be speaking."

"Any idea of what the sister will be saying?" Evelyn asked Marianne.

There was a little pause as Marianne listened to what Evelyn said, then she replied, "No idea yet, Evelyn. I'll be letting you know as soon as we know something. Here she comes now."

Marianne's face left the screen and the picture now showed a dais with a row of police officers standing behind it. A woman walked past them and up to the microphone. She was short. Wearing heels, she still barely came up to the shoulder of most of the officers she walked past.

She was pretty, too. Not as pretty as Marianne. Certainly not as exotic. She had a round face and feathery reddish-brown hair and a little pointed chin. She had on black slacks and some kind of complicated shirt that wrapped around her and tied.

She adjusted the microphone down and said, "My name is Veronica Osborne and I am . . . was . . . Max Shelden's sister."

Gary's world whirled a little. Max's sister? He peered closer at the TV set. Was it little Pop-Tart? It had to be. Who else could it be? Max had only talked about one sister. He'd talked about her a lot, though. What a great kid she was. How smart she was. How funny she was.

Only once had he mentioned that she had been

the one to betray him, that it was because of her that he'd ended up at the Sierra School for Boys enduring treatment that no one would wish on a dog.

Gary shoved a tape in the VCR and hit record. He'd need to watch this again. Maybe more than once.

After the interview Marianne came back on. "There you have it, Evelyn. A plea from the dead boy's sister for any information that could help police figure out how his body came to be in that construction site." Marianne looked very earnest, as if it was terribly important that everyone know what happened to Max. She was right. People should probably know.

"Thanks, Marianne," the news anchor said. "Here's the contact information for anyone with any information on Max Shelden." The screen filled with an 800 number and a website URL, and Gary jotted both down.

What would they do if he called? He could tell them about the last time he saw Max. About the blood and the bruises and the way his head had rolled back. Gary wasn't sure how Max's bones ended up down in that construction site, but he was beginning to have an idea or two. Maybe he could share those, as well.

First, though, he wanted to be sure about the Pop-Tart. He turned the heat off from beneath the frying pan, washed his hands, and went to the trunk that he used as a coffee table. He cleared the top off and opened it up, then lifted out the blankets that were on top. Beneath that were several shoe boxes. He took out the brown-and-orange one at the bottom and opened it. Inside was a watch, a belt buckle, a ring, and a photo of a light-skinned African-American boy with a little blond girl on a beach.

He took the photo back into the kitchen, hit rewind on the VCR tape, and watched Veronica Osborne's press conference all over again, holding the photo up to the TV set.

It was her all right. It was Max's Pop-Tart.

A whisper started in the back of his head. The Pop-Tart was a betrayer. She was the first and possibly the worst, and fate had shown her to him. The universe had shoved her in front of his face. It must mean something.

9

It was over. How did politicians do that day after day? All those lights. All those cameras. All those eyes. It was horrible.

The second it was over, she'd escaped off the dais and found a quiet corner in a back room.

"You did great." Zach walked up to her.

"Yeah, right." Her heart was still racing and she could barely get the glass of water to her lips because her hand was shaking.

"Seriously, you were perfect. Concerned. Sympathetic. Calm." He leaned against the wall next to her and smiled.

She felt her shoulders relax a little. They were only halfway up to her ears now. "You just think I did well because the flop sweat hasn't soaked through my jacket yet."

He laughed. It was a nice laugh. A deep, rumbling chuckle. "It really sets off all those fight-or-flight reflexes, doesn't it? I look up at those banks of cameras and microphones, and my first urge is to rabbit right out the back door."

"Have you done a lot of press conferences?"

He shook his head. "No. That's why we have a PIO."

"A what?"

"Public information officer. The person who gives most of the press conferences and manages all the media contacts."

Veronica blew a breath out at her bangs. It felt as if they were sticking to her forehead. No way was she taking off her jacket; she hadn't been joking about the flop sweat.

"You ready to go?" he asked.

Veronica looked around. Everyone had gone back to their business. She'd gone from being the center of attention to invisible in about thirty seconds flat. She rather preferred the invisible thing. "Yeah. That would be good."

"Great. I'll take you home." He put his hand on her elbow and started to guide her toward the door.

"You don't have to. I'm sure you have better things to do."

He smiled down at her and her knees went a little weak. "I can't think of a single solitary one."

*   *   *

Veronica smelled good. It was one of those girl things, but it wasn't perfume. Maybe it was the shampoo or the body wash—a soapy, clean thing. Zach opened the door of the Crown Vic and lingered for a moment to get a sniff of her as Veronica got in.

She smiled up at him after she got in and he shut the door. She looked almost impossibly young and way too sweet for the way she'd grown up. Looks clearly were deceiving in her case; she wasn't half as vulnerable as she appeared. But knowing that did nothing to stop the clench in his chest when he looked down into those wide eyes. He gave her a quick smile back and walked around to the driver's side.

He slid into the seat and put the car in gear.

It really had gone as well as it could have. Zach hadn't expected anything else. The press would behave themselves in a situation like this. If they jumped all over the grieving sister, they'd look like a bunch of punks. Which would not be entirely inaccurate. Still, it required a certain amount of give-and-take. That was the way it was a lot of the time with the police and the press. The press used the police for stories and the police used the press to get information out. That was on a good day.

On a bad day? Well, on a bad day, the press trampled on the rights of the victims, leaked information, and muddied the waters of an investigation. It felt good to put one in the win column today.

"Do you think it'll help?" she asked, looking ahead into the darkness.

"We won't know for a little while, but I do think it could. It definitely can't hurt. Sometimes you have to jog people's memories a few times. It's been a long time." The other possibility, of course, was that no one had seen Max in the Sacramento area because he hadn't come here after he ran away from the Sierra School. The possibility was definitely there and growing stronger.

"Someone other than my dad, right?" She turned to look at him.

He gave her a rueful grin. "I can't promise that, Veronica. The evidence will take us wherever it takes us."

"But right now, there's nothing that points to my dad. Nothing specific. And this might drum up something that leads away from him."

"Sure, it could." Or it could lead right back to him. Zach would cross that bridge if he came to it.

Her need to protect her father wasn't surprising to him. He'd dealt with too many beaten and abused kids whose first instinct was to protect the very people who'd harmed them. Which wasn't to say it didn't mystify him at times.

She settled back in her seat, adjusting her seat belt again. "Okay, then."

* * *

She fished the keys out of her purse before he pulled into the visitors' parking area at her condo complex. "Thanks." She opened her door and started to get out as soon as the car came to a stop.

"Hold on a second." He was around the car before she could get all the way out. "I'll walk you to your door."

"It's Curtis Park. I'll be fine."

"Humor me." He stood there, hands shoved in his pockets, shoulders hunched a little against the fall chill. "You just did a press conference that aired on all the local news stations. Crazies come out of the woodwork after those sometimes."

"Isn't that precisely what we're counting on?" As if she didn't know how to deal with it. Even sane people were crazy when you got them into an emergency bay. The actually crazy people went to Bat Shit One in a nanosecond.

He didn't budge. "There are crazies and then there are crazies."

That was true enough. Plus, he smelled good. She was almost as much of a sucker for that as she was for the dimple thing. She sighed. "Come on, then."

She saw him scanning the landscaping on either side of the sidewalk as they walked from the parking lot to her condo. They were almost at her door when she heard the screech of tires in the lot, then a thud, like a car going up over a curb.

She had already turned and was heading back to the lot when he grabbed her arm. "Me first."

Like he was going to know what to do if someone had hit something and needed medical attention? Still, the remark about the wide variety of crazies stuck in her head, so she nodded. They'd gone less than a dozen steps when they heard the slam of a car door and a voice yell, "You stupid slut, what the hell did you think you were doing?"

Veronica walked into the parking lot several steps behind Zach and said, "Hi, Dad. Nice to see you, too."

George Osborne's Buick was halfway up on the curb. Osborne had missed the lamppost by inches. Zach shook his head.

Osborne stood on the sidewalk, swaying as if a strong wind was buffeting him around. "What the hell did you think you were doing?"

"I might ask you the same thing," Veronica answered, her voice calm. She stayed a few steps back, wary and careful. She'd given Zach the impression that her father had never been violent with her, but she was acting like someone who knew how to avoid getting a punch thrown at them.

"I sure as hell haven't been shooting my mouth off on TV about things I don't know anything about."

Osborne took a few staggering steps toward them and Zach shifted so he was between Osborne and Veronica. He'd been convinced from the start that Osborne knew more than he was saying. Maybe he'd let something slip now, something Zach could use.

"What *do* you know, Dad? Do you know something about what happened to Max?" Veronica stepped forward now. Well, well, well, it seemed as if the dutiful daughter had been harboring a doubt or two herself. Underneath the dutiful daughter was a realist. He'd suspected that all along and was damn glad to be proved right.

"What the hell do you mean by that?" Osborne lurched another step toward Veronica.

"You said I was shooting my mouth off about something I knew nothing about. So I was wondering . . . do you know something about it? Is that how you know I'm barking up the wrong tree? Did Max come to you and Mama for help?"

"If that brat had darkened my doorstep again, he would have been back at that school so fast his nappy little head would have spun off his scrawny little neck." Osborne spat on the ground for emphasis.

"But you know something, don't you, Dad?" Veronica's voice sounded strained. "What is it? Won't you tell me? It's been so long. Can't we finally let Max lie in peace?"

Zach thought that Veronica was getting through to him, that Osborne might actually tell them something that would help them blow this case open.

Then something about her last sentence roused his anger again. In Zach's experience, there were two kinds of drunks: lovey ones and angry ones. He didn't enjoy being slobbered on, but he'd rather get a man hug than a right cross to the jaw.

"I'm not the one who's not letting him lie in peace. You're the one out there sniveling and begging for information. Offering rewards. Making promises. He's dead. He's been dead a long time. Leave it be."

Veronica's jaw tightened. "I can't."

Osborne threw his hands in the air. "Well, don't come crying to me about it. I warned you. Leave it be."

"Or what, Daddy? What will happen if I don't? Did you have something to do with this?"

"Why, you little brat! How dare you accuse me? You think I killed the bastard? Well, then prove it." Osborne advanced on his daughter. He wasn't a big man, but she was a tiny woman and he loomed over her. He clenched his fists at his sides. A vein bulged in the side of his neck.

Veronica stood her ground.

Zach moved between them. "It's time for you to leave, Mr. Osborne."

Osborne turned his attention to Zach. "Who the hell are you?" he slurred.

"Detective Zachary McKnight from the Sacramento PD, Mr. Osborne," Zach said, keeping his voice level and calm. "We met the other day."

"Oh, that's right. You're one of the monkeys that tore apart my house, aren't you?" Osborne squinted one eye as if that would help him make out Zach's features better.

"I think it's time for you to leave, Mr. Osborne." Zach stood very still.

"Oh, you do, do you?" Osborne poked Zach in the chest. "You gonna make me leave?"

Zach sighed. He didn't like to be poked in the chest. He especially didn't like to be poked in the chest by a drunk who had just screamed obscenities at his own daughter in public.

"Don't touch me." Zach grabbed Osborne's finger, twisted it back and around, and Osborne fell to his knees.

"Stop it!" Veronica pushed at Zach's arm. "You're hurting him."

Zach looked at her in surprise. "I wouldn't be if he'd stop struggling." All George Osborne had to do was settle down and he'd release him.

"And how likely do you think *that* is?" Veronica glared up at him, hands on her hips.

Zach looked from her down to Osborne on his knees in front of him. Not very fucking likely. Osborne was definitely a fighter; he'd stop struggling when he was dead. Zach released the older man's hand and stepped away. "Get in your car and go home," he told Osborne.

Veronica helped her father to his feet. He rewarded her by batting her hands away. "This is your fault, you stupid bitch."

"I know, Dad," she said, examining his hand. She didn't even react to the name-calling. Zach would bet she'd heard that and worse many times before. No wonder she could handle the drunks and crazies who paraded through the emergency room. She'd been raised with it.

Osborne snatched his hand away from her. "You're meddling in things you know nothing about."

"Then enlighten us," Zach broke in.

"Fat chance, asshole." Osborne turned and walked back toward his car, hand cradled against his chest. It probably hurt. It might even end up a little swollen, but Zach knew he hadn't broken anything. Anger made him very careful, and he was very angry right now.

What kind of man spoke to his daughter like that? What kind of abuse had he dished out for years to have her react like that? Or more to the point, to not react to it at all.

Veronica was walking after Osborne. "Let me drive you, Dad."

"I don't need you to fucking drive me, Ronnie. I was driving long before you were born." Osborne didn't even look behind him.

"I know, but you're hurt. Let me take you home." Veronica caught up with him on the sidewalk and took his arm.

"Leave me be. I'm fine." Osborne shook her off, damn near shaking her off her feet. She stumbled a bit and Zach rushed to steady her.

Most men would have balked at the look she gave him. He'd faced down worse, though. "You okay?"

She rolled her eyes as an answer, then turned back to her father. "Dad, I don't think you're in any shape to drive home."

"Too damn bad. I'm doing it anyway." He opened the car door, awkward with his left hand, and slipped inside.

As her father started the engine of the big Buick, Veronica stepped back onto the sidewalk and watched him peel out of the lot. "Fabulous. What if he kills someone on the way home?"

As if to prove her point, another car—actually a white pickup truck—nearly rear-ended the Buick when Osborne stopped short at the stop sign at the end of the street.

"His hand isn't hurt that bad," Zach protested.

"No, but he is that drunk. My dad can hold his liquor. If he's swaying and slurring his words, he's got quite a load on." She turned and marched toward her door, fumbling for her keys inside her purse.

Zach pulled out his cell phone. "I'll call it in and have someone pull him over before he can do any harm."

Veronica threw her hands in the air. "What the hell did I ever do to you?"

Zach paused. Did she want him to leave her father on the road or get him off the road?

"Who do you think they're going to call after they pull him over?" she asked.

He'd heard that tone way too many times from his older sisters, and realization dawned. It must have shown on his face.

"That's right. His dutiful, loving daughter, who has already maxed out two credit cards bailing him out of jail." She unlocked the door to the condo and started in, leaping back as a small black cat darted out the door. "Damn it, Shadow." She called after the cat, then turned again on Zach. "Now look what you've done. Have you ever tried to find a black cat at night? It's about as easy as getting a drunken father out of jail in the middle of the night."

So now her cat getting out was his fault, too? Jesus. "What was I supposed to do? Stand there and let him call you names?"

She marched right up to him, her nose practically at his chest. "Do you really think it's the first time?"

"Just because he's done it before doesn't mean it's right." He couldn't believe he was defending himself for defending her. How messed up was that? He'd been so right when he decided this girl was nuts.

She stopped for a minute, looking up at him with narrowed eyes, then leaned against the door frame. "Look. I get how crazy this looks. My father is a drunk. He's mean when he's sober and the booze does not improve that. He is, however, my father, and at this point he's the only family I have. As far as what's right and what's not . . . I'm sure you know as well as I do how little that applies to reality. My father is who he is. I can't do anything about it. I can only be the person I think I should be, and that person tries to be a decent daughter regardless of how fucked up her father is. Get it now?"

He did get it. She was correct. Fair and right didn't have much of a place in the world. It was part of why he was a cop: to help them come out on top a little more often.

"I'm sorry to have interfered. I'll just get going."

Veronica's hands dropped to her sides. She looked oddly deflated. "Thank you. I think that's probably best."

"Would you like me to check your condo before I go? Make sure it's all clear?" It's what he had come here to do in the first place.

She hesitated and then nodded. "Please."

It didn't take long. Nothing looked like it had been disturbed. The windows and doors were all still locked. No one was lurking behind the shower curtain, under the bed, or in her very tidy closets. He came down the stairs and found Veronica making tea in the kitchen.

"It's all clear."

"Thank you."

It was too strange. They'd gone from screaming at each other to detached politeness in one minute. Zach's heart was still beating a little too fast from his altercation with her father, and now they were Emily Posting it in the kitchen.

"I'll be going, then."

She nodded. "You'll let me know if anything comes out of the press conference, right?"

The last thing he wanted was more contact with Ms. Crazy, but he could hardly refuse to let her know if there were any leads. "I'll keep you posted as best as I can."

"Got it. Thanks again." She extended her hand.

Zach shook it and headed out the door, half convinced that the look in her eyes was regret.

*   *   *

He stood by the Crown Vic in the parking lot, trying to make sense of things. He'd made a connection with Veronica. He was sure of it. There'd been a moment when he'd half thought she was going to kiss him. They'd been leaning over her kitchen table; her lips had been tantalizingly close to his. He couldn't take his eyes off her face, off the delicate spray of freckles across her nose, off the full roundness of her lips.

If he'd leaned forward just a fraction, he could have kissed her. He could kick himself for not having done it; it wasn't like him to hesitate like that.

Then after the press conference, in the car on the way home, he'd felt her open up to him. Why it mattered to him, he wasn't entirely sure. He'd thought he'd wanted to win her trust to get whatever information she might be holding back. He'd wanted to solve his case, to keep his numbers up.

But somewhere along the line, that had changed. Now he wanted her to look up at him with those soft brown eyes and trust him. He wanted her to know that he was there to look out for her. He wanted her to realize that there was a man around who wouldn't let her down, who would be there for her, who would protect her.

No one had ever been there for her. She'd done

everything she'd done despite the people around her, not because of them. Zach couldn't imagine how that would feel.

He got into the car. Frank was right: he had it bad. When the hell had that happened? Had it been that first moment when he'd crouched next to her in her home and felt a surge of protectiveness in his chest as he told her that they'd finally found her brother?

Or had it been when they'd faced off at her father's house when he'd served the search warrant? Had it been her defiance in the face of all that overwhelming police presence? Lord knew he loved a plucky woman. He could probably credit his older sisters with that.

Veronica Osborne was a classic example of the caretaking adult child of an alcoholic. She undoubtedly knew it, too. There was too much intelligence under that freckle-faced girl-next-door exterior for her not to know it.

Zach turned the Crown Vic toward the station house. With any luck, the tip line would be ringing by now.

10

The whole situation still had her riled. Veronica laid the story out to Tina when she got to the ER.

Tina stared up at Veronica from where she sat at the nurses' station. "That's kind of sweet."

"The big police officer with the broad shoulders had my drunk father down on his knees begging for mercy!" Every time she thought about it, she wanted to scream. She just wasn't sure at whom.

Tina leaned back. "He does have nice shoulders, doesn't he?" She closed the patient file she'd been making a notation in and slid it into the rack.

"My father's an old man, and not a well one. It was completely over the top."

Tina's cell phone rang and she fished it out of her pocket. "Hey, yourself," she said.

Veronica knew that tone of voice. Tina had a new man.

"Here? Now? A nail gun? It's still in his chest?" Tina asked breathlessly and then listened for a moment. "Oh, you definitely know how to treat a girl. I'll be ready."

"Who was that?" Veronica asked after Tina hung up.

"Remember the EMT who brought in the asphyxiated chick?" Her smile broke out on her face like a ray of sunshine.

"The cute one who just moved here from Truckee?" The one who had argued with Tina and probably won her heart forever?

"The very one. He's bringing in a guy whose girlfriend attacked him with a nail gun." Tina leaned toward Veronica and whispered. "And the nails are still in place. I'm telling you, this guy knows how to make a girl hot."

"May I say again that you are one sick puppy?" Veronica shook her head.

"I wear it with pride. Oh, and about your police officer squaring off with your father? I think that's totally sweet. He was protecting you." Tina walked away, her purple Crocs squeaking with every step.

"I don't need protecting." She'd been taking care of herself for years. She didn't need anyone else to do it.

Tina paused in front of the curtain she was about to slip through. The usual smart-ass snap to her eyes wasn't there. "Everybody needs protecting sometimes, Veronica. Even you." Then she slid through the curtain to check on the guy who had apparently attempted to edge his own foot off while working in his yard. The curtain popped open and Tina peeked out. "By the way, did I tell you that I figured out why that asphyxiation patient looked so familiar?"

Veronica shook her head.

"It was Susan Tennant."

The name sounded familiar, but she couldn't quite place it. "And I should know her why?"

"You remember, she's the nurse who started that program for at-risk teenagers. The one down in Oak Park?"

That did sound familiar.

"We heard her speak once, at the Radisson. It was part of a continuing-ed thing," Tina prompted her.

Ding ding ding. Ladies and gentlemen, we have a winner. Veronica did remember now.

But seriously? Susan Tennant and autoerotic asphyxiation? "She's the one who looked like it was, you know, a kinky consensual thing?"

"Yep." Tina nodded, her eyes big. "I swear, I thought she was practically a nun. You never can tell with people, can you?"

"You sure can't." Veronica walked away as the emergency room doors slid open and Matt Cassel came in pulling a stretcher right toward Tina. Even from the nurses' station, Veronica could see the nails sticking straight up out of the guy's chest.

Tina's eyes shone. There were all kinds of sweet in the world.

Lyle watched the rebroadcast of Max's sister's press conference. Would this story never die?

He could see why the police wanted her in front of the cameras. She was pretty in an approachable way. She looked good on camera, sympathetic.

Too bad she wasn't obese, with a wart on her nose. The story might have disappeared by now. Eclipsed, ironically, by Susan Tennant's murder. That was assuming the police didn't figure out that they were connected. But maybe they weren't. Maybe it was one big crazy coincidence.

Lyle poured himself a drink. It was going to be okay. The phone rang and he snatched it up before it woke his wife, who had already gone to bed. "Hello."

"My price just went up," the man on the other end said.

Wow. Matt wasn't sure how much more he could take. The cute little nurse in St. E's emergency room was Max Shelden's sister? What was the universe trying to do to him?

More than one shrink had told him that he couldn't run from his past, that it would catch up with him eventually. He'd thought they meant metaphorically. But first Susan Tennant, and now Max Shelden's sister?

He'd had nightmares last night. Dreams that he'd been the one who had tied up Susan Tennant and watched her choke on her own vomit. He had been able to smell her fear, feel the texture of the ropes he'd used to bind her. It *was* just a dream, right?

Had Tennant been able to smell the fear of the boys she'd tormented? Or had it never touched her? He'd never know now. He hoped the memories of it followed her straight to hell.

But now Max's sister was in front of his face. What did that mean? Maybe he didn't have to do anything about Veronica. Maybe the universe would take care of that, too.

After her shift was over, Veronica wanted nothing more than to go back to her condo, crawl into bed, and stay there until her next shift started. There'd been too much emotional turmoil lately.

But today was unlikely to be drama free. She had

to check on her dad. Maybe he'd have been drunk enough that he wouldn't really remember what happened last night. He rarely blacked out enough to have no memory, but the details were often hazy, so she could spin them into a gentler reality.

It wasn't lying. Not really. It was more of a creative reimagining of her life. She preferred it in soft focus. She wasn't doing it for him, after all. She was doing it for herself.

The only reason she didn't cut him out of her life completely was that she couldn't bear to be the kind of daughter who wasn't there for her parent.

She got behind the wheel of her car and checked her watch. Dad would be up. She dialed his number on her cell, but after five rings it went to voice mail.

She hung up without leaving a message. So much for getting away with a quick phone call.

She sighed and started the engine. She'd just check on him. She could be in and out in ten minutes. He could make his own breakfast and take out his own trash for once.

She clicked on the news as she drove, but it was too depressing. Suicide bombs. Floods. Oil spills. She started scanning through the music stations, but nothing caught her interest. Not the song she didn't recognize, the song she'd heard too many times before, or the creepy old man trying to tell her that he was her friend in the diamond business. She snapped the radio off and rode in silence, brooding.

She wished her father would tell her whatever he knew about Max's death and get it over with. All the comments about her not knowing what she was getting into made her suspect that he knew precisely what type of hornet's nest Max's bones had stirred up.

It could take weeks to piece together the dribs and drabs he was giving her. By then, the police would have lost interest. She was surprised they'd been willing to do as much as they had up to now. There was no public hue and cry over twenty-year-old bones; why would there be? Why should they care anyway?

She shifted uncomfortably in her seat. Zach Mc-Knight seemed to care. He should have been scrambling away from this case as fast as those powerful-looking thighs of his could take him.

And why was she even noticing his thighs? She had sworn off cops, kind eyes or not.

When she parked in front of her father's house no lights were on. It was a good thing she'd come by. If he didn't get up now, he was going to be late for work. Jobs were harder and harder to come by for anyone, and even more so for alcoholic wrench jockeys in their fifties. He needed to hold on to this job for as long as he could, because Veronica was damned if she was going to support him or make another loan to him from her savings.

Loan, her ass. She'd known when she'd written him that last check that she'd never see that money again.

She looked at the house with its sagging front porch and peeling paint. Someday, all this would be hers. The porch steps creaked under her feet. She'd never felt more like a princess. Not.

She knocked. "Dad? It's me, Ronnie."

No answer. Maybe he was in the shower. Or maybe he was still out cold. She knocked again. Still nothing. She fished her key out of her purse and let herself in, tucking the key back into her purse as she walked through the door.

She nearly slipped in the puddle of blood on the floor. It took her a second to register why she'd lost her balance, and another second to register the sight of her father lying in the pool of blood.

Her throat clogged up as if a scream had gotten stuck just above her larynx, but it never made it out. Carefully, ever so carefully, she touched two fingers to his carotid artery to check his pulse. Nothing.

She'd known there wouldn't be. Heads weren't supposed to be bent at that awkward angle. Faces weren't supposed to be that color of gray. Eyes weren't supposed to stare with glassy fixation at puddles of blood.

There was a protocol to these things, and Veronica

knew exactly what to do. She'd checked for a pulse. Now she called 911. She gave the address. She said her father had fallen. She did not scream. She did not become hysterical. She did not move the body.

The body. Not her father. The body. She said it out loud. Her father was gone. He'd been gone for at least a few hours. She knew that. The words felt strange on her lips. In fact, her whole face felt strange. Numb.

It was stuffy in the house and it smelled terrible. She knew that smell. She should have recognized it the second she'd opened the door. It smelled like vomit and blood and feces. It smelled like recent death. It was the smell she fought in the emergency room. It was the smell she'd fought in her mother's hospital room. She was too late to fight it here. This battle had been lost long before her feet had hit the first creaky step outside.

She squatted down on her heels. "Oh, Daddy," she said. "I'm so sorry. I'm so very sorry."

Zach's cell phone had rung less than an hour before he was due to be at the station. Veronica Osborne's father was dead. Dispatch thought he'd want to know.

Half an hour later he pulled up in front of George Osborne's house, chewing the Clif Bar he'd grabbed out of his pantry before rushing to his car. There were already two black-and-whites, one unmarked car, an ambulance, and a fire truck at the scene. People were crawling all over hell and creation, but no one was moving fast. No one bothered to rush when the subject was already dead.

Zach sighed and got out of his car, making sure his badge was clipped to his belt and visible. One of the uniformed officers held the crime-scene tape up for him to duck under. There were no news crews on the street yet, but they'd be here eventually. He was glad the uniforms had secured the scene in advance.

"Who's inside?" he asked the uniform.

"Little Hillary," the man said, dropping the tape behind Zach.

Little Hillary was a coroner's investigator named Nancy Martinez, who had earned her nickname from the black pantsuits she habitually wore. She definitely was not little, though. The "slimming" black didn't hide the width of her behind. She was good at her job, smart, efficient, and hard to rattle. Maybe that was why they called her Hillary, and it didn't have anything to do with the pantsuits.

Zach stopped at the doorway to put on booties over his shoes and stepped into the house. Little Hillary was crouched over the body of George Osborne where it lay at the bottom of his staircase in a puddle of blood, urine, vomit, and excrement. Zach took a second to let himself adjust to the smell.

"Let me guess," he said when he finally trusted himself to speak without gagging. "A drunk fell down the stairs."

Little Hillary looked up at him. "Good guess."

Zach gave a little bow, feeling as if he'd gone to the head of the class. "Thank you so much."

"It is, however, completely wrong." She stood up and walked over to Zach, by the door.

"Really?" There was a drunk lying on the floor at the base of a staircase. Being wrong was pretty surprising.

Before Hillary could explain any further, Frank arrived. He stepped into the house with exaggerated care and then sighed. "They got this many people out here for a drunk who fell down the stairs?"

"Apparently that's a bad guess," Zach informed him. "Or maybe it was a good guess that just happens to be wrong."

"Really?" Frank looked downright surprised. "Do tell."

"Do you two want to know what happened here or not?" Little Hillary asked. While she was known for her professionalism, she was not known for her sense of humor. Or her patience.

For Zach, the black humor was a coping mechanism. It was for most cops. And firefighters. And a lot of health care professionals. When you dealt every day with the tragedy and the detritus of the way human beings deal with each other, sometimes you had to choose between laughing and crying. Sometimes drinking was thrown into the mix. Drugs weren't unheard of, either, especially prescription pills. Anger-management issues were definitely a possibility. Zach generally chose to laugh. Or at least to crack bad jokes and hope that someone else would laugh at them.

"We are all ears," Frank assured Little Hillary.

"Your drunk didn't fall down those stairs on his own. He had some help." She gestured for them to follow her over to the body, then pointed up the stairs. "The trajectory is all wrong. If he had fallen on his own, he would have landed closer to the bottom of the stairs. To land where he did, he would have needed a push."

The stench worsened with every step they took toward the body. "You're sure he was drunk, though." How many hours would it have taken George Osborne to sober up from last night? Zach wasn't sure. "How long has he been here?"

Little Hillary gave him a long, measured look. "Perhaps you might want to wait until I tell you what I know, and then ask questions. It might save all of us quite a bit of time."

She sounded like an impatient elementary school teacher. "No problem." He stuck his hands in his pockets and waited.

"So not only did your guy get a push down the stairs, somebody had a moment or two with him beforehand." Little Hillary crouched down and lifted Osborne's shirt. "See this bruising? That's a boot mark. Or maybe a dress shoe. We'll be able to get you a shoe size."

"Somebody kicked the crap out of him and then threw him down the stairs?" Frank crouched next to her and glanced up the staircase.

"I'm pretty sure they knocked him unconscious, then dragged him up the stairs and threw him down. Look at his shoes. The backs of the heels are all scuffed up. Someone staged this. They wanted us to come in here, smell the booze on this guy, shake our heads, and walk away." Little Hillary stood up and looked over at Zach. "Now do you want to ask your questions?"

A voice behind him said, "So my father was murdered?"

So much for asking who found the body. Apparently the answer was standing in the doorway to the kitchen wearing the scrubs she'd worn to work the night before.

His heart sank. This was a lot of loss for one small woman in a short period of time. How much could those narrow shoulders carry?

She walked into the room and turned to Hillary. "You're saying my father was murdered."

"I'm afraid so. I'm so sorry." Little Hillary looked sincerely regretful. She probably was. Overhearing the cops and the coroner's investigator talking at the crime scene was not the approved way of informing a family member that someone had met with foul play.

"Maybe you should go back into the kitchen," Zach suggested. "Let us finish up here, and we'll come and let you know what's going on. Is there someone we can call? Someone who can come and sit with you?" Someone needed to get her out of here.

She didn't even turn around to face him. "Do you know the time of death?"

"Around midnight last night. That's my best guess for now," Little Hillary told her.

Veronica's knees started to buckle. Zach caught her by the elbow, keeping her upright. She pulled herself up and snatched her arm away from him with a glare.

"That was only a couple of hours after I saw him." Her voice broke a little. "I shouldn't have let him go." She looked at Zach. "I told you it wasn't safe."

Murdered. They were saying her father had been *murdered*. It didn't make any sense.

She'd seen him and assumed he'd lost his balance on the stairs, hit his belly on the way down, and his cirrhotic liver and half-destroyed spleen had him vomiting up blood and bleeding to death in his own home. Alone. She blamed him for his own death instantly.

She added another rock to the weight that seemed to be crushing her heart.

She couldn't look at the cops or the coroner's investigator or her father any longer. She retreated into the kitchen.

By reflex, she pulled a coffee filter out of the drawer and began to spoon coffee into the cone.

"Veronica."

She'd known Zach would follow her, but she needed a minute or two to pull herself together. She didn't want that low voice, full of sympathy, cascading over her.

"Veronica," he repeated. "Are you okay?"

She laughed. Her favorite coping mechanism. They'd probably all think she was stark raving mad.

Maybe she was.

"No. I'm not okay. I'm several million miles from okay." She started running water into the coffeepot, her hands rock steady. She was every bit as much of an addict as her father; she just happened to be addicted to adrenaline. A stiff shot of whiskey in his morning coffee had always stilled the shakes in her father's hands. She needed a good shock to her system to make her strangely calm.

"You need to stop." He needed to stop using that deep, gentle voice. She knew precisely what he was doing and it was pissing her off. She turned to say so, but he went on, "This is a crime scene. You need to leave everything alone. In fact, you need to get out of the house while we process this place."

She froze. She hadn't thought about that. She backed away from the counter. "I'm sorry. My fingerprints are going to be all over this place anyway, though. I'm here a couple of times a week."

He nodded. "Got it. Still, let's get you out of here. Is there someone we can call?"

She glanced up at the kitchen clock. Tina would already be in bed. Monica would already be at work downtown. She would be here in a heartbeat if Veronica called her, but what could any of them do? Nothing could bring her father back from the dead.

She looked down at her hands. "I'll be fine. Where should I wait?"

"It would probably be best if you went home. Someone will be by as soon as possible to tell you what we know." He took a few more steps into the kitchen. "I am so sorry, Veronica."

She hated the sympathy in his voice. She hated the fact that his broad shoulders looked like a perfect place to lay her head and cry. She hated more than anything that she wanted him to take her in his arms and let her cry out all her hurt and sadness and regret.

His hands began to reach toward her. She looked up into his eyes and for a moment, her breath caught.

"Hey, Zach, Martinez is done. Okay with you if we move the body?" Rodriguez came into the kitchen and Zach's hands dropped back to his sides.

He turned to his partner. "Sure. If Martinez says we're done, we're done." He turned back to Veronica. "You okay to drive?"

She nodded.

"You sure? It's normal to be a little shocky right now. I can get one of the uniforms to drive you. No problem."

"I'm fine. It's only a couple of miles, anyway." It would probably be better if she walked home. She could use the time to clear her head.

"You're sure?" he asked again, glancing over his shoulder at the activity going on behind him.

She nodded.

"It might be better if you went out the back," he suggested.

Oh, yeah. People didn't like to see their loved ones being zipped into black plastic body bags. She'd escorted many family members out of ER bays to keep them from having to see that. Again, she nodded.

She looked around for her purse. It wasn't on the kitchen counter, where she usually set it when she came by the house. She bit her lip and tried to remember where she could have put it. She'd come into the house, she'd seen her father . . .

"What is it?" he asked. "What do you need?"

Dammit. Did he have to be so intuitive? "My purse. I don't know where I set down my purse."

He held up a finger and went back into the entryway. He was back in a second or two, holding her bag. It looked ridiculous hanging from his big hand, like a child's toy, really.

One of her coworkers, an older nurse named Jan, said you could tell how many people a woman was responsible for by the size of her purse. The bigger the purse, the more people she carried on her shoulders. Veronica's purse was pretty small. She supposed it was about to get a little bit smaller. At least she could throw out the business cards she carried around of all the bail bondsmen.

"Thanks." She took the purse from him and headed toward the back door.

Zach opened the door for her, but just as she was about to step out, he grabbed her arm. "Hold it," he barked. "Don't move."

"What the—"

He pointed to the step.

He'd grabbed her about a nanosecond before she walked through a perfect boot print on the back step.

"Martinez," he called into the house. "Can you get somebody out back, please?"

11

"Somebody was back here for a while." Phong Lee, the crime-scene tech, looked at Zach from underneath the oak tree in the backyard.

"Anything you can tell me about him?" Zach asked. The likelihood of the murderer being a woman seemed vanishingly small. It would take a good-size man to have hauled George Osborne up those stairs. He'd seen plenty of buff women at the gym, but he doubted any of them had the strength to haul the dead weight of a fully grown man up a staircase and then hurl him back down.

Lee shrugged. "I'll look at some charts and get you some approximate weights and heights when we get back to the lab. At this point I'm figuring a dude who's about six feet tall."

"I'm also pretty sure it's not the same person who kicked the crap out of your vic before he threw him down the stairs."

Now, that was interesting. "I'm listening."

"I didn't get a good look at the body, but Little Hillary said something about a dress shoe." Phong pointed over at the step. "Not too many dress shoes with waffle soles. That looks like a work boot."

"So we've got two perps? One inside, and maybe one keeping watch back here?" That didn't make sense. Why post a lookout back here? You should be watching for someone coming to the front door.

"That's up to you to figure out, Detective. But I don't think whoever was back here ever went into the house. Near as I can reconstruct, he hunkered down here under this tree for a good long while." Phong pointed to where the ground had been disturbed. "Then he went up to the back door, stood looking in, spent a little time crouched under that window, and then took off."

"So some kind of voyeur?" Who the hell would watch someone being murdered and do nothing about it? "Thanks."

Zach headed back into the house, which was buzzing like a beehive.

Frank was standing in the kitchen, talking to two crime-scene techs. He turned to Zach as he came in.

"So what are you thinking? You think this homicide is linked with the kid's bones turning up?"

Zach blew out a deep breath. "On the one hand, I can't imagine that they are linked. There's what? Twenty years between the two? On the other hand, I can't imagine that they're not linked. It's way too much of a coincidence."

"I got the same set of questions." Frank chewed on a toothpick he'd pulled from his pocket. "I don't like coincidence in a homicide investigation any more than you do, but I'm having trouble figuring out why a really old set of bones would get someone killed. It's not like we're hot on anybody's trail at this point."

"Is someone pulling all his phone records?" Zach asked.

Frank nodded. "I got some uniforms doing a door-to-door, too. Maybe somebody saw something or someone. A car. A guy. Something."

It was the kind of neighborhood where somebody might indeed have seen something. On the other hand, it was also the kind of neighborhood where people went into their houses, shut the door, and watched some TV once they got home. It was a long shot, but one that was worth taking.

Zach's cell phone buzzed in his pocket. It was the ME again.

"I got some more information for you. On your old bones."

"We'll be right over."

Veronica headed right to her bathroom, shedding clothes and belongings as she went. She dropped her purse and keys by the front door. Next she kicked off her shoes. Her scrub top and pants followed. Her panties and bra hit the floor right by the shower.

She stayed under the hot water until it ran out. Her skin was pink and raw, but still she didn't feel anything. The heat of the water and the scent of the soap were dulled, as if she was experiencing them from a distance. This was shock, she knew that. Giving it a clinical name didn't change anything, though. Sometimes knowledge was not power.

She pulled on flannel pajama pants and a tank top and went to the kitchen. She wasn't hungry, but she knew she would need her strength. She poured herself a bowl of cereal and milk.

In all those movies and books, when someone died the place was flooded with casseroles and cakes. The likelihood of that happening with her dad's death seemed slim. When her mother died, a few neighbors had brought over some food and so had her nursing school friends. Her father had been less than gracious about people's offerings. He'd spent years alienating pretty much everyone in the neighborhood, so they were more likely to throw a celebratory party now than to offer their condolences.

Veronica laid her head down on her folded arms on the table, next to her untouched cereal. She wished that her father had been a different man. She wished that the neighbors would be devastated and that his friends would feel the pain of loss.

She wished that she wasn't the only person on the planet to mourn him. Of all the many times that she'd felt alone in her life, this was the worst.

She finally sat up and ate her frosted mini-wheats, thinking about what she should do next. There were arrangements to be made, but she wasn't sure when they'd release her father's body. How was she supposed to plan a funeral when she didn't even know when she'd have the body?

Who was she fooling? Who was going to come to a funeral for her father, anyway?

So, no funeral planning. Tuck that thought away. If she was the only person sitting in the chapel when it was time, that was okay. Her heart clenched up a little, but it would be okay.

There were probably people to notify. His boss at work, for one. He'd need to know that George wasn't coming in. She glanced up at the kitchen clock. He was already way late. She looked up the number for the Jiffy Lube and dialed.

It took a few requests before she was connected to the manager, but she made it eventually. "Hi, my name is Veronica Osborne. I'm George Osborne's daughter. I wanted to let you know that he, uh, won't be coming in today."

"He sick again?" the manager asked. His voice was cigarette raspy. "Or I guess I should say hungover."

Her voice caught as she said, "Well, no. My father passed away last night."

"Excuse me? Did you say he died?" She couldn't blame him for the incredulity in his voice. She felt pretty incredulous herself.

"I'm sorry, yes. I know the news is shocking—"

"And who did you say this is?" he interrupted.

"His daughter, Veronica." Patience, Veronica. Patience. Don't snap.

"I didn't know George had a daughter."

She laid her head back down on the table and gently bounced her forehead against the wood. It was so good to know that her father talked about her so often that his coworkers didn't even know she existed. She knew what her father would have said if she had complained about that to him. He'd point out that he was there to work, not to socialize—whether he had a daughter was none of their damn business. She supposed he was right. But that didn't make it hurt any less.

"Yes. George had a daughter. Me. He won't be in to work today. He won't be in to work ever." She hung up.

Maybe she'd put off making any more phone calls. She brushed her wet hair into a ponytail and climbed into bed, exhausted. Each limb felt like there was a ten-pound weight hanging off it. Maybe she could sleep her way through this.

Fifteen minutes later it was clear that she would have no such luck. She lay watching the ceiling fan make lazy circles above her. Every time she closed her eyes, all she could see was her father's body lying at the bottom of the stairs in a pool of blood.

She thought about taking a sleeping pill, but didn't want to feel groggy later. She was barely putting one foot in front of the other as it was. She couldn't just lie here, though. She had to do something. But what?

She ticked through all the things that normal people did at times like these. There was no one to notify. No arrangements to be made. Wasn't there paperwork? There was always paperwork. She didn't even know if her father had a will, much less who his attorney might have been.

Maybe there'd be something at the house. She looked over at the clock. Surely the police were fin-

ished. She kicked off her blankets and went to find
her purse. She found Zach's card and called him.

"McKnight," he answered on the second ring.

"Hey, it's Veronica."

"What's up? Are you all right?" He sounded like
she called every day.

"Could I . . . I mean, would it be okay if I went
to my dad's house now? I thought I'd look for some
paperwork or something."

There was a pause. "You don't have to do that right
away. Why don't you give yourself a day or so?

"I need something to do. I can't sleep."

"Yeah. I know how that feels. Go ahead. I can't
imagine you'll hurt anything. Like you said, your
prints are all over that house. And Veronica?"

"Yes?"

"For what it's worth, I'm really sorry."

She could barely get the phone hung up before the
tears came.

"The bones are old. They're brittle and damaged. It
took a while to sort out what happened close to the
time of death, and what happened after the bones
were dug up and moved." Dinsmore shoved a stack
of papers across the table at Zach and Frank. "These
bones tell a story. I'm not sure it's one that anyone

wants to hear, but they're screaming it as loud as they can."

"And?" Frank asked, barely glancing down.

"And you've got a variety of breaks that occurred throughout this kid's lifetime." Dinsmore shoved his glasses up on his forehead and looked at the two detectives. "People started kicking the crap out of this kid when he was pretty young. They kept it up steadily until he was dead, and then some."

"Starting how young?" Zach asked.

"I'm guessing the first break—that would be the spiral fracture to his left arm—happened when he was about six or seven. It went untreated."

Zach winced. Spiral fractures were one of the most common child abuse injuries. They generally occurred when someone bigger and stronger twisted a kid's arm up behind his back. They didn't always get treated; trips to the doctor for broken bones brought questions that nobody wanted to answer. "Any hospital records on that one?"

Dinsmore shook his head. "Not that I could find."

"What else?" Frank asked.

"There were a couple of cracked ribs that had healed over pretty well." Yet another abuse injury that often went untreated. "Then there was the stuff that happened right before he died. I'm guessing that's what you'll be most interested in." Dinsmore slapped some

X-rays up on the viewing stand. "These breaks here in the arms were antemortem."

Zach stood up to look more closely. "Defensive wounds?"

"Quite likely. They'd be consistent with someone holding their arms up to protect their head while blows rained down on them."

Zach's stomach clenched. The kid had been what, seventeen? Eighteen? How bad could he have been, to have received that kind of beating? "What else?"

"Well, you've got these breaks to the ribs. They're also antemortem, but not by much. They'd be consistent with someone lying on the ground and getting kicked."

Zach flashed on the boot marks on George Osborne's torso, and looked at Frank. "There's our connection. It looks like we've got a kicker."

All fighters have their favorite moves. Muhammed Ali's was the jab. Felix Trinidad favored the left hook and Micky Ward was infamous for his double-hook. Bullies were no different. There were slappers and twisters and hair pullers, and there were most definitely kickers.

"I don't care for kickers," Frank said, his face serious.

Neither did Zach. Kickers tended to go for a guy when he was already down. Their victims would be lying prone, unable to defend themselves other than by curling into a ball and praying for it to end. That's when the kicker did maximum damage, whaling away on some poor guy who had already conceded the fight and was just trying to survive.

Max hadn't survived.

"Cause of death?" Zach asked.

Dinsmore shook his head. "It's not entirely clear. Based on the patterns of the injuries, I would guess internal bleeding. It would have taken a while, and it would have been painful."

Zach closed his eyes. Sometimes he hated knowing what people were capable of doing to each other. There were days when he dreamed about some job where the rancid underbelly of the human condition wouldn't be shoved in his face on a daily basis. On the other hand, he didn't think anyone could stay completely insulated from it all the time. Inhumanity reared its ugly head in everyone's life at some point. At least he had the opportunity to even the score a bit.

Dinsmore was still talking. "He was definitely dead before he was buried, though."

Fabulous. At least no one had buried the kid alive.

"And he wasn't buried down here in the valley. I'm guessing probably somewhere in the Sierras."

"Can you be any more specific than that, Doc?" Frank asked.

The Sierras. As in the Sierra School for Boys.

Dinsmore shrugged. "Not really. I could probably match soil samples if you brought me something to match it against, but I can't be any more specific with what I've got."

Frank looked over at Zach. "You ready to head up and talk to your buddy Stoffels? Maybe we could get some dirt for Dinsmore here. Kind of like an early Christmas present."

Yellow crime-scene tape still ringed the house, but there weren't any cops around. It wasn't the kind of crime where you'd need to post guards at the scene.

She ducked under the tape and pulled her keys out of her purse.

"Veronica, is that you?" a woman's voice asked.

Veronica turned. It was Mrs. Masi from two doors down. Mrs. Masi was in her seventies, but in great shape. She gardened and went for a walk every morning, rain or shine. She had a penchant for elastic-waisted Capri pants and polo shirts in pastel colors. Back when Veronica was a little girl, Mrs. Masi's hair had been brunette. These days, she kept it light ash brown. She had a few more wrinkles around her eyes, but otherwise she was pretty much unchanged. "Hi, Mrs. Masi. Yes, it's me."

"Oh, dear. Is what they're saying true?" Mrs.

Masi hadn't spoken directly to Veronica for at least three years. It had apparently begun with Mr. Masi asking Veronica's father to trim back a tree that was overhanging the street. Things had progressed rather quickly to what was, according to the police report, an operatic explosion of profanity on her father's part, including but not limited to some rather pointed suggestions about things to do to Mrs. Masi using tree branches.

"What are they saying?" Veronica answered.

Mrs. Masi trotted up the driveway. "They're saying your father's been murdered," she whispered, as if saying the words out loud might make the murderer pop out of the hedge.

"I'm afraid so."

Mrs. Masi put her hand on Veronica's arm. "How terrible. It's not a fit ending for anyone," she continued, and Veronica mentally added "even for your father, miserable scrap of humanity that he was."

"If there's anything I can do, anything you need, I hope you'll let me know." Mrs. Masi gave Veronica's arm a pat and went back down the driveway.

Veronica stared after her. It seemed like a genuine expression of sympathy. Wow. Things changed fast, didn't they? She would have bet that yesterday Mrs. Masi would have been all in favor of someone pushing her father down the stairs. Then again, maybe she was the one who'd had it wrong these past few years. A little nonplussed, Veronica let herself into the house.

She'd thought she had mentally braced herself sufficiently for the mess in the entryway, but she had been wrong. She reeled back, took several shallow breaths through her mouth, and then, skirting the mess, went upstairs to the room her father used as an office—Max's bedroom, originally.

Veronica sat down in front of the old metal desk and ran her hand over its surface. The desktop was relatively clear. There were a few bills and a bank statement, but Veronica wasn't looking for the recent day-to-day stuff. She opened the big filing drawer on the bottom-right side of the desk. There were tax returns going back way further than was necessary. Ditto with bank statements. There was a file for the car, and another one with owner's manuals for the refrigerator and washer and dryer.

She didn't see anything conveniently titled "will" or "open in case of death." She opened the drawers of the nearby filing cabinet. More bank statements; they seemed to go back forever. In the bottom drawer, she found a file with birth certificates for her, her mother, and her father, and several copies of her mother's death certificate, but no will.

Maybe he hadn't made one. Come to think of it, she wasn't sure her mother had had a will, either. She hadn't thought about it at the time of her mother's death; she'd simply assumed that everything would go to her father. But now what? What happened if her father died without a will? She'd have to look it up online.

She pushed back from the desk and bit her lower lip. Maybe there was a will filed with a lawyer. Didn't they keep copies of those things? She could look through some of the bank statements and see if her father had ever paid a lawyer anything. At least then she'd have a name and a place to start.

But there was folder after folder of bank statements. Where should she start? She pulled the statements from the year her mother died. It would make sense to make a new will after your spouse died, right? Not that she could count on her father to do the sensible thing, but it seemed like the right place to start.

Her father's bank statements were reassuringly boring. Money went in, mainly from jobs, occasionally from unemployment. Money went out to the mortgage company, PG&E, AT&T, and a few other sets of letters. There were pretty routine cash withdrawals and debit card charges at gas stations and grocery stores.

It stayed that way over the years from her mother's death until the present, so she started working backward. It didn't seem likely that her mother would have had a lawyer, but Veronica had long ago stopped expecting her parents to do what she expected. Their logic confounded her. There was a period of time when she assumed they were doing it just to screw with her head. Then she realized that she was simply not that important to them. They were erratic and that was pretty much all she could count on them to be.

The bank statements before her mother's death were pretty much the same, with the addition of a lot of medical bills. Those had eaten through her parents' savings pretty rapidly, though they'd had a tidy little nest egg set aside. Much more than she would ever have credited them with having.

She'd gone back ten years now. There were payments of all kinds, to doctors and credit card companies and car financiers, but no lawyers. She should probably just shut the drawers and walk away.

But what should she do then? She'd spent an hour and a half so far; what was another hour and a half?

She pulled another stack of file folders out of the drawer. They really did go back forever. Of all the strange things to keep . . . She didn't come across a single birthday card or Father's Day card, although she'd been dutiful about giving those. She didn't find one piece of personal correspondence. Just bank statements and tax returns.

She leafed through, watching her parents' nest egg

grow in reverse. It was like running a movie back-ward, watching buildings go back together instead of being blown up, or milk flowing up out of a glass into a carton.

Then abruptly, the bank account bottomed out again. She leafed forward. One minute there was no money, the next there was a bunch. Where the hell had that come from?

She slowed down. There were six payments that came over a six-month period that weren't from her father's job. Each one was for $9,500. The deposits had been made in cash. Where the hell had her parents gotten close to $10,000 in cash even once, much less six times?

She couldn't come up with a scenario that made any sense. Then again, she didn't even know what year she was looking at anymore. She flipped the folder closed. The year was 1991.

The year that Max disappeared.

12

"So Mohammed decided to come to the mountain," Stoffels said, motioning Zach and Frank into his house from his wheelchair. "Just as well; I don't travel as well as I used to."

Zach stepped into the log cabin and tried to keep his jaw from dropping. The ceiling of the great room soared twenty feet above their heads. A huge stone fireplace dominated one wall. The floor plan was open and airy, with the kitchen and dining area all in the big space. To the left, a spiral staircase went up to a loft area over what Zach assumed were bedrooms.

"Nice, huh?" Stoffels said, turning to admire his own house. "I built it myself, back when I was more mobile."

"It's incredible," Zach said, not exaggerating in the slightest.

Frank looked stunned. "You built it yourself? With your own two hands?"

Stoffels nodded. "On weekends and holidays and vacations. This is what I did."

Frank turned slowly around. "Now, this . . . this is a man's work."

"Oh, don't get him started." Stoffels's wife came out of a back room and into the kitchen, wiping her hands on a dish towel. She smiled at her husband, though, and came to stand next to him. "Do you boys want something to drink? Some coffee maybe?"

Zach shook his head. "No, thanks. We don't want to be any trouble."

"Well, at least sit down and make yourselves a little more comfortable." She gestured toward the dining area and they all sat down around the large plank table.

"We were hoping to talk to you about Max Shelden. Do you remember the case?" Zach asked Stoffels as he wheeled up to the table.

"Janice told me that was what you wanted to talk to me about. Have you met her?"

Zach shook his head. "We opted to come here and meet with you first, sir. She knew that we were coming, though."

Stoffels nodded. "I figured as much. If you get a chance, you should stop by and meet her. Never did I think that she would be able to make it here. Not that she isn't a fine cop; she is. Came with all kinds of credentials. But she's a woman and there's still a fair bit of chauvinism up here."

Zach could only imagine. He knew how much "chauvinism" there still was down in Sacramento. In his experience, the farther you got away from the city, the worse those things got, and they were pretty damn far away from the city up here. You wouldn't know it was only a day trip.

"Plus she's a cute little thing. Some kind of Asian something. I can't keep 'em all straight. She looks young, too, younger even than she is. She's done a heck of a job, though. Even the oldest of the good ole boys has had to admit that." He grinned over at his wife.

"About Max Shelden, sir?" Zach prompted. It had taken three hours to drive up here, and as much as he wanted to hear what Stoffels had to say, he'd like to sleep in his own bed tonight.

"Oh, yes. I do remember the case. That school had its share of runaways, but we found most of them right away. Have you been up to the school?" Stoffels looked up at Zach.

Again, Zach shook his head. "No, sir. You're our first stop."

"Well, you should put that on your itinerary, too. The school is quite a few miles from the road and, to be honest, I'm using the word 'road' loosely. It's basically a dirt track that twists up into the woods, and those woods are thick. It's easy to lose your way, especially in the dark. Especially if you're a city boy who's been dropped down into that place. Darn few of those boys had ever been out into the countryside.

"Most of the boys who tried to run didn't get far. We'd find them, scared and lost, covered with scratches and bug bites, sometimes a turned ankle, happy to be found. But we never found that Max kid, and it wasn't for lack of looking."

"How many people did you have out looking for him?" Frank asked.

Stoffels rubbed his chin and thought. "At first, it was just me and some deputies. That's usually all it took. After a day of not finding hide nor hair of him, we added the full search-and-rescue complement. People out here are fast to mobilize when someone's lost out there, especially a kid."

Zach knew how that went. Too many people got lost in the woods around here; campers and hikers and summer visitors didn't seem able to grasp how easy it was to lose one's way. Somehow they all forgot about the Donner party. This wasn't country to be trifled with.

"I'd never seen the folks who ran that school more antsy, either. It's as if they knew right from the start that we weren't going to find him." Stoffels's brow creased. "Of course, the old man was already half out of it. It was the younger set who were running things by that point."

Zach cocked his head. That was an interesting tidbit. "The man who ran Sierra wasn't all there?"

"Old Aaron Joiner had already started slipping by then. He still put on a good show most of the time, though. It wasn't until you watched him real close that you knew something wasn't right. That young man he had running things was a big help to him. They would have had to close the school down much sooner if it hadn't been for him. He really propped the old man up."

So much for interviewing Joiner, then. "Do you recall his name? The younger man who helped run the place?" Zach asked. Maybe the school officials would know something, although they should have shared that at the time of Max's disappearance. People had all kinds of reasons for what they would and wouldn't tell the cops, though. Sometimes distance helped a little.

"Oh, yeah. He's made quite a name for himself, that young man. I saw him in the newspaper not too long ago. His name was Burton. Lyle Burton."

The name rang a bell, but Zach couldn't remember from where. He glanced over at Frank, who gave a slight shake of his head. They'd look into it when they got back to Sacramento.

Frank and Zach stood together. "Thank you, sir. I think we'll go on up and check out the school grounds a little," Zach said.

"You boys know your way up there?" Mrs. Stoffels asked from the kitchen.

"No, ma'am, but we have a map." Zach patted his jacket pocket.

The Stoffels exchanged looks. "Why don't you let us lead you up there? It's not very well marked and we'd hate to have to call the search-and-rescue teams out for you two," Mrs. Stoffels offered with a smile.

"We really don't want to trouble you any more than we already have," Zach said. "But if you have the time, that would be great."

"Ray could use the fresh air," his wife said. "I won't take but a second to gather my things."

True to her word, they were wheeling Ray down his system of ramps and out toward his custom van within moments.

"If I could be so bold," Frank said as they approached the van, "how'd you end up in the chair?"

Zach shook his head. Frank asked people the most amazingly personal questions. Part of the amazingness was that people didn't seem to take any offense. Maybe it was because Frank's interest was so genuine. He just wanted to know.

"It's not an interesting story," Ray said as his wife

opened the van door and began to lower the wheel-chair ramp. "Sometimes I think about making up a story where I was shot by a violent suspect. It's just my damn MS, though. Started in my thirties and just kept getting worse."

He rolled into the van and Zach and Frank went to get into their Crown Vic.

"What's MS?" Frank asked.

"Multiple sclerosis." Zach tried to hide a smile. Frank was the tiniest bit of a hypochondriac. Not that he ever missed work for any of his imaginary ailments, but in the past two years, he'd been convinced he had diabetes and mad cow disease. Zach didn't mind; discussions of Frank's symptoms were better than hearing about his wives.

"What do you suppose the symptoms are of that?" Frank asked as they rolled down the Stoffelses' long driveway.

"I have no idea. You'll have to look them up when we get home." Zach kept his eyes on the road. It had already narrowed considerably. There was still room for two cars going in the opposite direction, but just barely.

"If we ever get home," Frank said, looking out the window. "You don't suppose the wheelchair thing is just an act and they're actually luring us out into the woods?"

"To do what? You think that Mrs. Stoffels wants to have her wicked way with you, Frank?"

He shrugged. "I'm an appealing guy. I've heard of more far-out scenarios than that one. Besides, maybe it's you she's taken a fancy to. Or better yet, Mr. Stoffels has."

"The inside of your brain is a very scary place, Frank."

"You have no idea." Frank tapped his forehead. "You should try living in here."

Mrs. Stoffels pulled off onto a dirt track. There was no way Zach would have registered it as a road, and it'd be hell if they had to turn around. The Stoffels wound through the woods for a couple of miles that felt like more, since they had to slow down to ten miles per hour in some places.

"Do you like the woods, Zach? 'Cause I'm not a fan of them," Frank observed as they kept winding through denser and denser trees.

"The woods are okay." Zach actually didn't mind them much. Nor did getting lost panic him. He always seemed to know in which direction he was facing. His mother said he had a compass inside his head, and it felt like that sometimes.

Frank grunted. The Stoffels took another turn onto an even narrower road. Zach noticed a mailbox lying on its side by the edge and decided this must be the driveway to the old school. They drove another mile and a half and then pulled into a clearing.

"Whew," Frank said. "At least I can breathe again. I felt like those trees were stealing all my oxygen."

"You know they actually *make* oxygen, right?" Zach got out of the car and breathed in the tangy pine scent, so different from the air down in the valley.

"I didn't say it was logical." Frank stepped out as well.

Mrs. Stoffels opened the van door, but didn't lower the ramp. "It's a little too rough out here for the chair."

The buildings had seen better days. Windows were broken and doors hung crookedly on broken hinges. Still, they were impressive. Most of them had bases of stone. Those would stand through anything. Zach turned in a slow circle trying to take it all in. The clumps of buildings, the overgrown paths between them, the encroaching woods.

Stoffels pointed to one building that stood apart from the others. "That's the administration building. Over there would be schoolrooms, and then back there are the dormitories." He identified the different clumps of buildings.

"The whole thing's connected underground by a series of tunnels. The place was heated with steam heat for years. Shoveling the coal was one of the chores the boys had to do."

"I can see why most of the boys didn't get far."
Zach began to walk toward the edge of the grounds.
He wished he knew what he was looking for; then
he'd know where to start. This case had had him wan-
dering in the wilderness from the start.

"They were beautiful buildings in their day," Mrs.
Stoffels said. "Most of the place was built during the
Depression. Joiner's father brought Hopi Indians
up here from Arizona to build the place. They were
amazing craftsmen. Their kids could go to school here
for free while they worked. Back in those days, it was
more of a private school and not so much a reform
school."

Zach nodded. It looked as if it had been built to
last through anything. You didn't see that much anymore.

"You think you boys can find your way back home
from here?" Mrs. Stoffels asked. "Ray gets cranky if he
doesn't get a little rest in the afternoon."

Zach smiled. "We'll be fine. Thanks for leading us
up here. You were right—I would never have found it."

"There used to be some signs, but they're long
gone." Mrs. Stoffels looked around, too. "Like a lot
of stuff."

As the Stoffels bumped out of the clearing and
down the driveway, Frank whistled the opening bars
to "Dueling Banjos."

"Very funny." Zach turned around and started to walk toward the administration offices. The porch steps creaked as he walked up them.

"Watch your step up there," Frank called after him. "I'm going to check out the classrooms."

Zach grunted his assent. He tried the door, which was locked. He laughed. The door was half off its hinges, but the knob was not going to turn. He was debating whether to kick it open when Frank shouted, "Zach, you better come take a look at this."

Zach headed back down the steps and strode toward the classrooms.

"I'm back here," Frank called.

Zach detoured around the building and found Frank standing over an open pit. The edges of the dirt were raw. It hadn't been dug all that long ago.

"I think I might have found where Max Shelden was buried the first time," Frank said.

Janice Lam stood next to Zach, arms crossed over her chest, watching the crime-scene techs work the area. "I thought my worst problem up here was kids screwing and smoking," she observed.

She was pretty much exactly the way Stoffelses had described her, a tiny Asian lady. Zach was guessing Vietnamese, but he could be wrong. Her long, dark hair was pulled back into a ponytail and she was chewing a piece of gum with a contained fury that frightened him a little.

"It looks like there's been plenty of that, too." The crime-scene techs had found a wide variety of beer bottles, half-smoked roaches, and a lot of used condoms. "At least they seem to be having safe sex."

"You're a regular Pollyanna, McKnight." She chomped a little harder.

Zach was starting to worry for her jaw. "I aim to please."

She turned and favored him with a bright smile. "Well, you did spice up a boring day, but frankly, I like boring. I wouldn't have left Modesto if I'd wanted things to stay exciting."

Modesto wasn't a big city with a lot of sexy crimes to investigate, but it did have a substantial gang problem. It would have been a tough place to police.

"In here!" someone yelled, and Zach and Janice hurried in that direction. One of the crime-scene techs was in a room in one of the outbuildings behind the administration building. The edges of the room were lined with metal racks that had been bolted to the walls.

"Yeah?" Lam asked. "What you got?"

"Just watch," the crime-scene tech said. "I've sprayed the place with luminol." Luminol was the stuff forensic investigators used to reveal latent blood on surfaces. A lot of times criminals thought they'd cleaned up everything, that there would be no sign of blood. Not a chance of that with this stuff around.

The tech turned out the lights and the place went pitch black. He turned on his black light, and the entire room turned an eerie shade of blue.

The whole place was splashed with old blood. What the hell had gone on at this school?

The press had gotten hold of the George Osborne story. Lyle sat in the study of his house, a glass of whiskey in his hand, and stared at the television. No one was saying homicide yet, but they were bandying "foul play" about pretty fast and loose.

He gnawed on his thumbnail. What else might they have figured out by now? The television news reporter, Marianne Robar, had made the connection between Osborne and Shelden very clear. That meant the police were also not overlooking that fact. Of course, why would they? No one likes a coincidence like that. Lyle didn't like it, either.

"Honey, dinner's almost ready," his wife called from the kitchen. Tommy, their eldest, would be home from soccer practice in a few minutes. He needed to pull himself together. He needed to put on a good face for the family.

"I'm going to wash up. Be there in a sec," he called back, hoping his voice sounded normal, not ratcheted up to the twenty-seventh degree of tension he was feeling.

If the cops or the reporters made the connection between Shelden and Tennant, *that* would blow the thing wide open. Then he'd have a real mess on his hands.

If they didn't figure it out, he'd still have to deal with the shriveled part of his soul, but he'd had lots of practice at that.

Something inside him had died the night Max Shelden died. Once you took someone's life for no good reason, you lost part of your soul and never got it back. Susan Tennant wasn't the only one who had carried a load of guilt and shame from what had happened up at that school that summer.

He had gone there with such good intentions. He'd gotten his degree in social work and he really had thought he was going to help people. A school for boys who were on the edge of getting in trouble? What better place for a young man to make a difference?

Lyle had never thought of himself as conceited, but he'd known what he looked like and who he was. He'd been tall and handsome and athletic then. He was still a strong man with a good build. Back then, he'd also had the kiss of youth on him. Kids loved him. Why wouldn't they? You could take one look at Lyle Burton back then and know he was a winner. Strong, smart, and handsome. It was a lethal combination.

Literally so, for Max Shelden.

But the kids at the Sierra School for Boys weren't like the kids he was used to working with at the local elementary schools and Head Start programs. These were angry boys, sneaky boys, lying boys. It hadn't taken long to realize that no one was going to hero-worship him there. Or if they did, it would be a facade behind which to hide duplicitous behavior.

You couldn't trust those boys farther than you could throw them. The only people you could trust were the other teachers and the guards. It came down to "us" versus "them" pretty damn quickly, and you could only trust someone from the "us" camp.

Lyle couldn't remember exactly when things had gotten out of hand. He honestly wasn't sure where the line that they had crossed was until they were obviously so past any line that any decent society would draw. It had started pretty simply. A boy had stolen food from the kitchen. All they'd wanted was for him to confess, and then they would have meted out some punishment—extra KP duty, maybe cleaning the toilets.

But the little shit wouldn't cop to it. He kept denying and denying. They'd separated him from the rest of the boys, left him alone for a while to think. He still wouldn't give in. They'd turned out the lights and left him alone in the dark. Still nothing. Then things had gotten rough. Lyle wasn't sure who'd taken the first swing. It wasn't him, but it had seemed so right when it happened.

Three grown men on one fourteen-year-old boy. By the time they'd been through with him, he would have confessed to assassinating Kennedy. It had been immensely satisfying.

Trouble was, it hadn't stopped there. After a while they'd stopped asking questions and gone immediately for the belts. Why waste time? The little shits weren't going to tell you a damn thing without some encouragement. The only thing they understood was a smack upside the head and a boot to the ass.

There had been no repercussions, either. Aaron Joiner was too old to notice what was going on right under his nose. He had left the running of the school up to his staff. And most of the parents were so glad to be rid of their juvenile delinquents that they barely wrote, much less visited. Lyle and his colleagues realized pretty early on that there was no one to stop them. The kids figured it out pretty damn soon after that.

It had been exciting to be that powerful. Sexually exciting. Lyle had felt the blood rush to his groin as some punk kid groveled on the floor in front of him, begging for mercy. And he wasn't the only one who felt it; he'd seen the flushed faces, the heavy breathing, the telltale bulges.

There hadn't been many outlets for that kind of thing up at the Sierra School. They were too isolated. The town—what there was of it—was miles away on dark, twisting country roads, and there was no guarantee of finding a willing woman once you got there. It hadn't taken long before some of the men were satisfying those urges in the most convenient way possible.

Lyle hadn't known at first. The boys didn't tell; they were too ashamed, too broken to say what had happened to them. And the men weren't bragging about it; they knew it was wrong. Lyle had figured it out eventually, though.

And he hadn't done a goddamn thing to stop it.

At the time, it had seemed like the little shits deserved it. They behaved like animals. They were treated like animals.

Now it made him sick.

He wasn't sure how Max Shelden had gotten so deeply underneath his skin. Maybe it was the way the other boys automatically looked up to him. He'd been a natural leader.

It had been the role that Lyle had assumed he would play and it irked him that this boy had usurped his place. The fact that the boy had less than zero respect for authority didn't make it any easier.

At some point, Max had become the focal point of Lyle's frustration. It had all culminated one horrible night that ended with the boy dead, and blood on Lyle's hands that he could never, ever wash off.

Lyle had tried to bury the man he'd become that night with Max Shelden's bones. He guarded against the violent tendencies that he now knew existed so very close under his skin. He stayed away from confrontation. He stayed away from direct contact with clients, heading instead for the administrative duties that he luckily had a knack for.

He stared at himself in the bathroom mirror now, and then down at his hands. It was as if Max Shelden was back, taunting him into more and more despicable acts.

Bui it wasn't his fault. These people were pushing him past his limits; he would never behave like this otherwise. He hadn't behaved like this for twenty years. He had been careful. So very, very careful.

And he was going to stay careful. He had way too much to lose.

He washed up, put a smile on his face, and went in to dinner.

13

It was late when Zach and Frank pulled into Sacramento. Zach was dog tired but wired from the road. Frank had fallen asleep near Auburn and snored the rest of the way into Sac. Zach had nudged Frank awake in front of his house and dropped him off there.

He'd thought about going home to his apartment, but the last thing he wanted was to have Veronica Osborne find out from a newspaper or radio broadcast that they'd discovered her brother's real burial place. He didn't think the media had wind of it yet, but even up in sleepy little Blairsden, they'd catch on soon enough. There were a hell of a lot of people driving up that narrow road into the woods. People were bound to notice.

Zach drove by Veronica's condo to see if the lights

were on. They weren't, and her Honda wasn't parked in its reserved spot. He did a quick tour of the parking lot to see if she'd parked it somewhere else, but didn't see it.

Where else could she be? A friend's house? The hospital?

The last one would be easy to check; it wasn't that far out of his way to his house. He wished he had a better reason to try to see her, something that didn't involve the death of one of her relatives.

He found her car in the employee parking lot of the hospital and shook his head. She shouldn't be at work, but he understood the impulse. It was better to keep busy; it was too hard to dwell in the valley of grief.

He remembered the night they'd come to tell them about his father. His mother had scrubbed the house from top to bottom that night, not that it had needed it.

He hadn't known what to do. He'd been twelve, too old to cry on the couch with his sisters, and too young to figure out a plan of action on his own. For a while he'd followed his mother around, trying to help her, but she had been too lost in her own grief to see him.

Finally he'd gone into his room, put on head-phones, and blasted Kiss as loud as he could. He'd stayed that way all night, blocking out everything with the angriest music he could find. It had set the tone for the next few years of his life. It hadn't been good times for any of them. Not for years and years.

He parked the Crown Vic near the emergency entrance and sat for a few minutes, letting his head loll back on the seat. He closed his eyes experimentally, but they popped back open. It was probably just as well. He didn't look forward to the images from that school popping up in his dreams, and they undoubtedly would. Some people had done some very bad things up there.

He got out of the car and headed into the emergency room to find Veronica.

"Veronica, earth to Veronica." Tina tapped her on the shoulder and she damn near jumped out of her scrubs.

"What?" she snapped.

"Go home." Her friend stood before her, arms crossed over her chest. "Do it for me. Do it for the patients. You're going to kill somebody tonight."

"I'm just a little tired."

"You shouldn't be here. If Nurse Ratchet wasn't such a rat bastard, she would have sent you home the second she heard about what happened to you today." Tina's eyes narrowed.

Nothing had happened to Veronica that day. Something had happened to her father. Since she didn't know when she'd be able to have a memorial service or whatever, it made sense to save her time off for that.

She hadn't counted on her brain turning into tapioca pudding.

She never had managed to get to sleep. It had become double unlikely after she'd stumbled across the bank statements with the big cash deposits. Who would have paid them that much cash? And for what?

She had the bank statements in her bag now. All day long, she'd battled over whether to take them to McKnight and Rodriguez. She knew she had to do it, but it felt like such a huge betrayal. Of what, though? Of her father's sainted memory? Hardly. As for her mother, she wondered if her mother had ever known anything about it.

"Go home," Tina repeated. "Now. I already called Monica; she's going to come in and cover for you."

Veronica dropped her head. She was tired now. Maybe she'd finally be able to sleep. "Okay. I'm going."

"Praise Jesus." Tina leaned on the nurses' station and gave Veronica an appraising look. "Should I get someone to drive you home?"

She must look even worse than she felt. "No."

Tina's brow creased. "Do you want me to come over after I finish my shift?"

That offer was more tempting, but Veronica knew Tina had her own life to live. "I'm fine."

"And how come you didn't call me?" Tina wasn't moving, even though call bells were starting to buzz.

"What could you have done? There was nothing for anyone to do at that point. He was dead. He was going to stay dead."

"Gee, I don't know. Maybe I could have done some of those things that best friends do for each other. You know, comfort each other? Make each other cups of tea? Pour large slugs of whiskey into the cups of tea?" Tina's arms stayed folded. "I might even have given you a hug." Tina wasn't of the sweet, maternal school of nursing, she was more of a tough-love kind of girl.

The reasoning that had seemed so solid this morning was starting to seem shakier and shakier. If she'd called Tina this morning, she wouldn't be carrying around bank statements and feeling like they might explode inside her purse any moment.

So she'd go home, get a little sleep, and then head to the police station to turn over the bank statements. That seemed like much more solid reasoning.

"But now you've missed your opportunity. I probably won't hug you until you get married." Tina sighed and uncrossed her arms.

Veronica gave her a rueful smile. "That could be an awfully long time, given how unspectacular my dating life is."

"Perhaps it just got a little more spectacular," Tina said, looking over Veronica's shoulder.

Zach McKnight was striding into the emergency room, looking like he'd slept about as much as Veronica had.

She was sitting at the nurses' station, a coworker in classic lecture pose in front of her, feet spread and arms crossed. Veronica was in classic acquiescent pose, nodding. The coworker spotted him first. It was the same nurse she'd been working with the night he'd come to return Max's photo. Her name was something that started with a T. Terry? No. Tina. They both turned to stare at him as he walked up to the desk.

"It's awfully late," Tina said. "Are you off duty, Sergeant?"

"I suppose I am, technically."

"But you're never really off duty, right?" Tina gave him a smile.

Zach smiled back. "I imagine it's kind of the same for you."

She nodded. "Oh, yeah. If the kid down the street falls off his bike, I'm called for a consult. If somebody's mother's heart is beating too fast or too slow, I'm called for my opinion. It keeps things interesting."

"That it does." Zach turned to Veronica. "Do you have a few minutes?"

"She has quite a few. I'm sending her home. She shouldn't be here in the first place," Tina answered.

Veronica smiled at her friend. "Maybe you'd like to come with me and answer any other questions Sergeant McKnight has?"

"Don't push me. I just might," Tina said. Her pager went off and she glanced at the number. "I've got to go. Get out of here, Veronica. I mean it." Then she was gone.

An awkward silence stretched between them and Veronica said, "She thinks I'm worthless tonight. She might be right. I guess I should have stayed home."

Zach generally didn't have trouble talking to women; he'd grown up in a house full of them. He knew the rhythms of their speech and the give-and-take of their motions and he knew how to fit into their dance. He felt inexplicably tongue-tied right now, though. "It's hard to know what to do. Nothing seems right."

Her brown eyes flew open. "Exactly! That's exactly what it's like. I had no idea what to do with myself. Which reminds me, I have something to show you."

"Maybe you ought to let me tell you what I came here to tell you first." *Maybe you'll fall into my arms and let me comfort you.* That seemed like a nice idea. Not the part where he gave her devastating news, but the part where he could be her shelter in the storm.

The idea was so appealing, it took him a few seconds to realize she was saying something to him.

"We might as well walk out to my car. I'll just be in the way here now that Monica's shown up."

He nodded and followed her to the door of the locker room, then waited while she retrieved her purse and jacket.

"So what do you have to tell me that brought you over here?" she asked as they stepped out into the night.

The air was crisp and cool, with the hint of a scent of rain on the breeze. Zach watched it lift her hair for a moment and resisted the urge to smooth it back for her. "There's no easy way to say this. I'm pretty sure we found where your brother was originally buried."

She stopped. "So he wasn't in that construction site the whole time, waiting to be dug up and found."

Zach shook his head and shoved his hands in his pockets. He didn't look at her, instead focusing on the tree branches tossing in the wind in front of the moon. "No, ma'am. That was a dump. We've known that from the start."

Her eyes were trained on him, unwavering. "So where was he buried?" You had to love a woman who didn't back down from the truth, no matter how unpleasant it was.

"It looks like he was buried on the grounds of the Sierra School."

She shook her head. "Then how the hell did he end up in that construction site?"

It was an excellent question, one that Frank and Zach were asking each other continually. "It appears that someone dug him up from the original grave and put him in the construction site."

"Why?" She stood still, as if the news had literally stopped her in her tracks.

"We're trying to figure that out," he said. "First and foremost, somebody clearly wanted him to be found and was tired of waiting."

She chewed for a second on her bottom lip and then started walking again, her stride brisk. "It doesn't make any sense."

Zach fell into step beside her. "I imagine it will eventually. It's going to take some time, though."

"Something had to have happened." They were at her car now. She stopped by the driver's-side door, digging in her purse for her keys.

Zach leaned against the side of the Honda. "Trust me, we're looking into that, too. We'll figure out how your brother died."

She looked up at him, almost surprised. "Yes, of course. But something has to have happened now, too—or recently. Something that would make someone want to dig up Max and make sure he was found now."

"We're looking into that angle, too. Did your father mention anything recently?"

She shook her head. "How did whoever moved his bones know they were there, anyway? Did animals dig him up? Was there some kind of disturbance, an earthquake or something that uncovered his bones?"

Zach thought about that deep pit in the woods. It would have taken a hell of a natural disaster to uncover Max's bones, and it wouldn't have left a neat, precise hole in the ground.

She turned slowly to stare at him. "You mean whoever dug him up knew where he'd been buried all along?"

Zach still didn't answer. He couldn't; it was an ongoing investigation. As much as he wanted Veronica to know everything he knew, he couldn't divulge specific details of the case to her.

"Somebody up at that school killed him?" she pressed, taking a step closer to him.

"We don't know that. He could have run into someone in the woods after he ran away. We have a lot more questions than answers at this point." That was for damn sure.

She thought about that for a second. "But he never came back here to Sacramento?"

"It seems unlikely." Even that was up for grabs. He could have come down here, not found any help, and returned. It didn't seem likely, though.

"So my dad wasn't involved." She sagged, as if the

only thing keeping starch in her spine had been her fight to clear her father's name.

Zach supported her. "We don't think so. At least, not directly."

She didn't seem to hear that. She pulled the keys out of her purse and stared at them, as if she no longer knew what to do.

Zach had seen it before. It was a combination of exhaustion, shock, and being emotionally overwhelmed. It was always hard to watch, but this time it damn near broke his heart.

"Veronica?" he said. She didn't respond immediately. "Ms. Osborne?"

She looked up at him blankly, as if she was surprised he was still there. "Yes?" She looked back down again at her keys.

"How about you let me drive you home?"

"My car's right here." She looked up at him, glassy eyed.

"I can see that." He held out his hand, and miracle of miracles, she dropped the keys into his palm. He shepherded her around to the passenger side of the Honda, his hand at the small of her back, way too aware of the soft swell of her hips. He unlocked the door and she got in, automatically buckling her seat belt. He hurried back to the driver's side, pulling his cell phone out as he went.

He hit the speed dial. "Frank, it's Zach. I'm going to give Ms. Osborne a ride home."

There was a pause. "Dude," was all he said.

"Don't," was all Zach replied.

"Whatever. Watch yourself."

"I always do." Zach folded himself into the car, barely squeezing his knees behind the steering wheel. He adjusted the seat back and the mirrors.

"I live over in Curtis Heights," she said.

"I remember. I've been there before."

"Oh, yeah." She settled back into her seat and into silence.

A couple of times on the ride over, she turned to him and opened her mouth as if she was about to say something, but then fell silent again.

He parked her car and shepherded her up the walk to her condo, opened the door, and walked in behind her.

She dropped her purse on a table by the door and kept going. "I need to take a shower."

"Sure," he said, and watched her go.

He headed into the kitchen to see if there was anything he could make for her to eat.

Gary watched the news coverage of George Osborne's death, including a clip from the Pop-Tart's press conference. She did a nice job of looking innocent, didn't she? But she didn't fool him. She had been set before him, just as the others had.

He packed the photo into a little box, careful to wear his gloves, and addressed the box to the Pop-Tart. This would be a little reminder of what she'd done.

Veronica stood under the spray of the shower. She had to focus hard to remember it all. Leaving the hospital. Zach telling her that someone had deliberately moved Max. Realizing that her father had had nothing to do with it. Not that he would care about having his name cleared.

It was as if the craziness of the last few days hit her all at once. Finding Max, just to learn that she'd lost him two decades earlier. Defending her father against accusations she feared might have merit. Finding her father's body. It all crashed in.

That was the problem with denial. Once it was gone you were stuck with reality, and that totally sucked. She'd like her cloak of deniability back. Instead, all she had was a shower that was starting to run cold and the smell of something cooking in her kitchen.

She brushed her wet hair back, pulled on her pajamas and slippers, and headed downstairs. She found Zach cursing under his breath as the omelet he was trying to flip broke.

"I can never do it, either," she said. "I always end up making scrambled eggs with stuff in them."

He turned and smiled. "My sister makes it look easy. I can't tell you how many times she's tried to teach me, but I just can't get the hang of it."

"Your sister Rhonda? The nurse?" Veronica sat down at the table.

He shook his head and turned back to the pan. "Nah. My oldest sister, Nancy."

"How many sisters do you have?" It must be so good to have siblings. What would it be like right now to have someone who could understand what she was thinking and feeling? Someone who had lived it with her, someone with the same blood coursing through their veins.

"Three sisters, all older. No brothers," he answered. "Estrogen practically flows like a river in my mother's house."

"So it was just you and your dad versus all those girls?" she asked.

He slid the eggs onto a plate and turned. "Not really; he died when I was twelve. My mother remarried, but not until I was seventeen, and by then all my sisters were out of the house. At least, officially."

"What does that mean?"

He set the plate down in front of her and went back to the stove. "Everyone lives within a five-mile radius of Mom, and the house is still nerve central. They're there all the time. Two of them have kids now and they're there all the time, too. Luckily there are a few boys in that mix. It's bedlam."

It sounded like paradise. "And you? Are you there all the time?"

"I'm there enough."

She started to eat and looked up, startled, when he set the salt and pepper shakers in front of her.

"I didn't know how much you liked. It's probably pretty bland," he said.

In all honesty, she'd barely tasted it. She sprinkled some salt on it now. He was right; it was better that way. In fact, it was really good. She applied herself to the business of eating.

She looked like a teenager, and she smelled like shampoo and lotion. She'd stumbled down the steps in flannel pajama pants and a worn gray hoodie with frayed cuffs, a pair of knock-off Ugg boots on her feet. Having been charged with buying real Uggs for his niece for Christmas, he knew the real from the fake. He definitely knew the difference in their prices.

She still looked a little like she was sleepwalking, though. He finished making his own eggs and sat down across from her at the table. "Feeling better?"

She looked up from her plate. "Not really. It's kind of a bumpy landing, you know?"

He nodded.

She pushed back from the table and looked down at her empty plate. "So is this part of your usual duties? Do you always drive people home and make them omelets?"

Busted. "Nope."

"But you did tonight." She dabbed her lips with a napkin.

"Yep."

She was silent, waiting for him to say more. There was a stillness to her that he hadn't sensed before. She was used to listening to people, used to waiting for people to get their stories out. Finally, he said, "It seemed like the thing to do at the time."

She smiled. "How many times have I heard that in the emergency room? Sometimes I think people should dial 911 the second someone says that."

He smiled back. "I'm hoping that this won't require stitches."

"I guess we'll see about that." She stood up, leaned across the table, and brushed her lips over his. "Thank you," she whispered.

He threaded his hand through her hair and brought her lips back to his.

This time it was more than a gentle brush, it was a

revelation. It was sweet and hot, and made his chest feel as if it had tightened and was going to explode simultaneously. It made it seem like a good idea to clear the table with one sweep of his arm and take her right there. An even better idea was to carry her upstairs in his arms.

They broke apart and she stared at him, her hands braced on the table on either side of her plate. "Wow. I'm pretty sure that's definitely not on the list of standard protocol."

"It's a unique situation. They can't cover everything in the manuals."

"So you're telling me that you're winging it?" Her pupils were dilated.

He nodded as his heartbeat returned to normal from its jackhammer beat. "Do I need to apologize?" He would if he had to, but he wouldn't mean it.

Her eyes narrowed a little while she thought. It was cute, kind of like watching a kitten decide what to claw next. She shook her head and stood up. "I sort of started it."

"Yeah, but I'm pretty sure I finished it."

"We can argue about who gets to take credit later." She started clearing the plates from the table.

He picked up his own and followed her to the sink. "I like that you're thinking credit rather than blame."

She scraped her plate into the sink and put it in the dishwasher. "We're both grown-ups."

Zach wasn't sure about that; he felt more like a teenager when he was near her. She made the blood ring in his ears and sweat break out on his palms.

"Which means we both know that we're in an intense emotional situation here, and that things happen and don't necessarily mean anything." She took his plate from him, scraped it, and put it in the dishwasher next to her own.

His shoulders stiffened. Not mean anything? A kiss like that? Sure, and the Sistine Chapel was just a painted ceiling. "I'd argue that."

He saw the corner of her mouth twitch up in a smile.

She put the omelet pan into the sink to soak and turned toward him. "Thanks for breakfast."

He might not be the sharpest knife in the drawer, but he knew his cue to leave. "It was my pleasure. Call me if you . . ." If she what? Wanted him to carry her upstairs and make love to her until neither of them could see straight? "If you need anything."

"I will." She just stood there, her hands gripping the counter behind her.

"Lock the door after me, okay?" Something was going on, something he didn't have a handle on yet. He didn't think she was necessarily in danger, but someone *had* murdered her father and tried to make it look like an accident.

She nodded.

"You've got all my numbers?"

She nodded again.

"All right, then." He headed toward the door, not looking back over his shoulder although his neck was practically seizing with wanting to. "See you."

He went outside and waited until he heard the locks snick into place. As he started to head out to the parking lot to call Frank for a ride, he kicked something and looked down. There was a box at his feet, with Veronica's name on it.

14

"You okay, Gary?"

Gary jumped and whirled, immediately assuming a defensive posture, fists up and ready to strike. Mr. O. had come up behind him, had startled him. That wasn't a smart move.

"Whoa, man. Sorry," Mr. O. said, his own hands up, palms forward. "I didn't mean to scare you. I just wanted to check on you."

Gary dropped his fists. "Sorry. I didn't hear you. I don't . . . I don't do surprises well."

"I noticed." Mr. O. snorted a little. "Are you okay?"

Gary pondered the question. He was tired, that was for sure. Being a janitor by day and an avenging angel by night didn't leave a lot of time for sleep. Or exercise. Or regular meals. He was tired and his stomach was starting to gnaw. Gary's system was all out of sorts, which made him extra jumpy. "Just kind of tired."

He realized that he must have been slumped against the wall. He'd meant to just lean for a minute, but he'd started to drift off.

"What's going on, man? You have a lady friend who's keeping you up nights?" Mr. O. gave him a playful punch on his arm.

Gary chuckled. Right. He'd never had anything remotely like a lady friend. Well, maybe that wasn't quite true. It was the Pop-Tart who'd kept him up last night, wasn't it? She was almost like a lady friend, wasn't she? He nodded. "You got me."

Mr. O.'s eyebrows shot up. "Really? Good for you, Gary. It's good to see you coming out of your shell." He walked off toward the teachers' lounge.

Gary rubbed his face hard, trying to get the blush he felt on his cheeks to fade. Could the Pop-Tart be his lady friend? She was pretty, there was no doubt about that. He liked that she was small, almost dainty. He looked at his hands and tried to imagine what they'd look like touching her.

He couldn't see it. He couldn't see them holding hands. He shut his eyes and tried harder to imagine it.

Instead of seeing them holding hands or seeing his hands caressing her face or her hair, he saw them wrapped around her throat. That he could see quite clearly.

That was definitely the way he wanted to touch the Pop-Tart.

"He kissed you? That's it?" Tina stared at her, all agog. She had come directly to Veronica's condo after her shift, and they were sitting on the couch drinking the tea that Tina had wanted to make her before. And, yes, it had a healthy dose of whiskey in it.

"Well, yeah. What did you think? That I'd sweep all the dishes onto the floor and do him right on the kitchen table?" Lord knows, she'd considered it. She was pretty sure he had, too. She'd seen the heat in his eyes and felt it in his kiss.

"Well, it would make a much better story than 'he kissed me over the dirty breakfast dishes and then we talked and he left.'" Tina raised her arms over her head and stretched.

A better story, true. A better choice? Hardly. "Good story or not, I'm just telling you. I'm considering giving up giving up on cops."

"Way to stand by your guns, missy. One hot kiss and you're a melted puddle of tough-talking nurse." Tina laughed her dirty laugh. It was somewhere between a throaty chuckle and an outright guffaw and it make Veronica feel better deep down in her heart to hear it.

Still, it was more than just that incredibly hot kiss that had her reconsidering. "He seems different."

"He's clearly a better kisser than the last one. What did you call him? Lollipop?" Tina took another healthy sip of tea and yawned.

Veronica shuddered. Lollipop. Or maybe it had been Lizard Tongue. Either way, it hadn't been a compliment. Veronica had felt like he was licking her mouth like a piece of candy on a stick, and not in a good way. "That's not the only thing."

Tina snickered. "It sure isn't. I've watched that man walk away. He has quite a few other things in his favor."

"Not just that, either. He doesn't seem to have the control issues that usually come with cop territory. He treats me like I'm a . . . person."

"Person, eh? Sounds really romantic," Tina teased.

Veronica frowned. No, but maybe romance wasn't what she wanted anymore. Maybe it had never been what she wanted. She'd found it awfully easy to dismiss guys for any number of small faults. Bad kissers. Torn fingernails. Dirty cars.

A few, she'd dismissed with good reasons. The ones who drank too much. The ones who seemed like they might explode at any second. She'd attended enough

Al-Anon meetings to know that she didn't need to marry her daddy. "You know what I mean."

To her surprise, Tina smiled. "I do. And it's about time."

"Speaking of which, it's about time for you to go home to bed. You look like you're about to fall asleep right here on my couch."

"It *is* really comfy. You could just throw a blanket over me. I really like that fleecy one you keep at the foot of your bed." Tina smiled, then yawned.

"I will if you want, but you know you'll be happier if you go home."

Tina got up. "You're right. You're sure you're okay?"

"I'm sure." She always was, after all.

"Lock up after me, okay?"

Veronica laughed despite herself. "That's what Zach said."

"So what is it?" Zach pressed Little Hillary in the crime lab.

She looked up at him and smiled. "It's a box, McKnight. What does it look like?"

"You know what I mean." *Now* she's got a sense of humor? He glared at her.

She straightened up. "Stop breathing down my neck, okay? It's not going to make anything go any faster. You want this to be solid evidence?"

He nodded.

"Then back the fuck up and let me do this right," she said politely.

He knew she was right, but it didn't make it any easier. He backed away and leaned against a desk next to Frank.

"So tell me again," Frank said, rolling a toothpick in the side of his mouth. "Where did you find this box?"

Zach didn't want to go into it with Frank in too much detail. It felt . . . private. It had only been a kiss, but it had been a damn fine kiss. "On Veronica Osborne's porch."

"And you found it when?" Frank's voice was as calm as if he was asking Zach what the weather report was.

"When I was leaving her place." Accurate but not overly informative was often the best way.

"So someone left it on her porch while you were there?" Frank's eyebrows lifted.

"Yes, Frank. Someone left it on the porch while I was inside her condo." That part was embarrassing. Big, strong, protective police officer doesn't even know it when someone leaves a box on the doorstep because he was too busy sucking face.

Frank continued, "And you didn't hear it because you were doing what?"

"Cooking eggs."

"And that's not a euphemism for . . . you know?" Now Frank did look at him.

Who would use that as a euphemism for sex? Probably Frank. "No, Frank, it's not a euphemism for anything. I made her food."

"You're losing your touch, big guy." Frank smirked.

Little did he know. Zach smirked back. "Whatever you say, Frank."

"The package is clean, guys," Little Hillary said. "No prints on the outside. Someone either wiped it clean or wore gloves."

"What's inside it?" Zach asked from over at the counter. He wasn't going to crowd her again. That was for sure.

"Come over here and look, you lazy bums. Do I have to tell you everything?" She put her hands on her hips and looked exasperated. Or maybe that was just how her face was. She looked exasperated a lot.

They walked over to the table. Little Hillary had pulled a photo out of the box, the same photo that Veronica Osborne had given them. It looked old, though. The edges were yellowed and some brown spots had formed in the lower-right-hand corner.

"Not exactly news-flash material," Frank observed.

Disappointed, Zach started to turn away, frustration growing in his chest.

"Don't you want to hear what's on the B side, big

guy?" Little Hillary asked. "It's got a good beat, and I think you can dance to it."

Zach turned and she flipped it over. On the back of the photo, someone had written in a big loopy scrawl "Me and Pop-Tart. Summer 1990."

Zach eyed the boxes of files without enthusiasm. There were more than twelve banker's boxes stacked in his office, each one stuffed with moldy paper that chronicled the rise and fall of the Sierra School for Boys. He was hoping to find a list of staff or students who had been there when Max was. That would give him and Frank another set of leads to follow while the crime-scene techs still crawled around the property up in the Sierras.

So far there'd been more than one room that had a lot of blood sprayed around and a basement room that the techs were referring to as Semen Central. The place was like a chamber of horrors. Child molestation statutes of limitation were all over the map in California, but aggravated rape had no statute of limitations whatsoever. This case could get ugly fast.

"So are you going to tell her about the box?" Frank asked.

"I think I have to. Somebody was on her property. She probably shouldn't be staying there."

"The department's not going to pay for her to be relocated or even stay in a hotel," Frank observed.

Zach knew that. The state had driven off a cliff more than a year ago, fiscally speaking, and they were still doing the frantic Wile E. Coyote air dance. "I'll talk to her. We'll work something out."

He put on a pair of gloves and opened up the box of files closest to him, and the smell of mildew wafted up at him. He couldn't read the tabs on most of the manila folders; the writing had been faded by time and the elements.

"When are you going to tell her?" Frank asked, opening his own box and making a face at the smell.

"I figured I'd stop by after work." He glanced up at the clock. It was midafternoon already.

"She expecting you?" Frank pulled out a stack of folders and set them on his desk.

Zach pulled out his own stack. "I have no idea."

Frank gave him a hard look. "Ladies like it if you call first."

"Which wife did you learn that from?" The papers inside the folders seemed to all deal with insurance and maintenance on various vehicles. Zach peered at the signature lines, trying to make out a name. He supposed it could be Aaron Joiner. These were no help.

Frank thought for a moment. "I think I learned that from Mary." He sighed. "She always was a class act."

Zach shook his head. Frank still had a soft spot in his heart for wife number one. "Well, if Mary said it was the right thing to do. I'll give her a call before I leave and let her know I'm on my way over."

Zach pulled out a folder from another box and flipped it open. It was marked STAFF DIRECTORY. He held his breath as he checked the date.

"Found it!" Zach's fists pumped in the air.

"What? What'd you get?" Frank sat up alertly.

"I found a box that has records from 1990 and 1991." A sweet moment of success.

"Nice!" Frank rolled his office chair over.

Zach pulled out a stack of folders and handed them to Frank, then placed another stack on his own desk. "You look through those and I'll look through these."

"What exactly are we looking for?"

"Anything, I guess. We'll have to start looking for current addresses. At least we'll have some idea as to who exactly was at that school the same time Max was." Zach opened the first file. The papers were hard to read. The type had faded and some of the ink had been smeared by damp.

"Hey, Zach," Frank called from his desk. "Does the name Susan Tennant mean anything to you?"

Zach pushed back from his desk and thought for a second. "Yeah, sure. She was that weird autoerotic death that Josh and Elise caught, wasn't she?"

"Yeah. That was what I was thinking, too. Guess what?" Frank peered at him from over his reading glasses. "She was the nurse in residence at the Sierra School for Boys the year that Max was there."

A chill ran up Zach's spine.

Ryan Arnott opened his door for the second time that night, and was again confronted by a face from the past. Just like the first time, it took him a second to place the face. What the hell? Was it some sick school reunion?

A right hook broke his nose and he went down like a bowling pin. What the hell!

Panic set in but before he could begin to fight, his legs and hands were bound. He was pretty sure that whatever was happening wasn't going to be good. "Don't do this, man. Leave now and I won't say anything to anybody."

The man just grabbed Ryan by his bound ankles and pulled him down the hallway toward the bathroom, letting Arnott's head bang against the floor. Arnott's insides turned to Jell-O. He tried to struggle, but between being bound and the blood from his broken nose pouring back into his throat, he wasn't getting anywhere.

"Help!" he screamed, even though he was way too far from his neighbors for anyone to hear.

The man shoved a washcloth in his mouth to silence him, then walked away.

Arnott heard the water going on in the tub and tears streamed down his face. He was pretty sure he knew what was coming. The man came back and loomed over him. Arnott tried to plead through the washcloth, but he could only get out muffled whimpers.

Finally, the man spoke to him. "I remembered you as being taller," he said as he dragged him toward the tub.

Zach had taken Frank's advice and called Veronica to ask if he could stop by after work. He hadn't said why, and he felt a little bad now since she had clearly put on mascara and lip gloss.

"So let me get this straight. You brought me to my house, made me eggs, kissed me until my head spun, walked out the door, picked up a package addressed to me, and took it straight to the crime lab?"

"Yep. That would pretty much cover it." Until her head spun? Good to know he wasn't the only one who thought that kiss was off the charts.

"The package wasn't addressed to you. Isn't there some law against tampering with other people's mail?" She crossed her arms over her chest, which was probably supposed to look intimidating, but which plumped up her breasts so they peeked out of the V at her neck-line. He'd happily get her mad any day for that view.

"Not applicable. That package never came any-where near a United States post office. Somebody hand-delivered it."

That shook her a little. She sank down in her chair. "Who would leave things on my doorstep? Who would even have a copy of that photo?"

He sat down across from her. "I don't know yet. I took it to the lab so no possible evidence on it was destroyed."

"And was there any evidence?" She looked hopeful, and he hated to disappoint her.

"No. Except that we know whoever did it was ex-ceptionally careful to make sure that there was no evidence on it. We're dealing with someone smart, someone organized, someone who's willing to take the time to do it right." Which did not sound like the person who had killed George Osborne. Whoever had done that had struck out first, and then tried to cover it up. But there'd been two people at that scene.

She shivered. He didn't blame her; it scared him a little, too. The vast majority of criminals weren't all that bright. Most people smart enough to be crimi-nal masterminds went into legitimate jobs and made their money without risk to their freedom.

Even your average sociopath generally tried to stay

on the right side of the law. Mostly, anyway. Prisons were full of people without consciences who also didn't have the education, the smarts, or much in the way of opportunities. The bulk of Zach's work was putting those people there.

"What am I supposed to do?" she asked. He could see by the set of her jaw that she'd decided to knuckle down and figure out how to get through the situation.

"Do you feel safe staying here?" He wasn't crazy about her being in this condo alone.

She glanced around her kitchen. "I'm not sure. I've been here all day and nothing happened."

"Is there someone you could call to come stay with you?"

She shot him a look. "I can just imagine that conversation. 'Hey, it's possible that a dangerous psychopath is stalking me. Wanna have a sleepover?'"

He snorted a little, then drummed his fingers on the table. "I could take you to my mother's. She has an extra bedroom. You'd be safe there."

She threw him another look.

Yeah, he hadn't thought so. He walked into her living room. "Crap, I forgot your couch is so small."

The thing wasn't much more than four feet long. There was no way in hell he'd be able to sleep on that.

She turned to look at it. "So?"

"So do I look love-seat length to you? Plus it's that patio furniture stuff. It's not even a real couch."

"It's a real couch and it's called wicker. It's made for indoors."

"Yeah, well, it's not made to be slept on." At least not by males over six feet tall and pushing two hundred pounds.

"No. It's made to be sat on." She clearly wasn't getting his point.

"So where am I going to sleep?"

She froze. "Uh, your apartment? Your mother's place? I don't know."

"No way. I'm staying wherever you're staying. That's a given."

"A given by whom?"

"Mainly me, but with a strong second from whoever decided to leave you that gift on your front porch."

He could almost see the wheels turn as she tried to put together an argument but couldn't. Finally, she said, "You know what? I need a drink."

"Thank God. I was starting to think you were a teetotaler. I could live with that, I guess, but it was going to be an issue eventually."

She laughed. "Which means you'd like one, too?"

"Yes, please."

He followed her into the kitchen. She pulled a bottle of Maker's Mark out of a cupboard, took out two glasses, put two pieces of ice in each, and then poured in the whiskey. She handed him one, picked up the other, clinked his glass and said, "Cheers." Then she took a long, healthy sip.

He raised his glass and did the same.

15

Here in the kitchen, with him so close and the whiskey warming her belly, Veronica finally let go. She was tired and lonely, and he was warm and strong. And he was a good man. He cared about the same things she did. Human dignity for everyone, and protecting children, and helping those who couldn't or wouldn't help themselves.

He also had shoulders to die for, thighs that made her breathe hard, a fantastic smile, an adorable dimple, and a butt that would have made Michelangelo weep. Oh, and man, could he kiss.

Who would it harm if she spent a night inside those strong arms, feeling safe and connected to another human being? She was so tired of being alone.

She'd spent her childhood alone because she could

never be sure what condition her parents would be in. How could she let anyone know that her father came home, got stupid drunk, screamed at his wife, smacked her around, and passed out? The shame of it was too much.

Even after years of therapy and a lot of Al-Anon meetings, she didn't want anyone to know any more about her family than she had to let them know. How could they fail to be repulsed by her after seeing where she came from? Or at least wary.

Not Zach, though. He'd met her father yet here he was, looking at her with those deep, dark eyes that warmed her even more than the whiskey did.

Veronica set her glass down softly on the counter and took Zach's hand. "You're right. You absolutely cannot sleep on that couch."

And then she led him to her bedroom.

Zach had been pretty sure what her intentions were from the second they walked into the kitchen. There'd been the slightest flush on her pale cheeks. Her eyes had been huge and dark. She'd bitten her full lower lip the tiniest bit, and then knocked back the whiskey as if she needed courage.

The woman was made of nothing but courage. Anyone who could spend a lifetime dealing with her excuse for a father deserved a combat medal. He could only imagine what her mother had been like. It had to have been a messy, violent childhood. Yet here she was, standing on her own two feet, never making excuses, never backing down. It made his chest swell every time he looked at her.

Then there were the attributes that made other things swell. The curve of her breasts, the fall of her hair, the delicious arc from her waist to her hips. The way she gazed up at him from under the sweep of her bangs.

In her room, she turned to face him, and he slid his hands to her waist, pulled her to him, and brought his lips to hers. She tasted like heaven. Her lips were so soft and so sweet, and when they parted he had to fight to keep his control. He wanted to throw her on the bed and devour her. He wanted to pour himself into her, screaming her name to the sky. He wanted desperately. Hungrily. Passionately.

But she felt so small in his arms, so soft and delicate, and he didn't want to hurt her. He gently laid her on the bed, following her down, his hand behind her head to guide her. Then he was looking down into her eyes. Her chest rose and fell beneath him, pressing her breasts against him, tantalizing in their warm, soft pressure. She reached up, tangled her hands in his hair, and brought his mouth down to hers again.

Her tongue swept against his lips and her hips rocked against him. He moaned. Her hands left his hair and began to work the buttons on his shirt, undoing them with quick movements. In seconds her hands were on his chest, running the length of him, gliding over his nipples. He kept kissing her.

He trailed his hand down her side and lifted the hem of her T-shirt. Her skin was so soft and smooth, like satin beneath his hand. She pushed him up with both hands on his chest, sat up, and stripped the T-shirt over her head.

"In a hurry?" he asked, trying like hell to look at her face rather than her chest.

"Aren't you?" She sat with her arms braced behind her, her lips swollen from his kisses. He could see her pulse beat in her throat. Her hair was tousled and her eyes were beyond huge. His heart beat so hard, Zach thought it might jump right out of his chest.

He unclasped her bra, slid it down her shoulders, and laid her back down on the bed. "Nope—no hurry at all."

Veronica apparently took that as a challenge; her hands went straight to his belt. As she started to undo it, he leaned down and circled one perfect pink nipple with his tongue.

She sighed and her hands slowed. Her back arched. He turned to her other breast, spurred on by the sound of her sighs. Her hips rose against his and he fought for control, raising his head and looking down at her. She smiled up at him.

Eyes locked on hers, his hand went to the top of her jeans, unbuttoning, unzipping. He toyed with the lace edge of her panties; her flesh quivered beneath his hand.

Then she was pushing him away again, stripping the jeans off her legs and the panties down her hips. She lay back before him, completely naked, completely delicious, completely clear about what she wanted from him.

But he wanted to look at her first. He wanted to memorize the silken expanse of her skin, her rounded belly, the curve of her hips, the perfection of her breasts. She was everything he'd imagined and more. Much, much more. In his imagination, she hadn't radiated this kind of heat. Her eyes hadn't held that hunger. She was so much better real than in his imagination, and she'd been pretty freaking good in his imagination.

He couldn't keep his hands off her another second. He glided his hands up her legs. Her thighs parted for him and his fingers slid into the hot, slick center of her. Her hips bucked and she arched her back.

She wanted this just as much as he did. He reveled in making her feel this way, in driving her on as she moaned beneath him, grinding herself down on his hand. He couldn't wait another second.

He stood and shucked off his jeans, then pulled a condom out of his wallet.

"*Hurry,*" she said.

After a few seconds that felt like a lifetime, he was covered and ready. She pulled him to her. He could smell her arousal. It made him want her even more. "You're sure this is what you want?" he asked.

She smiled. "Oh, yeah. I'm sure this is what I want. I really, really want it right now."

He obliged.

They lay spent and tangled in each other's arms. Veronica listened to Zach's heartbeat slow, the frantic tattoo of her own heart slow returning to normal as well.

"Wow," she finally said.

"Oh, yeah. Definitely wow." He pulled her closer and kissed the top of her head. "Completely and totally wow."

"Do you think it's because we're both so stressed? Or was that significant somehow? I mean, first times aren't always so amazing." They tended to be awkward, and occasionally embarrassing. Rarely were they wow worthy.

"I think that I refuse to overthink it, and I'm going

to stick to wow." His voice was a rumble deep in his chest that tickled her ear. His breath came more slowly, more evenly. He was falling asleep. How like a guy.

"Do you know what happened to Max yet?" She propped herself up on her elbow to look at him.

"Not exactly. We have some guesses." He propped himself up, too, so he was facing her. "I'm not sure you're going to want to know what went on up at that school. I'm not sure *I* want to know, but it's my job to find out."

She shuddered. "That bad?"

"And possibly worse."

"It was my fault, you know." She had to tell him. She had to tell someone. That hard rock of guilt in her chest was getting too heavy to carry by herself.

"What was?" he asked quietly.

"That Max was sent to that school. I was the one who found the marijuana. I didn't know what it was and I put it in my Fisher-Price kitchen. My dad found me playing with it and asked where I got it. And I told him. I don't know what I was thinking." That was a lie. She'd been thinking that Daddy was going to hit her the way he hit Max, and that it would hurt.

"You were a little girl. I'm guessing your thinking wasn't terribly complicated." He ran a finger along her jawline.

His touch made her want to melt into him, but her mind was racing, like a mouse in a maze, from one corner to another. "It hurts so much to remember. I've always regretted it. But to think that it was because of me that he was sent to the place where he was murdered—it's too much."

"You didn't send him there. You were a child. You didn't control anything."

That was exactly what she wanted to hear. She wanted to be exonerated of all the charges she was bringing against herself. It wasn't that easy, though.

"Do you think my father knew what they were going to do to him when he sent Max there?"

Zach sighed. "I doubt it. It doesn't add up. Besides, a lot of those schools are great. If it wasn't for a school like Sierra, I don't know what would have happened to me."

"You went to a reform school?" She pulled back to see his face better.

"My dad was killed in the line of duty when I was twelve. I kind of went off the rails for a while. I was pretty angry." He didn't look at her as he spoke. A muscle in his jaw tensed a little, but his voice stayed calm. Of course, he was good at that calm-voice thing. She'd seen him do it in quite a few situations now.

"I'm sorry," she said.

He reached over, still without looking at her, and took her hand. "It's okay. It was a long time ago."

"Doesn't mean it doesn't still hurt."

He nodded and ran his thumb along her hand. "True enough."

She thought for a moment. "Do you think it's possible that my father thought he was actually helping Max? Could he have been trying to do a good thing?"

Zach blew out a breath. "That's a tough one, Veronica. I wasn't there and even if I had been, I doubt I would have been able to figure out your father's motivations. He was . . . a difficult guy."

How diplomatic. Her father had been an asshole. "You don't have to pussyfoot around everything. I know who my father was. I know what he was."

"Doesn't mean I need to rub your nose in it." He pulled her to him and kissed her. She scooted closer so their bodies were pressed tightly together.

"That's true. I do need to know what happened to Max. I need to understand why someone would do something like that to him. He was just a kid."

He frowned. "You know as well as I do that people don't always have good reasons for what they do. You must see it all the time."

That was definitely true. The number of good intentions exposed as bad ideas in the emergency room was legion.

"It's no different with us. Oh, by the time they get to trial, they often have a reason for what they did.

But it always sounds like an elaborate justification to me. Most of the time, people act on instinct. They react without thinking. They follow someone they shouldn't follow, or give in to anger or fear or frustration or hatred. Reason doesn't play a big part in it."

That was a bleak view. "So you're telling me there's no real closure?"

"Hell, no. Closure, I believe in. It's part of why I do this job. I may not be able to tell someone why something happened, but I can find out what happened. I think it helps. Don't you think that being able to stop waiting for Max to show up at your door is going to bring you some kind of closure? Maybe not right away, but eventually?"

Veronica tucked her head against his chest. Would it? She didn't know.

"You don't have to decide right now, you know. You can think about it for a while. You could even sleep on it. How long has it been since you really slept?"

She wasn't sure. "Yesterday, maybe?"

"Yeah. You know, I always make my best decisions when I've had no sleep and have been living on an emotional roller coaster for several days."

She poked him in the ribs. "Hey, I decided to sleep with you on no sleep after riding an emotional roller coaster."

"And that was an excellent decision. But you

can't really expect to make a bunch of those at once, right?" He chuckled.

She smiled. "You know, you're kind of a sarcastic son of a bitch, aren't you?"

"Yep."

She sighed. "I think we're going to get along just fine. By the way, I think my father was blackmailing someone."

That woke him up.

Zach had decided to look over the bank statements the next morning. They weren't going anywhere, and he'd rather be naked in her bed.

"So this was what you wanted to show me?" he asked now.

"They're from the year that Max went missing." She sat back at the table, sipping her coffee. "I found them in my dad's stuff. I was looking to see if he had a will or anything."

He let out a low whistle. Six deposits of $9,500 each.

"Do you have any idea where your parents might have gotten that kind of cash?" He looked up at her, hoping there might be some other explanation.

"Not a clue." She took another long sip of coffee.

He set the bank statements down on the table. People got paid that kind of money in cash for a few things. Drugs, sometimes gambling debts. But more often, blackmail. And the timing was way too coincidental. "So you think your parents knew something about Max's death? Something someone paid them to keep quiet about?"

She bit her lip. "Not my mom. She was weak, but she loved Max. If she knew something, I don't think she would have kept quiet about it. Plus, she was still hoping he'd come home. Even as she was dying, sometimes she'd cry out for him."

She stopped speaking for a second, then she swallowed hard. "I think my dad knew something. All that stuff about me not knowing what I was getting into, and now this money . . . I think he knew something, and I think someone killed him because of it."

"So who do you think your father was blackmailing?" Zach set the bank statements down on the table.

She wavered. Blackmail was such an ugly word. Was her father capable of that? He would have made some kind of excuse for it, rationalized it somehow. She could practically hear him now: Whatever he knew wouldn't bring Max back, so why shouldn't he profit from it in some way? He'd make it sound pragmatic and reasonable. Or his other favorite, he'd make it someone else's fault. Pretty much everything that went wrong in George Osborne's life was someone else's fault.

Veronica likened it to what she liked to call the "some dude" phenomenon she saw in the emergency room. Half the people who came in were there because of the actions of "some dude." Or the equally infamous "two dudes."

"I don't know who. I don't know why. I don't even know for sure that he was blackmailing anyone. Was he capable of it?" Veronica put her head down on the table, pillowed on her arms. "Yeah. I think he was."

"I'm sorry," Zach said softly.

She snorted a little. "Me, too."

16

"So what can you tell us about Susan Tennant?" Zach asked. He and Frank were sitting in the Bean Conference Room with Josh Wolfe and Elise Jacobs, the detectives who had caught the Tennant case.

"Not a hell of a lot," Elise said. She was a tall woman with a café-au-lait complexion and a no-nonsense attitude. "Nobody saw anything. Nobody heard anything. She was quiet, kept to herself. She seemed to have spent every waking moment running her foundation."

"And she ended up tied up in her house, choking on her own vomit?" Frank asked.

"It sounds so pretty when you say it like that." Josh Wolfe leaned back in his chair. He was a big man. Nearly six foot three and well over two hundred pounds, but without an ounce of fat on him.

"I'm like a poet." Frank smiled at him. "How's married life treating you?"

Josh had recently gotten married to a psychologist he'd met during the course of a case last year. "It's nice. Really nice." He smiled.

Frank kicked Zach under the table. "See? I'm not the only one who likes marriage."

"No one likes marriage as much as you, Frank," Elise said. "So why do you think our dead nurse is related to your twenty-year-old bones?"

Zach explained about the connection between Susan Tennant and Max Shelden.

"So because she worked at the school when he disappeared, you think she had something to do with his reappearance?" Elise looked skeptical.

"He didn't just disappear. It looks like he was beaten to death and buried right on the school grounds," Zach pointed out. "Someone dug him up and brought him down here to Sacramento. Someone who knew exactly where he'd been buried."

There had been no other holes dug around the school. Whoever had dug Max up had gone to the exact spot.

"Susan Tennant wasn't the only one who worked there at the time," Elise said.

"She's the only one who turned up dead less than twenty-four hours after Max's bones appeared." Zach countered.

"Okay. You've got a point there," she said.

"We've been doing some research on her," Josh said. "We saw that she'd worked at the Sierra School. She left there late in 1992."

Zach and Frank exchanged looks. Zach said, "That's the year after Max Shelden disappeared."

"Here's the thing," Elise said. "She left there after the school year had already started, which we thought was sort of weird. Especially since she didn't have a new job lined up. She came back to Sacto, moved in with her folks, and promptly had a little nervous breakdown."

That was interesting. Zach leaned forward. "What kind of nervous breakdown?"

"She took a lot of pills. It's unclear whether it was really enough to kill her or not. Parents found her, had her stomach pumped, and slapped her into a comfy little institution for a couple of months. She got out and has lived a life of exemplary service ever since." Elise tapped the eraser end of a pencil on the papers in front of her.

"Serving at-risk teenagers the whole time?" Frank asked.

Elise nodded. "The kind of kids she probably got to know up at the Sierra School. We were wondering if something had happened up there that precipitated her quitting the job, trying to off herself, and then dedicating herself to the health and well-being of others. I mean, this chick didn't even date from what I can tell."

"You think watching a kid get beaten to death might be a precipitating event?" Frank scratched his chin.

"Sounds pretty precipitating to me," Josh said.

Zach couldn't argue.

"I still don't get why the bones suddenly showed up here." Elise drummed her fingers on the tabletop.

"We don't either," Zach admitted. "But something stirred somebody up. That's for sure."

"So what do you want to do now?" Josh asked.

What Zach wanted was a good long look at their case files. "How about we pool our evidence here? Maybe there's something at Susan Tennant's house that'll tie her to our case."

"Might be worthwhile," Elise mused. "I thought we were working some freaky sex thing. I wasn't looking for anything to tie her to your nasty bone thing, but maybe there's something. We searched her house, her office, her van, and didn't find anything interesting."

Zach's head shot up. "She had a van?"

"Yeah. She used it to transport kids around. Good-size passenger van." Josh pulled a photo out of one of the files and slid it across the table to Zach.

Zach looked over at Frank. "A van would be handy for moving a set of old bones around."

"It would at that," Frank agreed.

"And that construction site is only a few blocks from Tennant's teen center. She'd have to drive past it nearly every day on her way to and from work," Zach pointed out.

Frank gestured for Josh and Elise to pass over their files. "Let's see what you got from the van."

Veronica opened the door and let Zach in. She wrapped her arms around his neck and started kissing him.

"I can't stay," Zach managed to gasp out.

"Are you sure?" Veronica looked up into his eyes. Her pupils were so dilated there was practically no iris left and she was breathing hard.

Zach smiled. Damn, it was nice to know he wasn't alone in this. "I'm not happy about it, but I'm sure. I think we might have a break in the case."

"What kind of break?" Wow. She came down to earth fast. Zach tried to still his own breathing to catch up with her.

"A connection to another case. It's all pretty circumstantial now, but we've met with the detectives on the other case. We're pooling information now, and that's how we're going to trip this guy up. There'll be something someone heard. Something someone saw. Something left behind. Something will turn up—then we'll nail the son of a bitch." He felt it in his bones. This was the big break. This was where the case was going to crack wide open.

"Another case? Someone else has been murdered?" The look of horror on Veronica's face made Zach slow down. He forgot sometimes when he was dealing with civilians.

"Maybe you should sit down." He guided her toward the love seat.

"I think that was one of the first things you ever said to me. If it's going to be one of our inside jokes, I think we need to work on it a little." She sat down.

He felt that funny buzzy feeling in his chest. Inside jokes. That was something steady couples had.

"So," she said. "Who else is dead?"

"So far we've found one other person connected with the Sierra School who died recently under suspicious circumstances."

"So far?" Her head jerked up. "Do you think there're more? What the hell's going on?"

He held up his hands to slow her barrage of questions. "I don't know yet. I don't even know that it's connected to your brother or your father, but it's too much of a coincidence not to look into it."

"Who is this person? Can you tell me?" She tucked her knees up underneath her. She looked so small.

Zach hesitated. Susan Tennant's death had been reported on the news, but its connection to Veronica's father and brother was not common knowledge. Who would she tell, though? "You understand this is an ongoing investigation, right?"

She cocked her head to one side. "I deal with confidential information every day. I could lose my job if I talk about a patient. So if you're warning me to be quiet about something, I get it."

Good. "Susan Tennant," he told her.

She froze. "The nurse who ran that program for at-risk teens?"

He nodded. "Did you know her?"

"I worked on her. She died in my emergency room. I was one of the people trying to resuscitate her." Veronica got up and started to pace.

"Tina recognized her; we'd been to a seminar she gave a year or two ago." She twisted her hands in front of her as she paced. "She'd dedicated her life to helping kids. What connection did she have with the Sierra School?"

"She was the school nurse there the year that Max attended. She left pretty soon after he disappeared."

"How could she have had anything to do with what happened to Max?" Veronica asked, still pacing.

"We think she was the one who dug him up and put him in that construction site. Her clinic is only a few blocks away."

Zach wanted to grab her hands and still them. He wanted to pull her down next to him and hold her. She wasn't ready for that, though. She was still processing what he was telling her. He had to let her do it her own way, even if it was killing him.

She gave him a startled look. "Why on earth would she do that?"

He shook his head. "We don't know. We might never know. One thing for certain, though, she wanted him to be found. She wanted Max's bones to tell us their story—and unless I miss my guess, she died for it."

Gary sat in his truck outside the St. Elizabeth's emergency room entrance. The Pop-Tart had driven here in her little Honda. It was parked a few spaces over right now. It had been pitifully easy to follow her and equally as easy to sit here and watch her car. When the time came, it would be simple to find an opportunity when she was distracted and alone. She was so tiny, it would be easy to take her down.

It figured she was a nurse. Another whore. It hadn't taken long before she was spreading her legs for the cop. The thought of it disgusted Gary.

Now she was inside, pretending to be some angel of mercy. She was as bad as Susan Tennant. Maybe even worse. She was where it had all begun.

He started up his truck and pulled out of the parking lot. He had watched the staff go in and out of the employee entrance and he understood the rhythm of the place. When it was time, he'd be ready.

It felt good to be back in the emergency room. Tina was right; they were both adrenaline junkies. Thank goodness they'd found a socially acceptable way to get their jollies.

She told Tina, "Okay, I gave the drunk in number four his discharge papers. Supposedly his girlfriend is coming to pick him up. Let's hope she's had less to drink than he has. The kid in number seven is ready to go, too. His forehead's stitched up and the doc lectured him on playing capture the flag after dark." She slapped the two charts down on the counter, rubbed her hands together, and asked, "Who's next?"

Tina stared at her. "You got some, didn't you?"

Veronica tried not to look up. She could feel the smile spreading across her face. "Got some what?" she asked innocently, but a giggle escaped.

"You know what. A little something something. Was it the cop with the cute butt?"

"Maybe I did. Maybe I didn't." The smile was going to split her face.

Tina clapped her hands. "Oh. My. God. I need details. Now."

Veronica shook her head. "Do I look like the kind of girl who kisses and tells?"

"That good? So good you can't talk?" Tina clasped her hands under her chin.

Veronica looked up at her. "So good I can barely walk."

"Girlfriend! Yes, yes, oh yes!"

"That's pretty much what I said. With a few 'oh Gods' thrown in for good measure." She laughed.

"Oh, it does my heart good to hear that. If there ever was a woman who needed to get laid, it was you."

"Who got laid?" a male voice asked behind her.

Veronica whirled around. Matt Cassel was standing behind her. When had he gotten here?

"I'm guessing it's you, based on how hard you're blushing." He moved past her to set a stack of papers on the nurses' desk. "Hey, Tina."

"Hey, Matt." Tina smiled back.

"Girl talk, dude. You're not included," Veronica laughed as he walked away.

"We got another one." Frank walked into Zach's cubicle holding a piece of paper the next morning.

"Another what?" Zach grabbed the paper from Frank's hand. A man had been murdered in his home in Placerville. There was no sign of forced entry. When he hadn't shown up for work or answered his phone, his coworkers had gotten worried. One of them had gone over to the man's house during the lunch hour.

He'd found his friend facedown in his bathtub with a broom handle stuck up his ass.

The man's name was Ryan Arnott and he'd taught at the Sierra School for Boys from 1989 to 1992.

"How we doing with tracking down any of the other teachers from Sierra?" Zach asked. "Is there anybody else close by?"

"Yeah—this guy Lyle Burton lives right here in Sacto." Frank dropped a folder onto Zach's desk.

The name connected in Zach's memory. "Are we talking about the Lyle Burton who's about to become head of the CPS?"

"One and the same." Frank crossed his arms over his chest.

Zach rubbed his forehead. The name had come up someplace else, too. He pulled out the list of calls to and from George Osborne's phone the night he was murdered. There it was: a two-minute call to the home phone of Lyle Burton. He shoved the paper across to Frank and pointed to the name with his pen.

Frank's eyebrows climbed halfway up his forehead.

Zach glanced up at the clock. It was only eight. "Bet he's not in his office yet, but why don't we make an appointment and see if we can stop by for a chat today?"

"After we go to Placerville or before?" Frank asked.

Zach sighed. He'd hoped for a lead in this case; now it seemed like he had more than he could handle. "Placerville first. Then Burton. I don't think he's going anywhere. Did we get any traction on tracing that money, by the way?"

"Cash deposits from twenty years ago? The guys in Financial laughed in my face."

Veronica had had Joe, one of the security guards, walk her out to her car at the end of her shift. She felt ridiculous. The sun was already up and it looked like it was going to be another cloudless California fall day. She'd promised Zach she would be careful, though.

Matt Cassel was hanging outside the door, clearly waiting for Tina. Veronica waved as she went by.

"Thanks, Joe," she said as they got to her car.

"No problem. All you gotta do is ask." He hitched up his uniform pants and started back toward the hospital.

She got into her car. Asking for help didn't come naturally to her. Her instinct was always to try to take care of everything herself. She'd been told it was pretty typical of adult children of alcoholics. She'd had to assume caregiver responsibilities for her mother too early, and now it was an ingrained habit.

She drove home on autopilot. When she arrived, another little box was sitting on her doorstep.

She whipped out her cell phone to call Zach and got his voice mail. She stared at the box, tempted to skirt it like it was a dead rat. And then what? Hide inside her castle waiting for her McKnight to come save her? The very thought galled her. She went inside to get a pair of gloves.

They'd gotten nothing from the other box, and probably wouldn't from this one. But someone was trying to tell her something. It was time she started to listen.

"So you think this case is related to your old bones in the construction pit?" Sheriff Ian Bell gave Zach and Frank a disbelieving look.

Zach didn't blame him; it seemed pretty preposterous. But too many coincidences were stacking up. "Maybe, maybe not. It seemed like we shouldn't ignore it, though."

The man thought for a minute and then nodded. "I can see that."

He started up the steps to the house tucked back from the road. "None of the neighbors saw or heard anything."

Zach looked at the thick stands of pine trees between the houses and the distance between them. Hardly surprising that no one would hear or see anything. He glanced back toward the road. No streetlights, either. It was probably beautiful at night. Crisp and clear, with a thousand stars twinkling at you. It was an ideal place to commit a crime like this.

Bell lifted up the crime-scene tape and let them through the front door. "No sign of forced entry here or anywhere else. We're pretty sure he came in through the front door, though."

Zach looked at the blood spray on the walls of the entryway and figured Bell had it right. "What do you guys think happened?"

Bell scratched his bald head. "Looks like our perp busted Arnott one in the face right here. A find howdy do, don't you think? It'd be consistent with Arnott's broken nose, too."

Zach nodded as Frank shoved a piece of gum in his mouth. Lots of detectives had death scene rituals, little things they did to steel themselves against the smells and sights. Frank's involved Juicy Fruit. He offered a piece to Zach, who shook his head.

Bell took the offered stick of gum, though.

"Knocked Arnott right over. He wasn't a big man. Mean as a snake, but scrawny."

"You've had previous dealings with Arnott?" Frank asked.

"Nothing much. Some spats between him and the missus that got kind of nasty before they split up. He hasn't bothered her since she moved out. At least not as far as I know."

So he was an abuser but not a stalker. Give him a posthumous medal. "Anything else?"

Bell wrinkled his brow. "I'm pretty sure there was a DUI. Maybe more than one. I'll have to look it up."

There was an idea. Get to know the victim.

"No chance the ex had anything to do with this?" Frank asked.

Zach surpressed a smile. If there was anything that struck fear into Frank's heart, it was the idea that Doreen would try to exact vengeance on him. His thoughts had certainly turned to the victim's ex pretty damn fast.

Bell shook his head. "Doesn't seem likely. At least not working solo. She was an itty-bitty thing, and even with Arnott being scrawny, it would take a strong person to get all this done."

"What all did get done?" Zach pressed.

"Well, there was the original altercation in the hall-way. Actually, I'd be more willing to believe that Arnott answered the door and got sucker-punched." He pointed again to the blood spray on the walls as proof of that scenario. "Then it looks like whoever it was dragged Arnott down this hallway. After he trussed him up, of course."

Zach looked at the trail of blood that led away from the spot. It seemed as good a conclusion as any. In addition to the blood, there were drag marks in the carpet. "Those don't look like heel marks."

"Nope. We didn't think so, either. Our crime-scene guy thinks the perp dragged him by his tied-up ankles and let his head drag behind." Bell hitched up his pants.

"Anything special about whatever the perp used to tie him up?" Frank asked, chewing hard.

"Nah, just the kind of stuff you'd keep in the back of your truck to tie things down. Get it at any hardware store from here to Timbuktu."

Zach looked down the hall at the blood trail. "You guys done photographing and everything?"

Bell nodded. "Yep," he said and led the way down the hall. "Perp dragged him down to the master bedroom. Looks like he let him lie here for a bit." He gestured to a place where blood had soaked into the carpeting.

"Any idea why?" Zach crouched down next to the small pool of blood. A broken nose would bleed pretty hard, but eventually it would slow down. Especially if the victim was lying on his back, the way it looked like Arnott had been.

Bell shrugged. "Maybe he let him lie there while he filled up the tub. We're not sure."

Zach stood up. "Okay. Show us the rest."

All three men walked into the bathroom.

"This is where we found him." Bell grimaced. "Couldn't believe it when I saw it. Poor bastard. Facedown in the water. Pants around his ankles. Ass up in the air with a broom handle sticking out of it."

Zach grimaced, too. "Any sign of anything else sexual?"

Bell shook his head. "Our ME wants a little more time with the body, but after a preliminary exam he thinks the broom handle was, uh, inserted postmortem. As far in as it was shoved, there would have been a lot more bleeding otherwise. Of course, the water could have slowed that down, too. Damn cold."

Zach shuddered. What a way to go. "Arnott got any enemies besides the ex?"

"There's plenty of people who didn't care for him. But this?" Bell gestured to the tub. "This feels like an awful lot of hatred. It feels kinda personal, too."

It did seem like a lot of personal hatred. It also seemed very calm and calculated. There was no effort to make it look like anything other than what it was, either. Zach had a hard time believing that the same person who killed George Osborne had killed Ryan Arnott.

Susan Tennant, on the other hand? That seemed to fit.

He handed Bell his card. "Keep us posted, will you? I can't tell if this is related to our case or not, but I don't want to miss something for lack of looking."

"I hear you." Bell tucked the card away. "I'll make sure you get copies of all the reports."

They shook hands and Frank and Zach headed back to their car. "What do you think?" Frank asked.

"I'm not sure what to think about any of it at this point."

"Me, neither." Frank started the car and they headed back to Sacramento.

17

"I'll have to do a more detailed analysis to be certain, but it certainly looks as if the dirt from the back of Susan Tennant's van matches the dirt from Max Shelden's bones and the sample you brought back from the Sierra School site." Dinsmore pushed back from his lab bench.

All four detectives stared at each other.

"So Susan Tennant dug up Max Shelden and dumped him in that construction site?" Elise shook her head. "Why? What possible reason could she have for doing that? If our theory is that she spent her whole life trying to make up for letting him be beaten to death, why would she suddenly dig him up now? Why not when she first got out of the loony bin? Or after she started her foundation?"

"Why ask why?" Frank offered her a piece of Juicy Fruit. "At least we know who, which is a damn sight more than we knew yesterday."

"True that," Josh said, staring off into the middle distance. "It also doesn't tell us who killed her, though."

"No. But it might give us a motive, and that's not a terrible place to start." Zach suggested.

Josh nodded. "Okay. Let's say she had her reasons. Whatever they were, she wanted the world to find Max Shelden now."

"And as a nurse, she probably knew that we'd figure out he'd been murdered," Frank chimed in.

"I'm guessing there're quite a few people who don't want us digging into what happened up at that school, and to Max Shelden in particular." Elise drummed her fingers.

That was an understatement. "We started a list," Zach said.

"Can we see it?" Josh asked.

Frank looked over at Zach. "I think it might be a nice time to share. They did give us the evidence from their van."

They all headed back to police headquarters and met up at Frank's and Zach's desks.

When Frank pulled out the 1991-to-1992 staff roster for the Sierra School, Elise tapped her finger on Ryan Arnott's name. "Why does he sound familiar?"

"Because they just found him drowned in his own bathtub, riding a broomstick in a very uncomfortable fashion." Frank leaned back in his chair and smiled.

"Ohhh." Realization dawned on her face. "He's that dude."

"Yep. That dude," Zach confirmed.

"So you think that's connected, too?" Josh had taken up a position half sitting on Frank's desk.

"We think it's possible. We don't have anything but the Sierra School connection to tie it in, and that's twenty years old. From what we heard, Arnott wasn't the most popular guy around, but that seemed, well, pretty personal."

And very deliberate. There'd been a basement room with a bathtub in it at the school. Zach had only taken a quick look at it, and the crime-scene guys were still processing information. He almost didn't want to know what they found, at this point.

"Bell up in Placerville is still going to be working the case, checking the ex-wife's alibi and all that, but we're keeping an eye on it," Zach finished.

"Totally different MO," Josh observed. "There's no ritual. Serials usually have a ritual."

"We noticed that, too," Frank said.

"Most serials have a sexual component, as well," Josh continued.

"Broomstick up the ass seems kind of sexual." Elise cocked her head and looked over at him.

"True that." Josh thought for a minute. "Nothing sexual with Tennant, though. It looked like it could have been some bondage thing at first, but they didn't find any sign of sexual trauma."

"Maybe our guy's a little light in the loafers," Frank suggested. "Maybe he only likes guys."

"Maybe he's not a classic serial killer," Zach said. Just because the FBI said most serial killers behaved a certain way didn't mean they all did.

"Any other cases you got simmering on the back burner that you think might be related to ours?" Elise asked.

Zach slid the file on George Osborne across the table. Josh flipped it open and started to read, Elise reading over his shoulder. "This is even less like Tennant than Arnott is," she said after a few minutes.

"We noticed that, too. He's the Shelden boy's stepfather, the one who had him sent away to the Sierra School in the first place. What with the timing and all . . ." Frank let his words drift off. The other two detectives didn't need him to lead them by their noses.

"This is a mess," Elise said. "A right nasty mess."

*   *   *

Lyle Burton was a decent-looking guy in his late forties. He had an athletic build and a hard jaw. Zach guessed he might be a little thicker in the middle than he'd been in his twenties, but he still looked fit and strong.

He had a good firm handshake, too. He sat down behind his desk after shaking both Zach's and Frank's hand and asked, "What can I do for you gentlemen?"

"Mr. Burton, were you ever employed at the Sierra School for Boys?" Zach asked.

Burton's eyes widened in surprise. "Why, yes, I was. I was fresh out of college. It was one of my first teaching jobs. Why do you ask?"

Because your name keeps popping up every time I turn around. "I'm not sure if you've heard much about the remains that were discovered in a construction area in downtown Sacramento, but they belonged to a student who had run away from the Sierra School." Zach watched Burton's face carefully, and he knew Frank was doing the same. They'd compare notes afterward.

"You know, the name rang a bell. Shepherd or something, wasn't it?" Burton shook his head. "Terrible shame."

"Max Shelden was the kid's name," Frank said.

Burton's face stayed still. Almost too still. "I don't have any specific memories of the boy. Is there a reason you're talking to me about it? Surely the school has some records."

"The school's been shut down for a long time. Their records are spotty, to say the least. We found your name on a list of staff members and you were pretty easy to locate."

Zach made it sound as innocent as possible, but he was getting a very bad vibe from this guy. His face was too calm. His hands were too still. He was looking Zach a little too directly in the eye. Zach's gut screamed "liar."

Burton shook his head. "I'm sorry. There were so many boys, and it was so long ago. I'm afraid the name doesn't ring any bells."

"How about a picture, then?" Frank slapped the photo of Max and Veronica down on the desk. "Does this ring any bells?"

Burton looked at the photo for a moment and then shook his head. "I'm afraid not."

"How about when the boy's stepfather called you?" Zach asked. He wasn't going to bring up the grave yet.

Burton went very still. "Excuse me?"

"George Osborne. He called you and spoke to you for . . ." Zach checked his notes. "Approximately two minutes four nights ago."

"I'm sorry, I don't have any recollection of that call. Perhaps one of my sons answered and took a message. They're not always good about passing them on." Burton laughed.

Zach didn't laugh with him. He didn't say anything at all.

"Perhaps you could ask this Osborne fellow," Burton suggested.

"We can't. He's dead," Frank said.

"Oh my. How terrible." Burton pushed back in his chair and stood. "It was all so long ago, I'm not sure what else I can tell you."

Zach stood. "We're sorry to have taken up your time. You'll call us if you remember anything?"

"Of course. I'm afraid it was just too long ago." Burton smiled.

Zach was pretty damn sure something smelled in this room.

Fuck. Fuck. Fuck. Fuck. Lyle sat behind his desk, shaking. The cops had been gone for ten minutes and he still couldn't pick up a pen without it practically flying across the room. What was he going to do?

It was only a matter of time now. Somehow they'd put it together. There'd be a fingerprint or a hair. Someone would have seen his car.

He called his secretary and canceled his appointments for the rest of the day.

*   *   *

"You did what?" Zach stared at Veronica in disbelief. "You found another box on your doorstep, quite likely from a murderer, and you just picked it up, carried it inside, and *opened* it?"

"I wore gloves. I didn't contaminate it."

She didn't get it. If she got it, she wouldn't be sitting there all calm and pleased with herself.

"I don't think you understand what's going on here. This person has killed at least three people now."

Her head came up. "Three?"

"Yes, Veronica. Three. A former staff member of the Sierra School for Boys was found murdered up in Placerville last night. We're pretty sure it's linked." He hated making her shrink back into herself like that, but at least she was paying attention now.

"I didn't know." She looked down at the table.

"Can I see what you found?" There was no point in lecturing her further; the damage was already done.

He followed her into the kitchen. In the middle of the table, on a blue piece of paper, sat an odd-looking watch.

"What is it?"

"It's a watch that clips to your collar. It's something that you give to new nurses when they graduate. And it's engraved." She put a pair of latex gloves on and turned the watch over.

Zach bent down to look at it. It was engraved with the initials ST.

"I think this is Susan Tennant's watch," Veronica said. "Somebody left it for me. The same person who left Max's photo. Someone wants to make sure I know they're connected."

"You need to tell your girlfriend not to tamper with evidence." Little Hillary was not pleased to receive the undone package that had held Susan Tennant's watch.

"We had a conversation."

She looked up sharply. "So she *is* your girlfriend, then?"

Damn, he must be tired. He'd walked right into that one. "Can we just talk about the package?"

Little Hillary looked over at Frank, who held out his hand. She sighed, took her wallet out of her purse, and pulled out a twenty. "Someone finally got her hooks into McKnight. I never thought I'd see the day."

"You're betting on my love life?" Zach asked.

"Beats the ponies." Frank pocketed the bill.

Zach sat down. "The package please."

"There's nothing here. It's the same as the last one. Whoever wrapped it up wore gloves. The paper and the tape and everything else are things you can buy at any office supply store." Hillary shrugged. "I'll run more tests, just in case, but I don't think you're going to solve this one with trace evidence."

"Little Hillary's right," Zach told Frank when they were back at their desks. "This isn't going to be solved based on forensic evidence. Whoever killed Tennant and Arnott was too careful, and the evidence from the Sierra School is too damn old." Osborne's murder was a whole different ball of wax.

"So what do you suggest?" Frank asked.

"We're going to have to think this through ourselves." Evidence was so much easier. He'd much rather have a fingerprint or a DNA sample over motive or opportunity.

"We've been looking at the names of teachers. Maybe we should be looking at the names of students. I was thinking about how Arnott was killed. How very personal that was. And Tennant was killed in a way that was very intimate, too," Frank pointed out. "Maybe our perp isn't one of the staff members. Maybe it's one of the former students."

Zach went very still. "But why now? I keep coming back to that. We're agreed that Susan Tennant dug up Max's body and dumped it in that construction site. Why do it now, after all these years? And if that's what sparked somebody into a revenge killing spree, again, why now?"

"I don't know, buddy. I don't know that we'll ever know. And even if we find some explanation, it might never make any sense to us. I just know that looking at students feels like the right direction to go right now."

Zach pulled another box of files toward himself. "Lets give it a try."

"That's a lot of names." Elise Jacobs looked at the list and back up at Zach. "A lot of names."

It had taken Zach two hours to find the roster of students for 1991, and there were approximately thirty boys. "I know. It's why we need help."

"What are we doing with them?"

"Running down addresses and current disposition. Seeing if any of them could make a good suspect."

Elise nodded and looked over at Josh, who shrugged one shoulder. She turned back to Zach. "We're in."

A few hours later, Elise laid her short list down on Zach's desk. "I've got three names."

"I've got two." Josh set his list next to his partner's.

"We've each got one," Zach said.

"Seven total," Frank said.

"Pretty fancy math skills there, Rodriguez." Elise clapped him on the back.

Frank smiled. "I did it all in my head, too."

"You guys want to take these three and we'll take the other four?" Zach asked.

Elise picked up their list of names. "Sounds good."

*   *   *

Gary was getting more and more uncomfortable as he followed Lyle Burton—the Devil. As Burton made another turn, Gary couldn't believe his eyes. The Devil was turning onto *his* street. What was he doing?

Gary went past his street to the alley that cut behind his house and parked his truck. He slipped through the back fence, then into the house. The Devil was ringing the front doorbell. What the hell was he doing here? Was he marking Gary himself?

Gary took a couple of deep breaths to calm himself, then opened the door.

"Hello, Gary. Do you remember me? My name is Lyle Burton. May I come in?"

Gary stepped back and let the Devil into his home, into his sanctuary, into his haven. He let him take two steps in, shut the door—and then crashed the wrench he'd been holding behind his back onto the Devil's head as hard as he could.

When he dragged the Devil out to the shed it left a nasty smear of blood running down the hallway. That would be hard to clean up. Sometimes it was impossible to get that much blood out of a carpet. Damn him, he was ruining everything!

Quickly he bound the Devil's wrists and ankles

with duct tape. Then he sat down on the bench in the shed to catch his breath.

As he sat there, the Devil began to regain consciousness. First he moaned. Then he tried to roll to his side. Finally his eyes opened and he tried to sit up. Gary watched as realization dawned on the Devil's face. He looked up at Gary and said, "You're never going to get away with this."

"Who said I ever expected to get away with it?" Gary stood up, swung back his leg, and kicked the Devil as hard as he could in the ribs.

Zach and Frank approached the third house on their list.

Frank knocked on the door. Jimmy Lopez, a beefy-looking Latino with a bit of a beer gut, opened it. He squinted at Zach and Frank and their badges. "What do you want?"

It wasn't the friendliest greeting, but it was late and nobody really liked the cops showing up on their doorstep. "Are you the Jimmy Lopez who attended the Sierra School for Boys in 1991?"

Lopez glanced behind him and then came out onto the porch. He shut the door behind him. "I am. What about it?" He crossed his arms over his chest.

"We'd like to know your whereabouts for a couple

of nights." Zach whipped out his notebook, ready to write down information.

"You want to know where I was when the nurse and the teacher were murdered, don't you?" Lopez's eyes narrowed.

Zach stilled. "We do. You know about them?"

Lopez shrugged. "It's been in the news. Kind of hard to miss. They aren't names I'd forget. Ever."

"So you were acquainted with both the victims?" This was farther than they'd gotten with the first two men they'd spoken to.

Lopez snorted. "Acquainted? I guess you could put it like that, if you call getting acquainted being tortured by someone."

"So you held a grudge against these people?" Frank asked.

Lopez narrowed his eyes. "Look. I wouldn't cross the street to piss on those people if they were on fire. They did things to us kids that you read about happening in prison camps. But let me make your job simpler. Whatever night it was, I was here. With my family. You want to know anything else, you can contact my lawyer."

Lopez went back inside and slammed the door in their faces.

*   *   *

Gary changed clothes. The ones he'd been wearing had gotten sweaty and bloody. He'd need to be clean and fresh for tonight. The Devil coming to his doorstep had been a sign. It was time to finish this.

He'd left the Devil bound and gagged in the shed and he'd deal with him when he got home. Or if he was dead when Gary got home after dealing with the Pop-Tart, it would already be done. The bones would be satisfied. They would be avenged.

He put on a uniform that was close to the ones he'd seen the staff wearing at the hospital, got into his truck, and headed to St. Elizabeth's.

"Matthew Cassell?" Zach asked the man who opened the door.

"Nah. He's at work, man. I'm his roommate. And you are?" he asked.

Zach held up his badge. "Sacramento police. Where does Cassell work?"

"Why do you want to talk to him?" the roommate asked. "He's a pretty straight arrow."

"We just need to ask some questions. So where does he work?" Zach didn't feel a need to explain their case to what looked like a thirty-year-old computer programmer.

"All over the place, man. He's a paramedic. He could be anywhere."

"A paramedic?" Zach turned to look at Frank. A paramedic, who could waltz in and out of a hospital anytime he wanted with no questions asked. "And he's working tonight?"

"I assume so. He's not here and his truck's not here."

Frank was already headed back to the car. "You call. I'll drive."

Zach called dispatch. "I'm looking for a paramedic."

"You hurt?" the woman on the other end asked.

"No. I'm looking for a specific paramedic. I'm hoping you can tell me where he is. The name is Matthew Cassell."

"Let me check." The line went silent. Zach drummed his fingers on the dashboard as Frank drove toward the freeway. Then she was back. "Looks like he's gone on break. He's heading over to St. E's."

"St. Elizabeth's?" Zach hung up and looked over at Frank. "He's going to St. Elizabeth's."

18

"So what's up with you and the hunky paramedic?" Veronica asked Tina as she logged in test results on the diabetic lady in bay number 4 who had passed out at the grocery store.

"You mean Matt? I'm kind of wondering that myself." Tina scowled.

Veronica looked up. Tina generally had quite a bit to say about her relationships; she didn't spend much time wondering. "What does that mean?"

"We went out. We had a nice time. He took me for sushi and then to the Torch Club. We danced a little. Made out a little."

It sounded like a good date to Veronica, but Tina wasn't smiling. "What's wrong with that? Sounds like solid first-date material to me."

"Yeah. The conversation was weird, though."

"In what way? Like he thinks he's been probed by aliens weird? Or maybe he was nervous and said stupid stuff weird?"

"Like he kept asking about you kind of weird." Tina leaned on the counter and looked at Veronica, her eyes narrowed.

"Whoa, whoa, whoa. I haven't been poaching. Don't be giving me the stink eye." Veronica lifted her hands up in protest.

"I'm not giving you the stink eye. I'm trying to figure it out. I know he likes me. He doesn't flirt with you when I'm around." She paused. "Does he flirt with you when I'm *not* around?"

"Nope. I've seen him hanging around the doors a few times as I'm leaving, but I figured he was just waiting for you. We've never spoken when you're not there."

"Okay. It was just strange. He wanted to know about you and your dad, and if you ever talked about your brother." Tina chewed on her lower lip.

"It has been in the news. Maybe he was just curious." A lot of people were. Veronica was getting plenty of second glances in the hallways and whispered conversations behind her back. The gossip would die down soon.

"You're right. I'm sure that's all it is." Tina smiled.

"I'm off to check on that little boy who broke his wrist on the soccer field, okay?"

"You bet. I'm going to run some stuff down to the lab."

"Can you wait a few? I'll have some stuff to go in a little while. I'll cover up here when you go."

"Sounds like a plan."

It wasn't hard to find Matthew Cassell. He was right next to his rig, parked in front of the emergency room ambulance entry. He had no reason to hide. He could hang out there watching Veronica whenever he wanted and no one would think anything of it.

Like now.

"Cassell?" Zach said as he approached from the front of the vehicle, having already signaled to Frank to go around the back in case the guy tried to make a break for it.

He straightened. "Yeah?"

"I have a few questions for you," Zach said as he came toe-to-toe with the man. They were about the same height. Cassell was in good shape, but Zach was younger. He was pretty sure he could take him, especially with Frank to back him up.

"About what?" Cassell looked him up and down, eyes narrowed.

"About the Sierra School for Boys and what's been happening to the former staff members."

Cassell raised one eyebrow. "So you finally connected them, did you?"

"When did you?"

"I didn't have to. They came preconnected for me." He turned away and started to get back in the ambulance. "Personally I'd rather not have any connection with any of the rat bastards, but there you have it. My connection with them was not exactly pleasant."

Zach grabbed his arm. "Not so fast, Cassell. We're going to want to know where you were at a few key points in time."

Cassell shook Zach's hand off his arm. "You're kidding, right? You think I had something to do with it? Hell, I was the one who tried to save Susan Tennant."

"It'd be a heck of a cover," Frank pointed out from behind him.

Cassell whirled. For a second it looked like he might be getting ready to fight them. Then he put his hands up in a gesture of surrender. "Whatever. You want to know where I was? Check the ambulance logs."

"Don't think we won't." The guy was too cool, too easy.

"Look, I don't blame you for being suspicious. I moved down here to finally get away from that place.

Every time I had to drive near there, I'd practically break out in hives. I thought I was losing my mind when one of my first runs here was the bitch who used to tie us up. And then to find out Max Shelden's baby sister was one of the nurses in the emergency room? I've been spending plenty of time with my therapist this week."

Frank climbed down from the rig, the log in hand. "It's not him. Not unless he can be doing CPR on a kid by a pool at the same time he's drowning Ryan Arnott in a bathtub."

Cassell turned. "Arnott? Arnott's dead?" He turned pale.

"You remember him, too?" Zach asked.

"You don't forget a man like that. I bet he plays a starring role in a lot of men's nightmares." Cassell ran his hand across his face.

Zach looked down at his list. "You remember another kid up there named Gary Havens?"

Cassell nodded. "Yeah. A little guy. Got picked on by everyone—staff and kids. He's got to be one damaged piece of goods."

Zach looked over at Frank. "Let's go check him out."

Veronica hurried down the corridor. It was a good shortcut to the lab. It was a little serpentine, but had a lot less traffic. Right now there was just a janitor mop-

ping with one of those big yellow buckets. Veronica
didn't recognize him. She tried to be on good terms
with all the janitorial staff. There were messes that got
made in the ER that she didn't want to ever touch. A
smile and a pleasant word occasionally got her out of
dealing with some nasty shit. Literally.

She looked for his name badge, but didn't see one
hanging around his neck. "Hey, are you new?"

The man looked around as if to see who she might
be talking to, though the two of them were the only
ones in the hallways. "Uh, yeah," he stammered out.

She pointed to his chest. "You forgot your ID card.
I don't care, but the security guards make a fuss sometimes. I can't tell you how many times I forgot mine
when I first started here. I think Joe was getting ready
to strangle me."

He looked confused for a second and then looked
down at his chest. "Oh, man. There are so many rules
to remember. I must have forgotten my ID down in
my locker. I'll go get it right now."

"Don't do it on my account," she said, smiling.
"I'm just giving you a friendly heads-up."

"Gotcha," he said.

"I'm Veronica, by the way." She stuck out her hand.

He stared at her hand for a moment and then gave
it a quick shake. "Gary," he said. "Gary Havens."

"Nice to meet you, Gary," Veronica said and

walked past him. She heard a quick movement behind her and then the sound of something whistling
through the air.

Then everything went black.

It was a good thing she was such a little thing. Even
so, Gary was sweating by the time he'd managed to get
Veronica out of the hospital without anyone seeing.

With the keys clipped to Veronica's belt, it had
been easy to locate a laundry cart, but dumping her
into it took some effort. He'd tried to act normally,
but every time he pushed the cart past someone, he
kept waiting for them to notice how heavy it looked
or the strange bulge where her legs pressed against
the side.

But no one did. Pretty much no one looked at him
at all. Give him a uniform and a mop, and nobody
ever looked. Some even made a point of looking away.

Not the Pop-Tart, though. She'd walked right up to
him, bold as brass. That had been his first sign.

Then she'd started talking about the security guard
wanting to strangle her. That made Gary think about
what it might be like to strangle her, to wrap his
hands around her throat, to choke the life from her.
He'd stared at her neck. Her skin was so white, so
pale. His hands would look dark against it. He was

strong. She wouldn't be able to do a thing. He could see it so clearly.

Then she'd started to walk away, and he couldn't let that happen. The two of them alone in an empty part of the hospital? How much more of a sign did he need? Once again, the bones had put him in the right place at the right time. The Devil had come to Gary's own home. Surely that was a sign that it was time for the end of all this.

He'd pulled out the leather-covered sap hidden in his utility belt and smacked her on the back of the head, right behind her right ear.

She went down like a ton of bricks.

"Last house," Frank said.

Zach looked down at the name on his printout. "Gary Havens."

"You think he'll be the one?"

Zach shrugged. "It's always in the last place you look."

"True enough," Frank said.

Elise and Josh had hit their last place and found that their last Sierra School alumni had been out of town for the last two weeks. Gary Havens was either their guy, or they'd be back to the drawing board tomorrow.

He knocked. No answer.

Frank rang the bell. They both stood still and listened.

"You hear that?" Frank asked.

"Hear what?"

"That thumping noise."

Zach had been vaguely aware of the noise as they walked up to the house, but it wasn't coming from inside, so he'd ignored it. "It's coming from somewhere in back."

Frank pressed the bell again. The thumping got faster.

"That's a little strange." Zach looked up at the house. There were no lights on and no cars in the driveway.

"Strange enough to check out?"

Zach hesitated. If they went onto Havens's property without a warrant and he was the perp, they could lose whatever evidence they found in court.

The thumping got more frantic. This time, it was followed by a crash.

"I call that exigent, dude," Frank said.

Zach nodded.

He motioned Frank to go first down the side of the house and crept along behind him into the shadows. Frank slipped the latch on the gate that led into the backyard and looked over at Zach. He nodded. Frank flung the gate open and Zach barreled through.

Nothing. Just an empty backyard. As he turned to tell Frank that, the thumping started again. This time, there was no doubt about where it was coming from. Zach motioned Frank toward the shed that stood at the back of the property.

The door was padlocked, but the wood was cheap and flimsy. Frank nodded at Zach, who lifted his foot and kicked the door in with one good blow.

On the floor they found Lyle Burton, bound and gagged and kicking his tied feet against the wall for all he was worth.

Veronica woke in the dark, being tossed around like a pea in a frying pan. She tried to put her hands out to brace herself but they wouldn't move. They were tied behind her back.

Where was she? What was going on? She tried to use her feet to push herself upright, but they, too, had been bound.

Panic rose in her throat, threatening to strangle her. She couldn't even open her mouth to scream. It had been taped shut.

She tried to piece it together. She'd been in the hospital. She'd gone down a corridor and seen the new janitor . . .

After that she got nothing.

She rolled again, cracking her head against something hard. Where could she be?

It was dark. It was moving. She smelled exhaust. Slowly her confused brain added it all up. She was in the trunk of a car.

She didn't know why she was there, who'd put her there, or where they were headed, but she knew that it wasn't good news.

"He's crazy!" Burton screamed the second Frank pulled the duct tape off his mouth. "You've got to stop him. He's nuts. He's killing everyone."

"You're talking about Havens?" Zach asked.

"Yes, Gary Havens! Put out an APB, call something in! He's killed twice and he's going to do it again." Burton began to weep. "Thank God you found me. I was going to be next."

"Next after whom?"

"I don't know. He kept talking about the Pop-Tart."

Zach froze. That was Max's nickname for Veronica. That's what was written on the back of the photo that had shown up on her doorstep: "Me and Pop-Tart."

Zach pulled out his phone and called Veronica's cell. No answer. She might not have it on her; she didn't always carry it when she was working.

He hung up, called information, and had them connect him to the St. Elizabeth emergency room.

"Emergency room. This is Tina."

Thank goodness. "Tina, this Zach McKnight. Can I talk to Veronica?"

"I hear you've been doing a whole lot more than talking, big guy." She laughed, a throaty chuckle.

"Listen, Tina, this is important. Veronica might be in danger. I need to talk to her. I need to warn her."

"Okay, keep your pants on. I'll go find her. I haven't seen her for a couple of hours, but she's around here somewhere."

Frank was undoing the rest of the ropes that had bound Lyle Burton. "So do you want to explain how you ended up here in the shed?"

"I had to find out who was doing it."

"Who was doing what?"

"Killing the staff from the Sierra School."

"Did you ever think about maybe letting us do that? It's our job."

"I couldn't let that happen, either. I couldn't." Burton began to sob.

Tina came back on the phone. "Something's wrong. Veronica's missing."

Zach shoved his hand through his hair. "What do you mean by 'missing'?"

"She's not here. Not where she's supposed to be.

Not anywhere that I can figure out." Tina sounded tense, but calm.

"Should I call her cell?"

"I already did and I can hear it ringing inside her locker, which means her purse is probably in there, too."

Crap. "What about her car? Is it in the lot?"

"It's not there."

"Would she have left without saying anything?"

"No way. That could get her fired. She'd let someone know."

"Okay. Have you seen anyone hanging around who shouldn't be there? Or someone new?"

"No. Well, there was a new janitor tonight who didn't seem to know what he was doing, but that's typical. What do you think happened?"

"A janitor? What'd he look like?"

"I don't know. Who looks at janitors? Maybe six feet tall. Brown hair. He was kind of an average white guy."

Burton was signaling frantically to Zach. "Havens is a janitor at a school."

"Tina, I've got to go. If you see her, call me."

"Find her, Zach. Find her now."

"I'm doing my best." He hung up and told Frank, "We have to assume that Havens already has her. Call in her car. Sounds like he's got her in her own Honda."

Zach turned his attention to Lyle Burton. "Tell me what you know, right now."

"He's been killing people based on . . . based on things they used to do to the boys back at the Sierra School," Burton stammered.

Zach stared at him. "Excuse me?"

"Susan Tennant used to restrain the boys if they got out of hand, got too wild, talked back, whatever. She'd put them in soft restraints. That's how you found her, right? She was tied up? Facedown?" Burton rubbed at his wrists where they'd been bound.

Zach nodded. "Go on."

"Ryan Arnott used to put the boys in ice baths. At first he said he did it to calm them down. Then he started using it as a punishment. Dunking them over and over until they begged." Burton's voice was shaking.

"And the broomstick up his ass?" Frank asked in a nearly conversational tone.

Burton looked up at him. "I think you can figure that one out?"

"So what would he do to Veronica? She didn't beat anyone. She didn't drown anyone. She didn't rape anyone."

"But she's the reason Max got sent away." Frank's eyes narrowed as he thought it through. "If Max blamed her for his being sent away, then Gary would blame her, too."

"I bet he's taking her to the school," Zach said. "He

blames her for Max having been sent there, so he's taking her there to kill her."

He flipped the keys to Frank. "You drive. I'm calling Janice Lam on our way."

"I'm coming, too."

They turned to stare at Lyle Burton.

"I'm deadly serious. This is all connected to me. He's killed two people after I've gone to see them. He took Veronica after I came here. I think somehow it's connected to me. If anyone can stop him, it's me."

"There's no time to argue and he might well have a point," Frank said.

"Get in the back and buckle your damn seat belt, Burton," Zach said as he shoved him toward the car.

Zach started making calls. The first was to warn Lam about what was going down.

"You want me to send someone up there to check things out?" she asked.

"Yes."

"I'll keep you posted."

The next call was to Josh Wolfe at headquarters. After Zach reported what was happening and where they were headed, he asked, "Any vehicles registered to Havens?"

"Hold on a minute. Yeah. A truck. White pickup. License plate 4C98765."

Zach froze. A white pickup truck. They were common as dirt, but he'd seen one recently. More than one?

The white pickup leaving the parking lot following George Osborne, the night Osborne was murdered. The white pickup sitting outside Veronica's condo before she disappeared.

He'd assumed it belonged there. He'd fucked up, and Veronica was going to pay the price.

"Crap, Frank. He's been stalking her for days."

19

Gary set the cruise control on the Honda. Once he'd gotten out of Sacramento there'd been almost no traffic, and it would have been easy to start to speed. He couldn't afford to be pulled over. He was pretty sure he'd heard the Pop-Tart kicking in the trunk. As long as he kept going, he didn't think it would be a problem.

He was still breathing hard, but from excitement now. It was all coming to a glorious conclusion. He'd take the Pop-Tart up to the school. He'd show her what kind of hell she'd sent her brother into, and then he'd make her pay.

He wondered how long it would take before someone found her body up there. Weeks? Months? Years?

It had taken them twenty years to find Max. It

would be sweet if it took them that long to find her. He might even go up and visit her sometimes.

He changed lanes, careful not to exceed the speed limit, and started to whistle.

"Anything?" Zach asked Janice Lam over the phone.

"No. Nothing's been disturbed since my crime-scene guys left. You want me to station someone up here? Just for tonight?" she asked.

"Absolutely." He hung up. "There's no sign of him yet. Do you think we have this wrong?"

Frank kept his eyes on the road, which was good considering how fast he was driving. "Do you?"

"No."

"Me, neither."

Zach called Janice Lam again. "Anything from your man up at the school?"

"Nope. He's not due to check in for another fifteen minutes, though. Want me to radio up?"

"Would you? Let him know we're almost there. I don't want to startle him and have him take a shot at us. I'll hold." He looked over at Frank. "Nothing so far. If we get there and Havens isn't there, what's our plan B?"

"We've already got a BOLO on him and Veronica's car. They'll turn up," Frank said.

A Be On the Look Out was no guarantee they'd be found, let alone that they'd be found before it was too late.

Janice Lam came back on the line. "Kaminsky isn't answering his radio." Her voice sounded tense.

"Keep trying him. We're almost there."

"I'm right behind you, McKnight."

Zach hung up and looked over at Frank. "Drive, Frank."

"I'm driving as fast as I can."

Gary bumped the Honda up the dirt track to the site of the old Sierra School for Boys. He wondered how shaken up the Pop-Tart would be back there, flopping around with no seat belt or any way to brace herself. He did want her to be conscious, so he drove carefully.

He'd worried that maybe he wouldn't be able to find it at one point, but it turned out that every turn and twist up the road to the place that had broken him was indelibly imprinted on his brain.

It was overgrown, but other than that, it was just like he remembered it.

Except for the police car parked in the clearing

when he arrived. The only time cops had shown up at Sierra was when somebody tried to escape.

Gary made sure the sap was still in his pocket and got out of the car. He was instantly blinded by the glare of a powerful flashlight. He held his hands up in surrender.

"Hey, I'm a little lost. Do you think you could help me?" he said, doing his best to sound like a regular guy with nothing to hide. He'd spent years perfecting the act. It was barely even an effort anymore.

The light dipped a little. "This is private property, sir. I'm going to have to ask you to leave."

"That's all I want to do. I'm trying to find County Road 15. I think I took a wrong turn." He smiled and let his hands drop a little.

"You definitely took a wrong turn." The light dropped farther. Gary could see the police officer's face now; he was young. Figured. "You need to go back to the main road, turn left, and then take a right when you get to 89. Road 15 will be on your left another mile or two down the road."

Gary turned to face where he'd come in. "So go right out of here and then right on the main road?" he asked, doing his best to sound confused.

"No. Turn left on the main road." The officer walked up to Gary and gestured back to the road. "And then right onto 89."

Gary let the officer take one more step in front of him as he pointed out the general direction, then he slammed him in the back of the head.

When the car finally stopped moving, Veronica nearly wept with relief. She had no idea how long she'd been thrown around in the back of the car, but she could barely think. The fumes from the car were making her head throb and her stomach lurch. She was terrified that she would throw up and die like Susan Tennant, choking on her own vomit. She tried to take deep breaths to calm her head and her stomach, but with her mouth taped shut, she felt like she could barely get enough oxygen in.

She had a blessed few moments after the car stopped. She could hear voices, but couldn't make out what anyone was saying. She had to have a plan. She had to *do* something. She couldn't lie here in the trunk and wait for whatever this lunatic had planned for her. She had no idea what was going on, but it couldn't possibly be good.

She squirmed around so that her feet were toward the back of the car and coiled her legs to her chest. Then she waited.

When the trunk finally opened after what seemed like an eternity, she stayed as still as she could. She waited until the silhouetted figure over her leaned in—then she kicked out as hard as she could with her bound feet.

The figure reeled back with a grunt and she felt a grim satisfaction. This might be the end of the line for her, but she wouldn't go down without a fight.

As fresh, clean air finally reached her starving lungs, she breathed in through her nose as hard as she could, struggling to her knees.

The figure was back before her then. This time, he had a gun trained on her. "You always were a nasty one, weren't you, Pop-Tart?" he said. He reached in and ripped the duct tape off her mouth.

She cried out in pain as the tape ripped her skin.

"Go ahead, scream as much as you want. There's nobody here to hear you. Trust me. I know. I screamed plenty when they had me out here. Nobody ever came to help. Not for me. Not for Max. Not for anybody."

Veronica sat back on her heels. "Who are you? What are you doing to me?"

"My name is Gary Havens and I was with your brother right before they murdered him. I couldn't help him then, but I can help him now. I'm making sure that all the people responsible for his death are finally punished." He sounded so reasonable, so calm.

"You killed Susan Tennant?" Veronica asked, still trying to make sense of what this madman was saying to her.

"And Ryan Arnott, too." He sounded proud.

"Did you kill my father?" she asked.

"No. That was the Devil's handiwork. I didn't have to take care of that particular person." The man reached in and hauled Veronica out of the trunk, heaving her onto the ground.

She cried out again as she hit the ground, unable to protect her head or her shoulders. "What are you going to do to me?"

"Whatever I want to." He reached down and cut the tape that bound her feet. "First, though, I'm going to give you a little tour."

"We need to stop here," Zach told Frank.

"It's at least another half mile up to the school," Frank said.

"That's why we need to stop. The element of surprise might be all we have. Pull over to the side and we'll hike the rest of the way in." Zach took off his seat belt and got out of the car as soon as it came to a stop, then opened the door for Lyle. "Is there a good way in? One he won't be watching?"

Burton nodded. "Follow me."

*　　　*　　　*

"This is where Ryan Arnott raped your brother." The man named Gary had shoved Veronica down a flight of stairs, gun constantly at her back. Her legs were still numb and stiff and she had stumbled more than once.

She backed away from the filthy tub in the basement room, feeling like she might vomit.

"Go ahead. Take a good look at it. This is where you sent him, Pop-Tart. This is where he went after you ratted him out to your bastard father."

Veronica looked away.

"I said look at it!" Gary screamed. He grabbed her hair and forced her to her knees, pressing her face against the tub.

"Arnott took quite a few of us down here. None of us talked about it afterward. We were all too ashamed. So take a good look, you stupid little slut. This is where your brother was raped." He hauled her up by her hair.

Tears streamed down Veronica's cheeks as much from horror as from the pain. "I didn't send him here. I didn't."

He backhanded her across the face. "Take responsibility for what you did. You turned him in. You might as well have signed the forms sending him here."

"I was a little girl. I didn't even know what I'd

found." She had just wanted to play with the things she'd found in Max's sock drawer. She hadn't known her father would see them. She hadn't known he would use them to get rid of her brother.

"You were evil then, and you're evil now. I want to make sure you know how evil before I cleanse us both of your sins." He forced her up the stairs and back into the cold night air.

Veronica gulped in more air, trying to breathe deep without hyperventilating, but the panic was nearly overwhelming. No one knew where she was. No one knew who she was with. She was going to die up here. Would they even find her body? Or would she lie up here like Max, alone in the wood for decades? Oh, poor Max. Her poor sweet brother.

"And now, as the pièce de résistance, let me show you where they buried him." Gary shoved her through the maze of buildings.

If she slowed even a step, he pushed her again, making her stumble. She fell once and he hauled her up by her arm. She felt as if it might come right out of her shoulder socket.

They finally came to an open pit in the ground. "This is where your brother was for twenty years. It took the Whore, Susan Tennant, to dig him up."

"Why would Susan Tennant dig up my brother's grave?" Veronica felt like her head was spinning.

"Apparently she didn't want the Devil to get his next promotion. That's all I could get out of her before I shoved the rag in her mouth. The one that made her choke on her own puke." Gary laughed. "I saw her do that to dozens of boys. I just didn't take the rag out, like she used to. I let it stay in and I watched the life drain out of her, and with it, my sins."

Veronica looked down into the pit. This was where Max had been for all those years she'd waited for him. This was where he'd been when she secretly lit a candle on his birthday. This was where he'd been as she'd scanned the faces of strangers on the street, hoping and praying that he would come home.

She began to weep.

"Oh, please. Do you expect me to be fooled by those alligator tears?" Then Gary shoved her in the back with the gun, and she fell into her brother's grave.

"Gary, don't."

Gary whirled around. He knew that voice. He knew it all too well.

"What are you doing here?" Gary asked the Devil. "How did you get here?"

"The police brought me, Gary. This has to end. Let the girl go. None of this is her fault." He still had that same deep voice. It made him sound like he was always right, but Gary knew better now. The Devil was never right.

"The girl is where it started. She's the beginning and she will be the end." Gary lifted his gun. Behind the Devil he could make out two more figures. "You know that I saw what you did that night, right?"

"I didn't know. Not until now. I didn't think anyone saw it except the people who were involved," Burton said.

"I saw. I saw the way you kept kicking him, even after he was down on the ground, even after everyone else stopped. You kept kicking and kicking and kicking with those big, thick work boots you always wore. They looked like the kind of boots that would have steel toes." Gary could almost hear the sickening crunch of Max's bones again.

"I was wrong, Gary. I shouldn't have done that. Things . . . things got out of hand."

"You killed Max." He wanted it stated for the record. He wanted everyone to know.

"I did. And I have spent every day since then regretting it, Gary. I can't take back what happened that night. I wish to God I could, but I can't." Burton's voice clogged with tears.

Gary regarded Burton with a detached air. "You were pretty quick to kill again to cover it up. I saw what you did to George Osborne."

Burton hung his head. "How the hell did you see that, Gary? No one saw that. No one was there."

"I followed you. I saw you punch him and kick him, just the way you punched and kicked Max. Kind of poetic justice, don't you think? That the evil stepfather died the same way Max did? Then I watched you haul him up the stairs and hurl him back down. Did you really think that was going to fool anyone? Have you ever watched a single episode of *CSI*?"

"You followed me?" Burton sounded surprised.

"You were marking people for me. Your face was in the paper almost right next to Max's. It was a sign. Max was asking me to follow you. I followed you to the Whore and I killed her, and I followed you to the Rapist and I killed him."

"No. Oh, no," Burton moaned.

"I like that you killed Osborne. He sent Max to Sierra and he had to pay for that." He kicked a rock down onto Veronica. "She has to pay, too."

"Why does she have to pay, Gary?" Burton asked. "What did she do?"

"It was her fault that Osborne sent Max away. She found the drugs in his dresser drawer and couldn't keep her mouth shut." He kicked some dirt into the grave and Veronica groaned.

One of the figures behind the Devil started toward

him, but the other grabbed his arm and stopped him. Gary pointed the gun down at Veronica.

"Steady there," Gary said. "I'm pretty sure I wouldn't miss from this distance. I could be the lousiest shot in the world and I'm pretty sure I would still take her head clean off."

"Let her go, Gary. She didn't do anything wrong." Burton took a step toward him.

Gary swung the gun back up and pointed it at Burton. "She turned him in. She was a rat. We had plenty of those up at the Sierra School. You made sure of that, didn't you? You rewarded us for ratting each other out. Rats got a little extra food. Rats got fewer chores and fewer beatings. You didn't let Arnott take rats down into his nasty basement, did you?"

"You're right, Gary. We did that on purpose. We wanted to keep you boys at odds with each other. It made you easier to control."

"We were just boys!" Gary screamed. "How hard could we have been to control? You didn't need to treat us like animals. You didn't need to turn us against each other so we wouldn't even have a friend."

"We thought we were doing it right, Gary. We thought we had to break you down in order to build you back up. We just . . . we got carried away."

"Is that what you tell yourself late at night when you can't sleep?" He spat on the ground. "There was something wrong with you—with all of you. But you were the one who led them. You called the shots. Old Mr. Joiner hardly knew what day it was, much less what was going on in his own school. Did he ever find out? Is that why you left so soon after you killed Max?"

Burton shook his head. "No. That wasn't it. I . . . I couldn't bear it. Every time I walked past that building, I could hear Max screaming all over again. Every time I went past where we buried him, I could hear him moaning. It was too much. I had to go." Burton was shaking now. He looked as if he wouldn't even be able to keep standing much longer.

"Oh, poor baby. So you actually had some tiny conscience and you got all tormented. Well, I don't feel bad for you. You're a murderer, plain and simple. You don't deserve to live—much less happily ever after."

A sudden glint shone in Burton's eye. "Yes. I am a murderer. I killed Max Shelden and I killed George Osborne. That's two people's blood on my hands. How many people's blood do you have on your hands, Gary? How many have you killed now?"

"Two." Gary's chin came up. "The Whore and the Rapist."

"Veronica would make three, then."

Gary nodded.

"Once you kill her, you'll have murdered more people than I have, Gary. Doesn't that make you a worse person than me?"

"No!" Gary yelled. "I did not kill out of anger. I did not kill for pleasure, or to protect my miserable hide. My kills were righteous. Those two deserved to know what it felt like."

"I don't think why you did it makes any difference, Gary. You still killed. And it's not like it was in self-defense."

"But it was defense." Gary breathed harder now. "I was defending Max."

"Max has been dead for twenty years. It's way too late to defend him, Gary. This had nothing to do with Max." Burton took another step toward him.

"It had everything to do with Max!" It was all about the bones, and what they were telling him to do. He didn't get pleasure from it.

"Really? How did it have to do with Max, Gary?" Burton sounded almost amused.

"His picture was in the paper. Right next to yours. It was like he was pointing you out to me. So I followed you and where did you take me? Right to the Whore! He was leading me. He wanted me to punish her." Gary calmed himself a little, thinking about how it had felt to watch the Whore die.

"Is that what you did, Gary? Did you punish her?"

"You wanted to punish her, too, didn't you? I saw you slap her." Gary smiled slyly. "All I did was punish her like she used to punish us. I tied her up the way she used to tie us up. Oh, excuse me—she *restrained* us. So I restrained her, too. I restrained her until she stopped needing to be restrained at all."

Burton shut his eyes for a second and swayed. Slowly he opened them again. "And Arnott? What happened there?"

"You led me to him again. It was like Max was using you to show me the way. Like he was whispering in my ear." It had been so comforting to have a friend again.

"What did you do to Arnott?" Burton asked.

Gary shrugged and looked away. "That was harder. I . . . I thought I would have enjoyed that more. I didn't, though. That was another lesson that Max was trying to teach me. That even though I had killed, I didn't have to be like them. I didn't have to be like you. It didn't have to turn me on."

"You were worried that you were going to be like me?" Burton took another step toward him.

"Yeah. You liked what you did up there at Sierra. You can pretend that you regret it, but I remember. I remember how red your face would get, how hard you would breathe. I remember how you would go to the Whore afterward. How you'd fuck her and fuck her and fuck her, sweating and grunting like a pig. It turned you on, didn't it? It made you feel like a big man to kick little kids around." Gary felt sick to his stomach remembering it.

Burton hung his head, his hands loose at his sides. "There's no use lying to you, Gary. You know what I am. You know what I've done. You've seen the absolute worst of me." His head came up. "But you're not very different from me, are you?"

"I am completely different." Bastard! He was nothing like the Devil.

"You've killed the same number of people I have. And maybe you're even a little worse. I'm not a rapist."

"Neither am I."

"Ryan Arnott would argue that if he could. Was he already dead when you shoved that broomstick up his ass, Gary? Or did you want to hear him groan as you rammed it in?" Burton asked.

"Do you know how many of us he raped? How many times?" Gary shot back.

Burton shook his head. "No, Gary, I don't. I intentionally tried not to know. That was wrong of me, too. I should have been the one protecting you boys, but I wasn't. Not only was I cruel, I let others be more than cruel. I have to live with that stain on my soul, too."

"Your soul's so black, it's impossible to stain it any

more. Do you have any idea of what that does to a boy? To be used that way? To be humiliated and shamed like that?

"And it didn't stopped there. Oh, no. Cruelty breeds cruelty. Shame breeds shame. Do you know what happened in those dormitories after the lights went out?" Gary shuddered. "It was like a torture chamber. Until Max got there. Max got us to stop that. Is that part of why you killed him? Because he got us to stop feeding on each other like starving rats in a cage?"

"That was part of it. He made you all harder to control. He was a subversive element," Burton said.

"He was a *child.* He was barely seventeen years old and he was more of a man than any of you. That's why you had to kill him, wasn't it?"

"Maybe so. But is it going to make *you* more of a man to kill his sister? The one person he loved more than anyone else? I heard him talk about her. The idea of going back and saving her from growing up with George Osborne was how he held on. And now you're going to kill her?"

"She deserves to die. It's her fault that Max died. It's her fault that he was here. She was the beginning of it all." Gary couldn't let the Devil's arguments sway him. He felt their flawed logic swirling through his brain, confusing him, making it harder to stay focused.

"Maybe so. Maybe so. I see your point about what

she did as a child being the beginning of it. But she's not *entirely* why he's dead, is she? We're all a little guilty, aren't we, Gary? Even you?"

Why did he have to sound so reasonable? "How could I be guilty? You had me so beaten down I couldn't even defend myself." Tears sprang to Gary's eyes as he remembered it.

"Exactly. You couldn't defend yourself. Do you remember what Max did, Gary? Arnott was coming for you again, wasn't he? He had a special fondness for you, maybe because you were so small. Or because of the way you wept afterward. Who knows what turned him on about you?

"He was coming for you again. And who stood up for you? Who tried to defend you?"

"Max," Gary whispered.

"That's right. Max. That was his last act of defiance. His last big stand. It was protecting *you*, Gary. Not himself. Not his sister. Not anyone else. So, in a lot of ways, he died because of you, Gary."

"No," he whispered. "No."

"Yes, Gary. What about the stain of guilt on *your* soul, Gary? What are you going to do about that?"

"Their blood. Their blood will wash me clean." He had to stay focused. He had to remember why he was doing this.

"I don't think so. I don't think that's what Max has

been trying to tell you to do. I think you know who needs to be punished for his death—don't you, Gary?"

"I couldn't stand it anymore," he whispered. "He would come for me and there was nothing I could do. He'd make me strip and stand there while he filled that tub with ice water. Do you know what that feels like? To know what's coming? To know what pain is just moments away, and not be able to do anything to stop it?

"But as bad as it was, as much as you wanted to get out of that tub, you knew what was coming next and you dreaded that even more. The way he'd shove himself into you. The way he'd grunt and thrust. And afterward . . . all the blood. He'd make you clean it up while he stood there and laughed. My hands would still be numb from the tub, I'd still be bleeding, and he'd make me get down on my hands and knees and clean it all up."

"I should have seen it and stopped it, Gary—but I didn't. It was Max who tried to stop it, didn't he? And that's the real issue here. Max died protecting you."

"No. No. It wasn't like that. It wasn't just me. He did it for all of us."

"Not that night, he didn't. That night he did it just for you, Gary. Arnott wasn't coming for anyone else. He was coming for you. The only person who stood between you and Arnott that night was Max, and he did a pretty good job of it. Gave Arnott a hell of a shiner before we subdued him. Do you remember that, Gary? Do you remember us all coming in to take him down?"

Gary nodded. "There were four of you. Four against one kid! You dragged him out of the dormitory by his hair."

"And where were you, Gary? Where were you while that was happening?"

"I was right there. I was watching. I saw what you did."

"And I saw what you *didn't* do, Gary. I saw you back in the corner, trying to hide behind one of the beds. Max was getting the crap beaten out of him for trying to keep you from getting raped again, and what did you do? You hid. You didn't lift a finger to help him."

"What could I have done? I was just one kid, and one of the smallest ones. Nothing I could do was going to stop you."

"Max was just one kid. Max knew he couldn't stop us. That didn't stop him from trying. And not even to save his own skin. To save *yours*. Did you do anything to try to save Max that night?"

Gary had started to shake. The gun wavered in his hand, moving from Veronica to Lyle and back again. "I couldn't. It would have been me you beat, if I had."

"So really, Max took your beating, didn't he? Those kicks, those punches, they weren't really meant for Max, were they? They were meant for you. But you were too much of a chickenshit. You hid back there in your corner and watched Max die for you. He died in your place. How do you think he must have felt about that, Gary?"

"I didn't ask him to do it."

"But you didn't tell him not to, either, did you?"

"No. When he stood up between me and Arnott, I was so relieved. I didn't think I could take it anymore. I was going to lose my mind."

"But you still did nothing. You hid and watched while the one person who tried to help you bled to death in the dirt. Isn't that right, Gary? Isn't that what you did?"

Gary began to cry. "I didn't know what to do. I wasn't brave like Max. Or strong. So I hid. He took my beating and I hid."

Burton's voice was smooth and silky, almost seductive in its calm. "So who really is to blame for Max's death, Gary? The little girl who didn't even know what she had found, or the coward who let Max die in his place?"

"Oh, no. No, don't say that. Don't," Gary moaned.

"I'm just pointing out the facts. Whose blood do you really think Max would want to be shed here? The blood of his baby sister? The little girl whose picture he kept by his bunk? Or the blood of the coward who let him die in his place?

"What would really bring everything full circle, Gary? Her blood or yours? What would the bones tell you about that, Gary?"

Gary began to back away from the grave, hands shaking, tears running down his face. "No. He wouldn't ask that of me."

"Are you sure about that, Gary?" Burton started walking toward Gary. "Are you absolutely positive? You watched him die. You watched him be buried right here, wrapped in a plastic garbage bag. Maybe that's why he led you here. So you could make amends to him on the spot where he died."

"Do you think that's what he wants?" Gary whispered.

"I don't know, Gary. He doesn't talk to me. His bones told me nothing I didn't already know. What are they telling you?"

Gary went still and silent, as if he was really listening. As if a voice might actually be telling him what to do. "No," he moaned. "Please, no."

Burton's voice was implacable. "And who was the last person I marked, Gary? Who was the last person I came to see? It was you, wasn't it, Gary? What do the bones say about that?"

*   *   *

Zach crouched, ready to rush Gary. The gun went from Veronica to Lyle . . . then Havens leaped to the side and disappeared.

"What the hell?" Frank yelled. "Where did he go?"

Burton fell to his knees. "Steam tunnels!"

Zach remembered Stoffels telling them the whole place was connected by steam tunnels. He took off running, found the hole that Gary had disappeared into, and dove in after him.

It was pitch black and Zach felt around himself. Concrete walls. A pipe running overhead. Soft scurrying noises like rats, and louder, the sound of footsteps ahead.

Zach pulled the flashlight off his belt and shone it around. The tunnel bent just ahead and he shut off the light so he didn't give away his position. He slowly made his way down the tunnel, trying to still his breathing enough to hear Gary moving ahead of him.

He was there. He was still moving. Zach reached the place where the tunnel bent, feeling the turn with his hands. He inched his way around the corner, not sure if he would be greeted with gunfire or silence.

Neither. He heard whimpering ahead. Havens was completely deteriorating.

"Gary, come back," he called.

He was answered with the sound of Gary scurrying ahead. Damn. Zach took a deep breath and moved forward, wondering if he should leave a trail to find his way out again. He hit another junction and had to choose left or right.

Which way had Havens gone? He was coming apart at the seams and Zach could use that to his advantage. The guy was back at the scene of his past torture. He'd come face-to-face with one of his tormentors. What was he thinking? He had to get into this guy's head.

"You okay, Gary?" he called into the darkness.

"What do you think, asshole?" Havens called back from the left.

Progress. Zach moved toward the sound of his voice. "I don't know what to think, Gary. I'm still trying to figure it all out. You've got it all figured out, haven't you?"

"I thought I had. I really thought I had."

"We all make mistakes, Gary." Zach continued down the tunnel and hit another intersection. "I've made plenty."

"I did not make a mistake. Max's bones told me what to do. I was helping him. I was finally helping him," Gary sobbed.

To the right this time. "And I'm sure he knows that, Gary."

"Do you think so?" Havens's voice was much closer now.

It was hard to tell in the echoing tunnel, but he sounded only a few yards ahead. "I do, Gary. I think he knows."

"I really tried."

Shit. Havens had stopped and Zach was almost on top of him. He flicked on his flashlight. Havens was crouched at a dead end. Part of the tunnel had collapsed. There was no way out, and Havens was pointing his gun directly at Zach's chest. The light from the flashlight temporarily blinded him, and Gary threw up his other arm to protect his eyes.

"I know you really tried, Gary. Max knows, too. We all know." Zach kept his voice low and calm. Every muscle was tensed, ready to spring. He just had to wait for the right moment.

"I felt like it was cleansing me. I spend all day cleaning, but I can never get myself clean from what they did to me. Their blood was finally making me clean."

"What those men did up here was criminal, Gary. We'll go after every single one of them. I swear that to you." That was no lie.

Gary's arm dropped a little. "You will?"

"Yes. They make me sick. No one should be allowed to prey on children like that." Zach took a tentative step forward.

"So you'll make them pay? All of them?"

Gary's gun hand relaxed a little. If it wavered another couple of inches to the side, Zach could rush him.

"I will, Gary. I'll make them pay."

Gary smiled. "Good." Then he shoved the gun into his mouth and blew the back of his head off.

20

Veronica had told the funeral director to set up only a dozen chairs. It would be too depressing to see row after row of empty folding chairs at the memorial service laying her brother and her father to rest.

She had spent the past week making the arrangements; she was too shaken to go back to work yet.

It had taken hours after Gary Havens had shot himself to finally get out of there. They'd found the Plumas County deputy who'd been waiting at the clearing handcuffed to a tree. He had a concussion, but was otherwise fine. Veronica had a dislocated shoulder and a lot of bruises, and loud noises still made her jump. If Zach wasn't in her bed next to her, she needed a light on. Recognizing the signs of PTSD, she was talking to a shrink. She'd work through it.

Lyle Burton would never be the same again, either. He had already made one suicide attempt in jail. Veronica wondered whether he'd ever make it to trial. He was a broken man.

She watched now as the chairs had filled within five minutes of the funeral director opening the doors, and the room was soon packed with people trying to find a place to stand as the employees scrambled to set up more chairs.

Zach's sisters were here with their husbands. His mother had come, too. There were friends from the hospital. Tina, of course, and Matt Cassel, her EMT boyfriend. Even some people she knew from Al-Anon were there.

"I can't believe all these people came," she whispered to Zach. "None of them knew Max, and if they'd met my father, they probably wouldn't be here to pay their respects."

"They know you, though." He put his arm around her and pulled her against him. "They're not here because of Max or your dad. They're here because they love you. It's why we're all here."

She stood on her tiptoes and kissed his cheek.

He was right, too. These things weren't for the people who'd died. Nothing could change anything that had happened to her brother or her father, or anything they'd done in their lives. It could change things for her, though. It could make a difference for her. Couldn't it?

She sighed. "Max has been gone for so long. He's been gone from my life longer than he was in it. And my dad wasn't much of a dad in the first place."

"So you can lay them to rest now. And you can say good-bye and go on with your life."

"It's never been completely mine before. I don't have to nurse my mom, or bail out my dad, or wait for my brother. The only person I have to worry about is me. I can go wherever I want."

"And where do you want to be, Veronica?" Zach asked softly.

She stepped into the circle of his arms. "Right here."

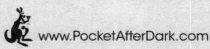